Torn

A Forbidden Age Gap Dark Mafia Romance

Carrington Cartel
Book 1

Chiquita Dennie

304 Publishing Company

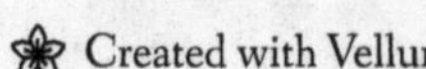 Created with Vellum

Disclaimer

This work of fiction contains strong language, graphic violence, and explicit sexual content and is only intended for mature readers. The story may contain unconventional situations, verbal abuse, grief, and encounters that may offend some readers. Please consider carefully before reading or try my contemporary romance work instead. Intended for mature readers (18+).

Introduction

Grab some wine and get ready for more spicy, sinful, sexy suspense.

Are you signed up for my newsletter?

Join today and find out all the latest in new releases, contests, giveaways, sneak peeks, and more.

www.chiquitadennie.com

The Carrington Cartel Series

Welcome to the Carrington Cartel, a duet series that features characters from Stuck in Love, and Fuertes Cartel. Gigi, Laurent, and Axel briefly appear in the Struck in Love series as an introduction. You do not have to read the entire series, but spoilers are included in this new series. If you want the entire reading order of Struck in Love Universe, check the next page.

Struck In Love Universe

https://books2read.com/u/49Zjnw
Ruthless Struck in Love Book 1
https://books2read.com/u/4AxKLo
Savage Struck in Love Book 2
https://books2read.com/u/bpED6g
Beast Struck in Love Book 3
https://books2read.com/u/3LpgdJ
Janice and Carlo Captivated by His Love
https://books2read.com/u/b6je6M
Brutal Struck in Love Book 4
https://books2read.com/u/4NQyE9
Stolen-The Fuertes Cartel Book 1
https://books2read.com/u/mvZlgV
Saved-The Fuertes Cartel Book 2
https://books2read.com/u/4DWwLd
Redemption Struck in Love Book 5
https://books2read.com/u/b5kZ8O
Betrayed-The Fuertes Cartel Book 3
https://books2read.com/u/4A5LGp

Torn: The Carrington Cartel Book 1
https://books2read.com/u/mqXare
Claim: The Carrington Cartel Book 2

Latest Releases from Chiquita Dennie

Saved: Fuertes Mafia Cartel Book 2
Refuel (A Driven World Novel)
Pressure (A Driven World Novel)
Until Serena (HEA World Novel)
Renew Book 4 (Jessica and Joseph)
She's All I Need
Red Light District (A Fantasy Romance Short)
The Carrington Cartel Book 1
Betrayed: Fuertes Mafia Cartel Book 3
Something Gained (A Romantic Comedy Book 1)
Upcoming Releases (2023/2024):
The Carrington Cartel Book 2
Fall For You (Satin Hill Book 1)
Bronx
Unveiled (Achille Cartel Book 1)
Nicco: TN Seal Security Book 3

Synopsis

When a cartel princess breaks a longstanding promise – her life isn't the only one in danger

Gigi has always known what her future holds. Marry into the Ramini family, strengthen the cartel and obey her father.

That was until her father assigned Axel as her personal protector.

A trusted associate of her father and a high-ranking member of the cartel, Axel is everything Gigi knows to avoid, instead she finds herself drawn to him.

Their desire for each other is danger, more dangerous than the cartel itself.

Because if anyone learns the truth, the consequences will be dire.

Chapter 1

Gigi

"Rise and shine, Gigi!" Aurora, our housekeeper, drew the curtains in my room.

The bright sunlight made me groan. I didn't feel like dealing with anything or anyone today. I was still dealing with a hangover from the party my father made me go to with him to meet Joaquin Fuertes. Too many times, I'd pretended to be sick. My excuses had run out, and time was ticking for me to finally step up as the leader of the cartel. Unlike most families led by men, my parents only had me, and being the daughter of one of the top families in Italy, I had no choice but to follow in the family's footsteps.

"Ugh. No, Aurora." I groaned, tightening the covers around my body. I heard her chuckles inside the room.

"Gigi, you know your father wants to have breakfast with you."

"So?" I tossed the covers back and sat up against my bronze monogrammed headboard.

"How was the party?" Aurora bent to pick up my dress and shoes off the floor.

I complained to her all the time about picking up behind me. I was a grown woman, yet she still treated me like a little girl. A smile remained on her face as she grabbed more of my clothes off the floor.

I shrugged and stretched my arms before lifting my cell phone from the night table. "It was boring as usual." I tapped on my messages, seeing I had lots from my best friend, Ginerva.

"Did you meet anyone?" Aurora walked into the bathroom as I lay across the bed, texting Ginerva.

"I met Sofia Fuertes and a few other mob wives." I stared at the photo of me getting out of the limo with Axel standing off to the side, watching.

Me: *Where did you get these?*

Ginerva: *Baby, you're plastered on all the papers.*

Me: *Fuck.*

Ginerva: *You can't panic, Gigi. This is your life.*

Me: *I know. I wish they'd leave me alone.*

"Oh, is she nice? I've seen a few of her movies." Aurora came out of my bathroom carrying the trash bag.

I closed out my message, jumped off the bed, and took it out of her hands. "Aurora, I told you to stop cleaning my room. You need to relax and go on vacation."

She waved me off and reached for the trash. Although she was in her early sixties, Aurora looked no older than forty. She always kept her gray hair in a bun and wore heels all day long, no matter the season. Aurora had been with my family since before I was born, and from the stories I'd been told, her husband was killed years ago. He worked for my father, so he brought her on staff when she needed a place to live. My mother wasn't fond of her because my father and I loved her and treated her like family. In Rosa's eyes, Aurora was the help who needed to stay in her place. I thought of Aurora as more of a parent than Rosa.

"One day." Aurora kissed me on the cheek and pulled the bag out of my hand. Her golden-brown cheeks rose in a smile, and I rolled my eyes.

"Gigi, time for breakfast!" Rosa shouted.

I grunted, walking toward the bathroom.

Aurora smacked me on the butt, then cupped my cheek. She had a gentle, wise, and beautiful spirit. "Be a nice little girl."

The warmth of her touch on my chin calmed me down. "Yes, ma'am."

"Who were you texting with?" Aurora pointed to my phone.

"Ginerva."

Aurora started to make my bed. "It's early for her to be texting. Everything okay?"

I walked into my bathroom, turned on the shower, and checked the temperature. "Yeah, she sent photos of me at the party last night," I yelled from the bathroom, preparing for my facial routine and gathering all my products.

"You looked beautiful last night." Aurora stood at the door of the bathroom.

I nodded and winked at her through the mirror as I brushed my teeth, and she shook her head.

"What is taking so long for you to come downstairs?" My mother burst into my room.

Aurora hurriedly shut my bathroom door, and I locked it. Removing my nightshirt and shorts, I hopped in the shower before she could come in and bug me. I was twenty-two, and she still treated me like I was five, wanting to dictate everything I did and who I saw.

Arranged marriages were a well-known tradition in the cartel lifestyle, and she was all about pushing me into the Ramini family. Something I refused.

"Hurry up, Gigi!" I heard banging on my door.

"Coming, Rosa!" I yelled.

"Keep disrespecting me, Gigi," Rosa shouted from the other side of the door.

"Keep disrespecting me, Gigi." I mimicked, lifting the lavender body wash and towel and lathering them across my arms and legs.

Rosa was the definition of a kept wife, one who only wanted to shop and throw parties. The goal of my marrying Dario Ramini was so he could form a cohesive unit with our gun business, ultimately signifying a stronger hold on all of Italy. My mother and Dario didn't understand that the De Luca Cartel would never relinquish or fold their power. Dario was an egomaniac, a pompous asshole, and a womanizer who only wanted to fuck me so he could tell his friends. He was twenty-five, the eldest of Ramini's sons, and power-hungry like his father. Edmundo Ramini trained his son to be like him regarding women, which meant treating them like objects instead of someone you loved.

I turned off the water, slid the door open, and grabbed the towel on the island near my vanity mirror. My father agreed to redo my room and bathroom if I went on a date with Dario and attended the party last night. I'd learned that to get anything out of him, I needed to show I wasn't weak.

Drying off, I removed my wrap and let my soft curls fall against my back, nearly to my ass. I turned, looking at the stretch marks on my thick curvy figure. Rosa constantly complained that I needed to lose weight before the wedding, but I loved my curves and thick frame. Not obese or stick thin, in the middle, with thighs, hips, and plump breasts women paid to get.

Coming from a mixed background, I inherited my mother's tawny skin and my father's green eyes, thin nose, and short height of five-six. I thanked my mom for giving me her beauty, even though she was evil on the inside ninety percent of the time. She acted like she'd never had a privileged life outside of my father's money, despite her family coming from a political background. Her father was a retired congressman, and when she met my father during his visit to America for a business meeting, it was arranged that she would marry him, and her life was uprooted to Italy.

Unlocking my bathroom door, I was met by my mother sitting on the edge of the bed. I tightened the towel around me and smiled sweetly.

"Morning, Mommy." I strode toward her, leaned down, and kissed her cheek.

She gripped my chin, forcing me to look at her. "Why do you insist on pissing me off, Gigi? Huh?"

I jerked out of her hold and stomped to the dresser drawer to grab a bra and panties, ignoring her fussing. "I don't know what you're talking about."

I scanned through my wardrobe, wondering what I was in the mood to wear and what would piss my parents off even more. Having a walk-in closet that expanded into another room was the best idea I ever had. I ran a hand across the dresses and shoes hanging in a color-coded sequence. The walls were painted a light cream to match my bedroom color scheme of cream and silver. The two-thousand–square-foot room was my safe haven when I needed to be alone, including a couch nook for reading and doing my class work.

"One of these days, you're going to piss me off too much, and your father won't save you." Mother stalked into my closet, standing with her hands on her hips. Her hair was pulled to the side, her face all made up, and her eyes dipped low in slits.

"Why are you in my room?" I pulled down a pair of black leggings, a white crop top, and flat sandals.

Stepping around her, I moved back into the bathroom and started to close the door, but she blocked me.

"This is my house, and you will follow my rules." Mother's mouth thinned with displeasure.

I opened my mouth to respond, and she held her palm up, stopping me. Closing my eyes, I took a deep breath to control my emotions before we got into another shouting match. "I need to get dressed."

A muscle flicked angrily in her jaw. She glared and finally moved out of the way.

I closed the door, locking it for good measure.

"Breakfast is getting cold," she called from the stairs.

Breakfast is getting cold... pfff.

I removed the bra I had just donned and replaced it with nipple tape, then threw my shirt on and slid my legs into the leggings. I grabbed my brush to comb my hair into a ponytail, then dabbed on a little lip gloss and eyeliner.

"Ready for the show." My mouth took on an unpleasant twist.

Leaving the bathroom, I grabbed my phone, shut the door, and trod down the spiral stairs, checking for missed calls or messages. I scrolled past the calls from Dario and tapped on Ginerva's message.

Ginerva: *Gigi, call me*

Me: *Sorry. Rosa started with me again.*
Ginerva: *Girl, you better stop calling her Rosa.*
Me: *She'll be fine.*

I stepped into the massive dining room with its twenty-seat table, million-dollar chandelier, and family portraits on the wall. Growing up, I thought we lived in a museum with the amount of artwork and statues lying around.

"My little girl finally graced me with her presence," Dad stated.

I smiled, heading toward him and kissing his cheek.

He grasped my hand, shaking his head at the leggings and crop top I wore. "Why do you continue to dress like this, Gigi?" He waved for me to take a seat at the table.

Aurora came in with a plate of food and laid it in front of me.

"Laurent, I think it's time she married Dario," Mother muttered, enjoying the gentle sparring for my father's attention.

I glared at her and jumped up from my chair.

"Sit!" Dad yelled, pointing at me.

"You promised I could finish school." A tremor touched my lips.

Mother's eyes were sharp and assessing. "Promises are meant to be broken," she said, sipping her morning drink of orange juice and vodka—more vodka than juice, I assumed.

"Listen to me, Gigi. You know I'm retiring, and we need protection." My father leaned back, his eyes cold.

Dario was only interested in using me as a trophy on his arm and trying to get in my pants. I'd prided myself on remaining a virgin and refused to lose it to a man like Dario.

My father's hand came down on the table. "The deal we have is not a hundred percent secure, and having the Ramini family—"

"I don't care about the Raminis!" I whirled to leave the room.

"Stop! Come sit back down." Father stopped me with a raised hand.

Tears welled in my eyes. I wiped them away and sat down with my arms crossed. One day, I wanted to open an antique shop and graduate with a degree in business. I loved finding out where things came from and how they were built.

I shook my head. "Dario is not a good man."

"He's the eldest boy of a great family, and your father made a good choice," Mother explained.

"Then you marry him," I mumbled.

"Do you think someone magically created all of this? You have to make a sacrifice like the rest of us," Mother chastised. She threw her napkin on the table, rose out of her chair, and left the room with her drink.

"She's right, Gigi. You're our *neonata*." Father smoothed my hair.

As usual, I became their baby girl in Italian when they wanted to manipulate me into doing what they wanted. I knew this was all a ploy to keep me under their thumbs and from leaving home.

"If you love me, don't make me marry Dario." I cradled my head.

"The decision has been made." Father slammed one fist against the table.

It wasn't often he was so upset with me, but I had to get out of this arrangement. "You want this life. I don't."

The last thing I wanted to do was sit down with Dario today.

"She's right here, Dario," Mother stated, re-entering the room. She was smirking with her arm looped through his.

I almost gagged at the fakeness as he kissed her hand and came over to me, trying to kiss me on the lips. I turned my head away.

"Gigi." My father warned.

Dario raised his hand. "It's fine, Laurent. In time, she'll fall in line." Dario pinched my cheek.

"Why is he here?" I questioned, ignoring his presence.

"Your fiancé wanted to see you today and take you out on a date," Mother informed me.

I shook my head. "Not happening." I moved away.

"It *is* happening. You want to move to America, correct?" Dad reminded me about the negotiation we made a year ago. If I married Dario and took over the family business, I could move to America. Even though I grew up in Italy, I was familiar with the lifestyle, having traveled occasionally and visited my mother's family.

"And you want someone to take over this business. Put Dario in charge and leave me out of this," I spat, renewing my efforts to leave.

Dario grasped my wrist. "I love you, Gigi," he said, taunting me.

"Let me go," I gritted through clenched teeth.

"Gigi, Ginerva is here," Aurora blessedly interrupted.

I nodded, and Dario removed his hold. I rolled my eyes at him, stomping out of the room.

* * *

As soon as I walked into the living room, I saw Ginerva sitting on the couch, typing away on her phone. I plopped down next to her and groaned in annoyance.

She closed the phone and sat up to stare at me, pulling her feet underneath her. "Aurora called me."

I removed my arm from over my eyes and smiled. Aurora was the only one who knew me and protected my sanity. "Were you in class?"

"No, I was shopping." Ginerva grinned.

I chuckled, knowing how she loved to spend her father's money. Ginerva Pauduano's family wasn't in the business directly like my father. Her mother, Piera, was a retired school teacher and her father, Marcuello, was a police officer. He was on my father's payroll, but treated Ginerva way better. She wanted to move to America, and he was fine with letting her live her life as a beautician. Her mom encouraged her to be independent and not become someone's wife without exploring the world first.

"Dario's here," I scoffed, lifting a hand to my forehead.

"Oh. You want me to put a hit out on him?" She bit her lip to stifle her grin.

"If that's all it took, I would say yes. But we both know my parents will find another family to ship me off to." My tongue nervously moistened my dry lips.

"You never told me how the party went." The warmth of her smile echoed in her voice.

I shrugged my shoulders and started to speak when a throat cleared behind me.

"Dario." Ginerva kissed her teeth.

"Ginerva." His smile was without humor.

They hated each other ever since Ginerva caught him having sex with another woman at our joined family dinner. I told her I wasn't bothered since I knew it came with the territory, but when we were alone in the limo, I tried to scratch Dario's eyes out for embarrassing me in public.

His long-time mistress was a girl we went to school with before she dropped out after having a baby. Rumor said it was his baby, but he refused to claim the child since it was a girl. The old rules of having a child out of wedlock mattered to our parents more than anything, and it would bring shame upon our families if he let her take his last name.

"Dario, leave me alone." I stood up to leave, get some fresh air, go shopping, anywhere.

"We have to talk at some point, Gigi." Dario followed, approaching me with a smirk.

"No, we don't." I tried to move around him to head out of the living room.

He grabbed my elbow, spinning me around. His expression was stony. "We're getting married, and you *will* be my wife."

I wanted to smack him. "Get your hands off me."

"That mouth of yours is going to get you into trouble." He thought I would obey him because he got along with my father.

"You heard what my best friend said." Ginerva cocked her head to the side, standing beside me with her arms crossed.

Dario glanced from me to her and back with a smile. Removing his hand, he raised it in surrender.

"How long have we known each other?" Dario slid his hands into his pockets.

"Too long," I replied, resigned.

He chortled. "Since you were twelve, and I was

fifteen. It's always been understood our bloodline would connect in marriage."

"You don't own me, Dario," I voiced firmly.

He leaned in closer, with his face only a few inches from mine. "Think again, my love. Once we get married, all of you will belong to me." Dario ran the back of his hand across my cheek.

I didn't miss the lust in his eyes. I slapped his hand down. "Understand something, Dario. I might be quiet and reserved, but you need my family's money more than we need you."

"Are you threatening me?" Dario snapped, his voice cold.

"Stay out of my way." I smiled, grabbed Ginerva's hand, along with my purse and phone, and left the house.

Despite living in Sicily all my life on my family's sprawling estate, it could be suffocating, with all the body-guards and people who showed up for meetings with my father, forcing me to be the dutiful daughter.

Chapter 2

Axel

I stamped my foot into the man's chest, with no regret at his screams. People never learned. I was the last face they saw as they took their last breath. Like this guy. The minute Laurent agreed to a deal with him—and gave an extension—he thought it would be a good idea to leave town. When I had to chase, I made the pain even worse. Time I felt was wasted because they thought I wouldn't catch them.

I cracked my neck, wiping the sweat off my brow as I slammed my foot into his chest again.

"Please don't kill me." He coughed as blood seeped down his nose, placing a hand on his stomach.

I took my lit cigar and twisted it into his forehead. "Shut the fuck up!" I yelled in a harsh, raw voice.

People like Kiran pissed me off when they interrupted my schedule. I had plans to check in on a big shipment Laurent wanted me to ensure would arrive on time after weeks of delays. And here I was because no one else could be trusted to get rid of this piece of shit.

"Hold his leg out."

My crew grabbed both legs and held them together as Kiran squirmed.

I removed my gun and placed it on his kneecap. My voice dropped in volume. "Where's the money?"

He closed his eyes, tears squeezing out as his lips trembled.

"Speak," I hissed.

He tensed. "I will get his money, I promise you."

My voice was icy. "Too late for that. Laurent saved you more than once."

"Come on, Axel. I just need a little time." His mind was languid, without hope.

"Time, huh?" Men like him would never learn—same excuses every time.

I fired the gun.

"Argh!" he screamed, gripping his left knee.

"Why should I let you live?" Their answer never mattered to me, but I allowed them to feel comfortable enough to think I wouldn't kill them.

Kiran groaned in pain.

My phone buzzed in my pocket, and I answered it, staring at the blood on the ground.

"Is it done?" Laurent asked.

I glanced at Kiran, pointed the gun at his head, and fired. "It's done." My skin grew hot, and my jaw clenched.

"Come to my office." Laurent didn't wait for me to agree before hanging up.

When I took on the role of enforcer, I made sure the disposal of bodies wouldn't fall back on the cartel or me. We had our hands in real estate and owned locations like this where situations would never be questioned.

"Clean this up." I pointed at Kiran's wallet on the floor.

"His family?" Lazaro asked.

"If they question his whereabouts, kill them."

He hesitated. "The women…"

Many would consider me evil for hurting women and children. I paused at the door. "Make the consequences clear if they go to the police."

"Understood." The words caught in his throat.

"Check his home for the money. If it's not there, burn it down," I instructed.

I exited the back of the room and jogged outside, climbing into the passenger seat of the chauffeured car Laurent expected his team to travel in when doing business. Most of the time I drove, but I'd had to get my hands dirty tonight and didn't have time to go home and change.

I reached down and picked up the clean shirt and jacket. "Take me to Laurent's."

"Yes, sir."

The car ride was silent while I looked out into the streets. I haven't slept for the last few days because of repeated nightmares. One of the reasons I did business at night was to keep my mind off what would otherwise creep into my thoughts. Laurent needed me to handle another situation, but I might be late with his last-minute call.

We arrived at his home a few minutes later, and I jumped out. "Keep the car running."

I removed my gun and checked the chamber, placing it back in my holster and walking up the stairs to knock.

"He's expecting you," Butler remarked.

I headed toward his office and lightly knocked before pushing the door open.

"Sit," Laurent said.

"What's this about?" I brushed a hand through my hair.

"How are you?" He eyed me up and down.

My brows scrunched in confusion. "Is there a reason for the visit?"

Laurent huffed. "Still the same Axel."

"How else should I be?" I looked at the clock on the wall.

"Did you get the money?"

My phone vibrated. I pulled it out, seeing a message from the team.

Lazaro: *Got it.*

"We have the money." I pocketed the phone.

Laurent's mouth thinned. "More business is coming our way."

"Okay."

"Things are going to change and get busier for you and me." His mouth hardened.

"Busier, how?"

"A few businesses I want to expand. With the upcoming marriage of my daughter and Dario, I think we'll be in a good place."

I paused at the mention of Dario and the deal Laurent made. "Anything else?"

"Are you sleeping at night?" he asked somberly.

My face wrinkled in contempt. "We're not talking about my personal life."

He reached for a cigar. "The anger you hold inside won't just go away."

My face grew warm with shame. "Unless you need anything else—"

A knock at the door interrupted me, and I turned to see the one person who never failed to piss me off.

"Oh, sorry. I thought you were alone," Gigi said, glancing from her father to me.

I looked away, leaning back in the chair.

"Give me a minute, and I'll be out," Laurent replied.

"Excuse me." She pulled the door closed.

"That girl will drive me to an early grave," Laurent complained.

I stood, finally ready to get back to what I loved most.

"I got word you killed some of Casella's men," Laurent stated.

"My job." Color stained my cheeks. I didn't like being questioned about my moves.

"A truce is in place for a reason."

"Then remind his people," I stated, leaving the office and shutting the door behind me.

Marching down the hall, I passed the kitchen, glimpsing Gigi laughing with Ginerva. She caught my stare and quickly turned away.

As soon as I got home, I poured a drink and lit a cigar to ease the adrenaline from the day.

* * *

"Axel, you need to eat your vegetables," Mother complained.

I laughed when my dad made a funny face behind her. "Leave the boy alone," he responded, brushing his lips against her cheek.

"He's spoiled because of you." Mother looked up at him with slight surprise in her eyes.

All eyes moved to the front door as someone knocked. My father rose out of his seat and answered with a nervous smile.

"Mr. Carrington," Father greeted, stepping to the side to allow the man entry.

At ten, I didn't understand what business needed to be conducted at eight at night, but Laurent Carrington was in my home. My father introduced him to my mother, then me, before motioning him to the back office.

My mother snapped her fingers to stop me from staring at the large men in suits standing outside the door. "Finish eating, Axel."

"I'm full. Can I go to my room?" I rubbed my eyes sleepily.

"Fine, but take your bath and go straight to bed."

She picked up my plate, sauntering to the kitchen. I slid out of my seat and plodded down the hall, staring up at each man. Neither said a word, but I heard whispering from the office.

"I can't do that. You're putting too much in without a trail," Father said.

I wondered what he was talking about.

"You can. I believe you're the best. Think about what I said." The door opened, and Laurent looked down at me and smiled. "I'll see you soon," he said, marching out of the house.

"Shit!"

I woke to another reminder from the past I couldn't forget.

I pushed the covers back, stumbled from the bed, and picked up my watch from the nightstand. It was two a.m. I strolled into the bathroom, reached for the light, and splashed water on my face. Seeing the bruises on my knuckles, I clenched and unclenched my fingers to ease the soreness. I popped open the medicine cabinet and took two Advil.

Banging at the front door instantly had me on red alert.

"The fuck?" I stomped out of the bathroom and snatched my gun off the dresser. In only my boxers, I yanked open the door with my gun raised.

"I tried to call but didn't get an answer." Fulgenzio studied my face, then the gun in my hand.

I set the gun on my front counter near the closet. "What are you doing here?"

"One of Laurent's businesses got hit."

Nerves rippled low in my stomach. "Which one?"

"The warehouse where he keeps some of the guns."

I raised a hand and stroked my jaw. "How much did they take?"

"Not sure. Laurent is pissed, and most of the team is there."

"You need to get back to the house. I'll drive myself."

"Yes, sir." He stepped back.

I shut the door and headed to the bedroom. I grabbed a pair of pants and a shirt before hopping in the shower.

Less than thirty minutes later, I arrived out front of the Temple—a nightclub owned by Laurent. He'd built storage units underground to make it easier to transport our merchandise.

Some of his men stood out front, stepping aside as I walked into the deserted club. I noticed Laurent yelling on the phone.

Lamberto took a shot from the bartender. "What do you know?"

I scanned around the room; it felt rigid. "I just got

here." Anger wedged in my throat. Laurent expected me to be ten steps ahead. "Is this the best time to drink?"

Emotion flickered in Lamberto's eyes. I was the only one to get away with questioning him. "It helps calm my nerves. Who do you think hit us?"

His face darkened as he searched the room. His men never saw him agitated. He endeavored to be in control at all times—like me.

"Too early to tell," I answered.

"You tell me the second something is found." Lamberto slammed the glass on the bar.

I scanned the room, picking up a single screw from the dismantled floorthey'd left behind. "Soon as we get the surveillance, we'll have a better idea."

"How much was taken?" Lamberto questioned.

"Laurent doesn't keep a lot here. Only enough for a quick sale," one of the guards said.

"From now on, we need to have extra men on sales," I replied.

"I agree, but Laurent only listens to you," Lamberto commented.

I looked behind as Dario came through the door. "How did this happen?" he demanded.

I shrugged. "I just got the message to come here tonight."

"So you didn't have people at the door?" Dario quizzed.

"That's not my job." I didn't run the day-to-day operations of the club.

Dario huffed, considering my comment. "Laurent is always bringing outside people around."

I clenched my fist.

"Dario, not now," Lamberto replied, clutching his elbow.

"He's the enforcer, right? So enforce security around here. When I take over, this won't happen," Dario emphasized, waving his hands dramatically.

"If that time ever comes, we can have a conversation." I ignored his vile stare at my statement.

"Look, they say it was only a hundred grand, plus a crate of guns," Lamberto said as the door opened to Laurent and his guards.

"Update me with better news," Laurent snapped, folding his arms.

"Fulgenzio told me we got hit, and Lamberto confirmed a crate of AK-47s and a hundred grand."

Laurent glared at Lamberto. "Any idea on who was in charge of the exchange?"

"Dario, you handle the clubs," Lamberto hinted.

Dario glared at him in humiliation. "I put Lazaro to monitor the exchange."

"Lazaro," Laurent responded, glancing at me for confirmation.

I nodded. "He was with me earlier."

Lamberto and Dario had harsh expressions.

"So he didn't come directly here to handle the exchange?" Dario inquired.

I observed the room, noticing the bottles of liquor arranged on the floor exactly where they should be after being brought in, and only a select few had access. "Nothing looks tampered with. If Lazaro is behind anything, I'll catch him."

"Bring him to me now," Laurent demanded, his brows pulling together in a frown.

"I can handle him, Laurent," Dario countered.

That suggestion piqued my curiosity. Lazaro took orders from me on a daily basis unless Laurent specifically gave a direction.

Laurent agreed and faced me. "Get reliable people down here, and I want the footage brought to me only."

Laurent turned and left the room.

"I'll send you the footage," Dario spoke over his shoulder.

Lamberto left the room, and I touched the hardwood floor where the crates were kept. Dario was jealous that Laurent always listened to my advice, and our first meeting had determined the outcome of our relationship.

"Axel, I want you to meet my future son-in-law, Dario Ramini," Laurent introduced.

I nodded in acknowledgment and focused on the meeting. I'd never been a friendly man and wouldn't start now.

Dario dropped his hand, and a few men chuckled at the situation.

"Gigi always talks about the help around the house," Dario taunted, arching a black brow.

Laurent interrupted the unspoken tension between us. "Gentlemen, we have some decisions that need to be made, and I wanted Dario here."

I listened as he paced the office.

"As you all know, Dario is marrying my daughter in the future, which means he will have a position in the family. He comes from a fine family. Edmundo Ramini is a longtime friend and business partner," Laurent explained.

"She's going to be the perfect wife and mother," Dario bragged.

"I want a grandbaby soon." Laurent laughed, causing some of his men to chuckle in response.

I grew bored at Dario kissing ass; most men came in by

working hard and building respect. Dario was trying to get into a top position without earning respect from Laurent's team.

"Anything new we need to be discussing?" I broke up the conversation.

"Axel, always about business. The main reason I requested this meeting was to introduce Dario as an adviser and as the Boss once he marries my daughter. I have a few deals coming up soon with the Casella family." Laurent paused and turned his head.

"They're not reliable, Boss," I said.

"Orson has always been on time with my father," Dario stated, a vein throbbing in his forehead.

"We're talking about the Carrington's. No offense, but your family doesn't have the reach that Laurent is capable of." Dario's eyes darted around the room.

"If you go in with Orson, you have to know the risks," I countered.

"Orson is well known in Italy. We could take the entire area, plus more if we work with Orson," Dario chimed in excitedly.

Laurent sat back in thought.

"Friends end up with more problems that turn into foes. I hate to kill unnecessary things," I mentioned, continuing to take in the conversations around me.

Since that day, Dario and I had been cordial but nothing more, and we hated each other's guts. Laurent was a smart man, but even he had to know that marrying Gigi off to Dario would result in more issues.

When I needed peace and clarity, I visited my parents' gravesite. That was the only place where I could cope with the grief that continued tormenting me after their deaths. It was paralyzing how little things reminded me of their laughs or the times I got into trouble.

I closed my eyes and took in the night air. "I bet you're pissed I came here again after what I've done."

People always said it got better with time, but each day, I grew angrier. Family tried to talk me into speaking with someone, but I felt no one could understand how this world worked. When you lived within the mob, you knew your time could be up at any moment, but I hated it came for my parents. All I had left of them were pictures and a gravesite.

After an hour of staring at their names, I hopped in my car and drove home. My phone rang as soon as I tossed my keys down and removed my jacket. Laurent's name popped up on the screen. Out of respect, I answered immediately and listened to Laurent explain he needed me to check in with Fulgenzio and stay close to the family. Threats had increased against the family, and he didn't want Gigi in harm's way.

I rubbed my forehead to relieve the stress. "I've checked in with Fulgenzio, and he says she only goes to class and hangs with Ginerva."

"She drives me crazy, like her mother."

I put the phone on speaker, removed my watch, and left my shoes at the door. I angled toward the kitchen and lifted a glass, pouring the rest of my brandy. "Boss, I don't trust Lamberto and Dario."

"Do you think I'm stupid?" Laurent probed.

"No." My mouth hardened.

"Good. I have my eyes open, Axel. Never fail to know that I see everything."

I placed the glass in the sink and left the kitchen. "I'll have the footage sent over to you."

"The wedding is coming soon. I need you on top of her security at all times."

I stalked down the hall to my bedroom. "Of course."

I ended the call, placed the phone on the bedside table, and removed my shirt and pants. Shower, then sleep.

Chapter 3

Gigi

A week later.

Ginerva spilled to me about her latest argument with her parents as I walked out of the school building. Everybody was used to the two guards who followed alongside me every day. I watched people, noting the normalcy of folks my age—cuddled up couples in love, doing the usual college routine—made me long for a simpler life.

"Are you done with class now?" Ginerva interrupted my thoughts at the end of the phone.

"Yes, thank God. Do you want to meet for lunch?" I let my guard open my door when we arrived at the car.

"How long will it take? My parents have plans and want me to join," Ginerva whispered.

Fulgenzio turned onto the road, and I put my books down, sliding the seat belt over my shoulder. I noticed a few girls laughing together, and a shot of envy ran through me.

"Hmmm..." I checked my watch. "Maybe twenty minutes if you want to meet at Capri Cafe."

"I think I can pull that off," Ginerva answered.

My phone beeped with an incoming call. "Hold on, Ginerva."

I pulled the phone from my ear and clicked over to my mother's call.

"Hello," she answered.

"Yes, Mother," I responded, checking my nails.

"I need you to meet me somewhere," my mother commanded, trying to run my life as usual.

"Where?"

She hesitated. "Fulgenzio has the address."

I groaned, looking up at him with desperate eyes. "What is going on?"

Often she'd inconvenience me by "bonding" through shared interests, but it was all for her ego. She wanted to be seen as the perfect mother in front of other people.

"Something I should have set up sooner." Her tone seemed truthful.

"I made plans with Ginerva." No matter my excuses, it never changed her mind. My heart beat faster.

Rosa said, "She can come too. I'll send her mother the address."

"Wait! Where is this place?" If Aurora was there, I knew she would tell me to give her a chance to show me her mothering skills.

"Keep an open mind, Gigi."

"That doesn't sound good."

"I'll pretend you didn't say that, but you'll have fun."

I exhaled heavily after she got off the phone. "Where are we going, Fulgenzio?"

He looked at his phone. "The address is a boutique."

"Shopping?" I asked nervously. Mother was judgmental about my clothes.

"Yes, Miss Carrington." Fulgenzio responded.

I relaxed a little. "I told you to call me Gigi."

He grinned and made a turn at the light. "Gigi."

"I'll tip you if we head to Capri's instead." Fulgenzio would never take a bribe from me, but I'd offered many times.

He chuckled. "Sorry. Mrs. Carrington wants me to bring you here."

I sat back in a daze while he passed through long lines of traffic. Mother sets up a situation to blindside me at the worst times to show off in front of her high-profile friends. So many dinners I've had to attend and act like the perfect daughter of Laurent and Rosa Carrington.

We stopped in front of a wedding dress shop, and my brows dropped when I saw my mother wave and open the door.

Rosa's smile was fake. "Hurry up, Gigi."

Fulgenzio started to get out of the car, and I motioned for him to stop. "Stay. I might need you to keep the car running."

He laughed, and Rosa glared at him, which caused him to stop.

I stomped toward the store, and my mouth dropped open as I saw a few cousins and friends sitting with champagne glasses. "What is this?" I motioned with my hand.

"Dress fitting," Mother answered.

A few family members whispered amongst themselves.

"Mother—"

"Stop worrying. You'll fit in everything or lose a few pounds," Rosa said, nudging me forward.

"I had plans." I forced a smile on my lips for appearances.

"Your plans can wait. We need to pick out a dress for your wedding." Rosa swept my hair off my shoulders.

The sales associate walked over to us with a tray of champagne, and I thanked her as I took one. My stomach was in knots at the thought of trying on gowns for a wedding I had no intention of fulfilling.

A rack of gowns came out from the back, and Mother pointed at what she wanted me to try on first. "Here, make sure you suck in your stomach."

I gave her my glass and took the dress out of her hands, heading to the dressing room to change.

"Can we get some more gowns wider in the hip section?" I heard my mother's request.

A few minutes passed before I emerged from the room, maneuvering the long sequined gown with a train and pearls embedded on the sleeves and corset.

A smile spread across my mother's lips. "You look beautiful, but maybe if you lose two or three pounds." She came to stand beside me and held out the train, staring at it with a perplexed look.

"I don't need to lose weight."

"Women in our business have to look a certain way, Gigi. Hold in your stomach." She tapped me on the hip.

"Seriously. I can't do this with you."

"The dress costs seventy thousand, not including the veil and shoes. If you think I'm going to have people talk negatively about how you look in pictures, you've lost your mind," she spat.

"We could try the off-shoulder silk gown," a sales associate suggested.

"How about we don't," I quipped.

Mother glared. "How about we try it on and see?"

I whipped around and went back to change.

The bell rang over the door, and I glanced behind me to see Dario entering.

"Gigi. Mrs. Carrington. Glad to see my soon-to-be bride is close to finding her gown. You look amazing, Gigi," Dario said as he shut the door.

His mother hugged me, then approached Rosa. "Gigi, I must say, my son is going to be very proud to walk down the aisle with you," Mrs. Ramini commented.

I bit the inside of my lip to avoid expressing my disgust. "Don't you know you're not supposed to see the bride in her gown before the wedding?" I snapped.

Dario covered his snarl with a smirk and reached out to hug me. "Behave," he whispered in my ear, pinching my side.

"She's technically right, but he brought his mother, and I didn't think it would hurt," Mother said, patting him on the arm.

"How many times do I have to tell you to stay out of my affairs?" A flame rose in my stomach.

My mother frowned. "Gigi, not today. You're standing in the middle of a dress shop in a gown. It should be a fun day."

"Yeah, fun." I grabbed the train and turned to change into the next prison apparel.

* * *

Mother picked out her favorites and told them I would lose three pounds in time for the wedding. Dario promised to help me lose the weight. I wanted to scream for everybody to leave me alone, but I played nice long enough to get out of there. I put my shades on and left with Dario on my heels.

"Slow down." Dario gripped my elbow, but I snatched it away.

"You can stop pretending to be nice. They're still inside gossiping." I turned, falling into a hard chest.

"Sorry." I glanced up into Axel's sharp, cold eyes.

"You all right?" His warm hand touched my hip.

I looked down at his hand, and he removed it swiftly.

"Why wouldn't she be?" Dario extended a hand around my waist.

"I don't know what to do with her." My mother's voice pulled me from my daze, and I stepped out of Dario's grasp.

"I can say the same," I mumbled under my breath. I went to the car and pulled out my phone to call Ginerva.

"Bored already?" Ginerva laughed on the phone.

I watched through the window as Dario and his mother talked with Axel. "Beyond bored. Guess where I am and who showed up?"

"Who?"

"Dress fitting for the wedding, and Dario brought his mother."

"Maybe you should try to make the best of things," Ginerva said.

I balked at the statement. "So, give up?"

"Not give up, but see if you can have input in what you want for the wedding and marriage."

"We're talking about Rosa Carrington."

Dario hugged my mother and opened the car door to speak to me.

"Hold on." I covered the phone with my hand.

"I want to take you to lunch tomorrow," Dario stated in a silky tone.

"I'm busy." I turned away.

"Gigi, either way, I'll see you tomorrow. Did you forget I practically grew up around your family, and your mother likes to impress?" Dario taunted.

My cheeks burned as his eyes swept over me. "Visit if you want. Doesn't mean I'll be there."

Ginerva giggled in my ear.

"Who are you talking to on the phone?" Dario asked.

"We're not married yet. You don't need to screen my calls," I snapped.

Dario moved back to let my mother get in the car.

"See you soon!" Mother waved at them.

"Yeah, Ginerva." I ignored my mother.

"Tell Ginerva you'll call her back," Mother said, turning to face me.

"Can't this wait for when we get home?"

Her brow wrinkled. "No."

"Talk to her," Ginerva suggested.

"Tomorrow. Don't forget." I reminded her.

I finished the call and stared off into the traffic. A headache was forming and would only worsen the longer I was in my mother's presence.

Mother turned up her nose. "You've embarrassed me, Gigi. I wish you would understand your place."

I pointed at myself. "My place?"

"As a mother and a wife, I am expected to teach you how to raise your household."

My next words spilled from my lips. "Aurora did that."

Mother shook her head. "School was a mistake. I might have to talk to your father."

She would use anything she could to manipulate me, like throwing school in my face. "You wouldn't dare."

"Give me a reason I should keep letting you slide."

"Mother—"

"Oh, *now* I'm 'mother?' What happened to Rosa?"

I sighed and caved to her ego. "I liked the silk gown with the ruffles.".

She grinned. "Good. That was my favorite." She lifted my chin and stared into my eyes.

"We still have time to change our minds, but you need to lose a little weight."

"I'd planned to go to lunch with Ginerva, but she's busy. Do you want to come with me instead?" I asked, playing into her hands. She hated when I gave others more attention than her, especially my loyalty to Ginerva and the number of secrets I dumped on her instead of my mother.

"Lunch would be good. My treat." Mother stretched her arm around my shoulder.

"You mean Dad's treat."

We burst into laughter. While the moment was nice, I thought back to when I was younger and tried to ask my mother about her life growing up in America. We rarely saw her family. I had memories of her flying back and forth and a few brief phone calls, but my father mentioned the deep hatred some felt at the marriage. If I'd grown up during their time, would I have had the courage to make those same decisions?

Chapter 4

Axel

The following day.

I pushed my sleeve back to check the time on my watch. It was unbearable dealing with Gigi when she was in her shopping mood. We'd spend all day going from one store to the next, carrying multiple bags.

Laurent Carrington elected me as the enforcer of the Carrington Cartel a few years ago when he caught me stealing from one of his men. I was nineteen, and trying to get money to survive after my parents died in a car crash. Well, that's what I was told, but I knew it was a mob hit.

The door opened, and Gigi walked out with Dario behind her. The soon-to-be-married couple clearly weren't on the same page.

I thought we would have a drama-free day without problems, but then I saw Dario grab her arm. She tried to smack him, and he caught her wrist. Gigi had her faults, but no one put their hands on her.

I started to get out of the car when the door opened and Gigi's friend came out. Dario released her wrist and stepped back, allowing them to come down the stairs before he got in a separate car. Dario pulled off while I held the door open for Gigi. Our eyes connected, and she briefly smiled.

I shut the door, then came around to get in the front passenger seat. Fulgenzio, her driver, started the car, heading out of the compound. I respected Laurent because he'd saved me and put me in a position to become my own man. Some of his men hated me, along with a few rival families, because I could have become the Underboss at thirty-four. But I liked not having to deal with the politics of the cartel world. My goal as enforcer was to make things go away without leaving a trace. I was good at that.

I glanced in the rearview mirror and saw Gigi and Ginerva whispering back and forth. Gigi still had a lot to learn, and it didn't help that she rebelled against her family's rules.

"Maybe you should tell your mother," Ginerva stated.

Gigi shook her head. "Be for real, Ginerva. My mother would throw me under the bus."

I could relate to being an only child, but how she handled her parents would never have been tolerated by mine. My father was strict but had an open-door policy that I could come to him about anything. Plus, my mother was my best friend.

"Either you speak up now, or you're walking down the aisle with that scumbag, Dario," Ginerva stated.

Fulgenzio approached a red light, and I turned in my seat to pause their conversation. "When we get in the store, try not to spend all day. I have another appointment I have to handle."

"Don't you work for me?" Gigi tilted her head and smirked.

I pulled my shades down slightly to make eye contact.

"I work for no one, Gigi." I slid them back up to cover my eyes and turned to face forward.

"That's what you get." Ginerva giggled and poked Gigi in the arm, who swatted her hand away.

I smirked in satisfaction. We usually kept things light between us. She knew not to pull that Carrington Boss role on me. All the other men cowered, but I pushed back. One reason could be her intimidating beauty. I found her exquisite, with her deep-set, concrete-green eyes, catlike facial structure, and tawny skin.

"The engagement dinner is soon, right? You might as well force their hand." Ginerva drew my focus away from Gigi.

"I don't know. It's like suddenly, what I want in my life doesn't matter. My father's making me do this."

We arrived at the mall, and I stepped out to open their door, helping them out. Gigi swished into the mall, with Fulgenzio in the front, while I stayed back. We constantly told Laurent that having detail stationed at locations would be better. I greeted our men with a nod, and they tipped their chins up in acknowledgment.

Gigi laughed about something, bringing my focus back to the women.

"And it's only pissing me off even more because they know this isn't what I want. I need to talk to him again," Gigi stated, entering the Louis Vuitton store.

A sales associate came around the counter, extending a tray of champagne for Gigi and Ginerva. "Miss Carrington, nice to see you again."

Gigi took the glass off the tray. "Miccuia, nice to see you again. Did you get my message about pulling some looks for me?"

"Yes, we have everything in the dressing room for you." Miccuia turned and placed the tray on the table.

"Ginerva, are you getting anything?"

"Probably. I have to pick something for my date next week," she responded, standing and following Gigi to the dressing room.

"Follow them," I commanded, sliding my hand into my pocket to take out my phone.

"Hopefully, she won't keep us here all day. Boss has a meeting tonight," Fulgenzio said, marching to the dressing room.

I scanned the text message from Mr. Carrington.

Boss: *Axel, make sure Gigi doesn't cause any problems. We don't need any bad press before the announcement.*

Me: *Gigi plays by her rules, but I'll try.*

Boss: *My daughter is special but extremely spoiled.*

Me: *You created a monster.*

Boss: *That I did.*

The dressing room door opened, and I lifted my head to see Gigi stroll in wearing a long silk ball gown. I didn't know all the different styles of dresses, but this one caused a flutter in my chest. Something about the curves of her hips and the sway of her arms when she planted them on her small waist. She was only five foot five compared to my six-one height, and it could be said she would bring any man to his knees with her full lips, voluptuous curves, and plump breasts. It would never work between us; not only was she Laurent's daughter, but she was young and had goals of living in America and seeing the world. I was there to protect—at all times—the Carrington Cartel. I would never hold her back from her future, and I refused to give up the pledge I made to

Laurent and the cartel, but I knew she and I had a connection.

Gigi turned left to right in front of me as she posed. "Do you think it's too much?"

My eyes locked on her delicate, manicured hands.

"Hello, Axel?" Gigi waved a hand in my face.

"Yeah, what was that?" I cleared my throat, not up to holding a long conversation after another sleepless night.

Gigi looked confused. "I said, do you think it's too much?"

She turned around to show the back, and she was bare from the top of her shoulders to the curve of her plush ass.

It annoyed me that another man would see her in the dress, but I quickly reigned in my thoughts. "Only you can make that determination."

There was an excited catch in her voice. "But I want a guy's opinion."

I knew what she was doing. "If you were mine, I would say yes; it's too much."

"Really? You don't think I look cute in the dress?" As usual, she fished for compliments from me to prolong a conversation.

"I think you need Ginerva's opinion more than mine."

Gigi sauntered over to me, closing the distance. "I want your opinion," she muttered, staring into my eyes.

She often tried to challenge me, and I ignored her little flirtations.

"Gigi, what do you—" Ginerva interrupted, breaking our intense gaze as we turned to look at her.

"Ginerva, do you think this is too much?" Gigi spun around, posing for her.

Ginerva looked from Gigi to me.

"It looks good on you, but your father will have a heart attack." Ginerva glanced at me as Gigi walked away to change.

"You're right. I have to be prim and proper." Gigi lifted the bottom of the gown, sauntering off.

"She's about to be engaged," Ginerva said.

My head whipped around to face her. "Very aware, Ginerva." I was unsure if she'd fabricated something between Gigi and me, but she was my boss's daughter and nothing more.

Ginerva smiled. Without hesitation, she said, "You like her?"

"She's the daughter of my boss. Not having this conversation."

"If it matters, I think Dario is only using her." Ginerva looked over her shoulder, then back at me.

"Not my business."

Ginerva shrugged and went back to the dressing room.

* * *

People murmured around the table, and laughter and shouts from some family members greeted Laurent and his wife. After a mundane afternoon of Gigi having us go in and out of four different stores, she finally picked a dress suitable for the evening that wouldn't cause an argument between her parents.

I stood next to Laurent, observing the crowd that included a few familiar faces. He'd told me to sit and relax for the night, but there was no time clock in my job.

Loyalty was something I would give willingly to Laurent, and that meant always being vigilant.

Tonight's celebration with Dario and Gigi seemed extremely fake. She sat beside him but kept her body turned toward her mother or talked to Ginerva. Every time Dario took her hand, she swiftly moved it out of his reach.

Dario and I didn't get along because I knew what kind of snake he was and how he was only doing this to become the Boss of all the families. Laurent was too blind to see Dario's intent to change his plans and put Ramini as the top family in charge once he retired.

Candles flickered on the tables, and the lighting was dim. A few servers arrived with food for the table, and Laurent stood up with a glass in his hand to make a toast.

"Everyone, I would like to say a few words," he said, reaching down to cup Gigi's chin.

She smiled, but it didn't reach her eyes. I clenched my teeth and felt a hand on my shoulder. I turned to see the Underboss, Lamberto.

"Come with me," Lamberto commanded.

I glanced back at the table, motioning for Fulgenzio to take my spot. We walked to the back of the restaurant, through the kitchen, and into the manager's office.

"What's wrong?" I crossed my arms over my chest.

"The delay in the shipment tonight. We need you to go check and make sure nothing is hindering," Lamberto said.

"Now?" My brow spiked at the statement.

"Laurent only trusts you, and I agree. This is a delicate situation." Lamberto fixed his eyes around the room and never on me.

"Why not send Lazaro or Sandro?" Some of our foot soldiers could check into something this small.

"They are there already, but if our shipment gets stolen, Laurent will be pissed," Lamberto said, his voice holding an edge.

I blew out a breath, running a hand through my hair. It was getting longer and would fall in my eyes if I didn't get it cut. "All right. I need to let Laurent know."

"I can do that," Lamberto replied.

"As Laurent's enforcer, I want to ensure he's protected at all times."

Lamberto held his hands up in surrender. Most times, I wouldn't push back on other people doing recon for situations like this, but Lamberto and I weren't on the best of terms. He'd wanted to be the Boss after his father retired and thought Laurent wouldn't last as long as he had in the position as the Don of the family. They were cousins, but not as close as regular family members.

I marched out of the office and back to the table, where everybody cheered Dario and Gigi while he held her hand up with the engagement ring.

Laurent kissed his wife, then grabbed her palm and kissed the back of her hand.

I bent down to whisper in his ear. "Lamberto told me about the issue. I have someone covering me while I check on the shipment."

Laurent nodded and clapped me on the back. "I trust you to ensure we are on the right track, Axel."

"Always, Boss." I stood to leave and caught Gigi's stare.

My commitment was to the family, and I couldn't abandon it for anyone—including her. Once a man fell in love, his senses betrayed him, and he was vulnerable to his enemies. We both knew she shouldn't stay with Dario, but he was a safer bet compared to the unpredictability of my life.

"Do you need backup?" Laurent asked.

I shook my head. "Lamberto told me Lazaro and Sandro are there."

I headed out of the restaurant, hopped in the awaiting Jaguar, and pulled a cigar out of my pocket.

"Those things will kill you." Turin flicked the lighter, and I puffed on the cigar, exhaling the stress away.

"Better than someone," I responded, checking to see if I had a text message from Lazaro.

"So, what are we supposed to be doing?"

Turin was the only person I could call a friend and brother throughout my time in the cartel. Many times we'd battled for survival and won to make it to the top. As soon as I came up, I brought him with me as my right hand. He was the one who brought me back from the edge whenever we needed to get rid of someone—a job that always unleashed my bloodlust. Where Turin was a straight shooter, I gave people false hope, thinking they would live until that last second—and then I slit their throat.

"Lamberto said something is up with the shipment."

"Does Laurent know?" Turin was the type to investigate every angle before attacking.

"He was the one that wanted us to check it out."

"Lamberto told you that?" Turin asked.

I rubbed my chin, puffing on the cigar again. "What are you saying?"

"Nothing. Lamberto hates us, so I'm surprised he even talked to you."

In Lamberto's eyes, Turin and I should be replaced because Laurent trusted us too much.

"Laurent probably told him to pull his panties out of his ass." I chuckled.

Turin laughed and sped up. It was only nine at night, so most of the streets were empty. Thirty minutes later, we reached the abandoned building Laurent bought a few years back. I went to open the door, but my phone rang. I put it on silent, slid it into my pocket, and shut the door after me. Lifting my gun from the holster, I double-checked the clip as Lazaro and Sandro approached.

"How's it going?" Lazaro asked, tugging at his beard.

"You tell me. Lamberto said you two were fucking up." I held my gun at my side.

"Axel, we just got the information," Lazaro replied.

"Which is?" I challenged.

A few rumors had circulated that Lazaro had gotten too high with power.

"Fifty caseloads of weapons should be here, and the guys who came only brought twenty," Lazaro pointed out.

"Whose job was it to double-check the order?" I glanced from Lazaro to Sandro.

"Lamberto told us it was fine," Sandero informed me.

My brow hiked at his answer.

"Lamberto told you to take whatever they gave you?" Turin repeated.

"Yeah, we were told to wait here," Sandro said.

"By Lamberto?" Turin was good at sniffing out liars. He'd rub his chin while he smiled at them to make them feel comfortable. Right now, he seemed relaxed, with no alarm bells, so I positioned my gun back in my holster.

"Are the men still here?" I queried, walking toward the building.

The place displayed a meat packing sign, the front for his money laundering. The land it sat on covered two acres and had mostly abandoned homes nearby. Turin opened the door, and Lazaro and Sandro came in behind us as we stared at our guys packing the guns.

"Stop what you're doing!" I demanded.

All voices quieted as I looked around the room from the doorway.

"Who are you?" responded a tall man with a large, round gut spilling over his pants.

I wanted to bust him in the mouth. "I ask the questions. My guys say you're short by thirty crates."

"I brought what I was told to bring," the fat fuck responded, waving me off.

I hated being ignored or dismissed. My response to their disrespect crept into my voice. "By whom, exactly?"

"Lamberto. It's all laid out in my form." His hand went into his pocket, and my men pulled out their guns.

His hands rose in the air. "Hold on, fellas. Let me grab the order sheet."

I motioned for my men to stand down. "What's your name?"

"Alvar. I work for the Casella family."

Alvar passed the paper to me. I looked it over and saw exactly twenty meat orders to be delivered.

"What does it say?" Turin asked.

"Lamberto and Laurent, what are you up to?" I muttered to myself. It wasn't like Laurent to go along with something Lamberto cooked up.

"Are we good?" Alvar asked.

I grinned, folding the sheet and giving it back to him. I clapped him on the back. "We're always good, Alvar."

He turned away, and I reached into my holster, cocked my gun, and shot him in the back of the head.

"What the fuck?" Lazaro shouted, jumping back.

"Pack up everything, and we will meet tomorrow," I instructed.

I stomped out of the warehouse, pissed because someone was lying to me, and I didn't know why. Patience was something I didn't have, thanks to the constant dreams every other night. Laurent was probably too full of excitement over the wedding to talk business right now.

I slammed the car door and Turin hopped in the driver's seat.

"Did you have to kill him?" Turin asked, shaking his head.

A van pulled up to the back of the door to dispose of anything left behind.

"*Merda!*" I cursed, slamming my hand on the window.

"Casella's family will want answers about Alvar," Turin pointed out.

"He's worthless to them."

"Axel Bresciani, you need to focus. We have enough problems with the other families trying to take Laurent's position when he retires." Turin said, his expression disgruntled. He backed up out of the gravel, turned the radio down, and sped away.

"I think something is going on and they want me here." I settled in my seat, recalling the last few meetings in my head as Turin hit the gas.

"Have you been sleeping?"

I ignored his question. "When we get back to the restaurant, I need to talk to Laurent." I took out my phone and turned it back on to see multiple missed calls and text messages. "Something happened." I clicked on Gigi's voice message.

Turin continued out of the area to get us back to the restaurant.

Gigi's screamed message came through the phone. "Axel, where are you? They shot at my dad and we're on our way to the hospital."

I quickly dialed her number.

Gigi picked up right away. "Something's happened to my dad."

I slammed my hand on the dashboard. "Fuck! Are you hurt?"

"No! I don't give a fuck... It's my phone," Gigi argued with someone. The phone call ended abruptly.

"Gigi! Gigi!" I tried redialing her number, but it went straight to voicemail.

"What happened?" Turin asked grimly.

Everybody was on my distrust list now. "Someone took a shot at Laurent."

"What! They know it's a death sentence to go after the boss," Turin spat.

My hand was itching to kill everyone. "Just hurry and get us to the hospital."

Turin fought through traffic, while my mind replayed the fear in Gigi's at the thought of her father getting hurt. Gigi was headstrong, spoiled, and opinionated, but she loved her parents. I prayed he pulled through because there would be hell to pay otherwise. The streets loved Laurent more than any Don we'd had in the past. No matter the deaths he'd sanctioned, people respected him.

Despite the back-and-forth between Gigi and me, she knew I was the only person she could rely on to handle this discreetly. Laurent had embedded the idea that I wasn't a lost cause after my parents were gone. He gave his time and advice freely, pushing me to look into a legit life. I'd always made it known he had my full loyalty wherever I was in life. Besides Turin, Laurent was the only other person who knew about my sleepless nights and graveyard visits.

Chapter 5

Gigi

One hour earlier.

After my father's toast, I held a fake smile on my face and grinned as people came up to us to extend congratulations on the engagement. Dario ate it up and ensured I played my role. Anytime I didn't speak or give him attention, he squeezed my thigh or hand under the table.

Like right now. As my father sat down to talk to my mother, Dario leaned over to cup my hand, and I moved it out of his reach. The public perception was that we were in love and happy, but behind closed doors, I couldn't stand the man. If I could get away with killing him before the wedding, I would. Everybody knew Dario was trying to position himself as Boss once my father retired. Many times he'd said it would be in my best interest to go along with the wedding because marriage wasn't about love but a partnership to get to the top.

I examined the guests and my eyes fell on *him* again, standing behind my dad as his protector and guard. Axel Bresciani was a six-foot-one, sexy asshole with a god complex I hated but loved at the same time. In the beginning, when my father brought him around, I was young and still in high school and had no business crushing on my dad's henchman. One look at Axel and all of his rules went out the window. I tried to always be in his presence, and he stared at me when he thought I wasn't looking. Whenever his eyes were on me, my heart pounded and butterflies erupted in my stomach. If Dario was around, Axel's mouth always curled in disgust. I never said anything and thought his jealousy was cute. But when I tried to flirt, he shot me down. I was younger at twenty-two, but I was also the daughter of his boss and technically untouchable. That only fueled my desire and need for him. I had a plan tonight to get him alone for a few minutes, but Lamberto approached and tapped him on the shoulder.

I sat back in my chair and played with my food.

"You can at least look happy," Mother whispered.

"I am happy. See?" I put on a fake smile, cupping my chin with both hands.

"Soon as this wedding is over, you'll thank me," Mother said, rubbing my arm.

"Doubt it," I mumbled, despite my best efforts not to bitch.

"Ladies and gentlemen, I'd like to make a toast." Dario rose out of his seat and knew more bullshit was about to come out of his mouth.

I would respect him more if he'd do like other husbands and stay away from the wives. Every other day, his mother planned something for us to do as a couple. I explained I had a life outside of her son, but she always called me a silly young girl.

"Laurent and Rosa, I truly want to thank you for creating a beautiful woman because my future wife is gorgeous, smart, and caring. I hope our life reflects the love our parents have." Dario smiled and raised his glass, and everybody clapped and cheered.

My mother jumped up in excitement and pulled me up by my arm to nudge me toward him.

"Don't make me look ridiculous. Kiss me," Dario growled in my ear.

I grinned, pecking him on the lips, and he gripped the back of my head to force his tongue down my throat.

"That's my boy!" Edmundo Ramini yelled loudly and whistled at us.

"Save it for the honeymoon, son," Father teased.

I jerked away, reaching for my purse to go to the restroom.

Dario gripped my elbow, turning me around to face him. "Where are you going?"

"To the bathroom. Is that okay, Sir?" I challenged. He knew I didn't like to be manhandled or treated like some dutiful wife. I wasn't married to his ass yet.

Dario smiled. "Of course, dear. Take my mother with you."

"I don't need a babysitter."

"Either she goes or you don't." Dario glared at me.

"Fine, I'll sit back down." I huffed, plopping down in my seat.

"More wine for everyone!" Father shouted.

"Laurent!" a gravelly voice shouted right before all hell broke loose.

Gunshots rang out and the guests screamed, running for safety. All I could do was watch as bullets tore through my father's chest and he fell backward. Someone grabbed my arm and pulled me to the ground.

"My father! Let me go!" I screamed, trying to get up to help him.

"Gigi! Shut up! We're under attack." Dario tried to soothe me as more gunshots echoed around the room.

"Get away from me! I want my mom and dad." I tried to push him off me, but he wouldn't budge.

Babies cried and women yelled for help. Time stood still until the gunshots stopped.

"Move! I want to see my dad."

"Your place is at my side," Dario said in a menacing tone.

* * *

When I came up from behind the table, I crawled toward my father. His eyes looked lifeless and tears stained his cheeks. There was so much blood that I didn't know how many times he was shot. I glanced around the room and couldn't see Axel, so I knew something was off about this hit.

Dario wouldn't let me ride in the ambulance. My mother agreed I should ride with him and show that our union was solid. The last thing on my mind was Dario or the public's awareness of how in love we were—which was a load of shit.

The nurses and doctors were taking forever to come and tell us what was going on with my dad. Dario's mother and father sat with my mom while we waited, and most of our family and friends were there.

Dario got in my face as I tried to call Axel. I ignored him until he snatched my phone from my hands.

"Give me back my phone." I tried to grab it out of his hand, but he slid it into his pocket.

Dario stood in front of me with his arm around my waist to show he was comforting me. "Who were you on the phone with?"

"None of your business."

"My love, do you really think you're smarter than me?" he challenged.

Our eyes connected.

If he wasn't so evil, he'd be a good catch.

There was a devil behind those crystal blue eyes; everything revolved around him and if you challenged him, you were an enemy.

I frowned uneasily. "I was talking to Ginerva."

A devilish smirk tugged at the corner of his stern mouth. "You expect me to believe that?"

"I don't care what you believe," I snapped

"Keep your voice down," he commanded.

"My father is fighting for his life and you want me to play along with your little game?" I glowered at him.

"As the future wife of the Ramini family, I expect you to do what I say," he said with his trademark haughty grin.

"Whatever, Dario." I walked around him and went to sit beside my mother.

"If anything happened to him, it would be all over the news," Mother muttered.

I wiped the tears off my face and rested my head on her shoulder.

"What were you talking with Dario about?" she queried.

"Nothing."

"You should be over there with him. It will look better to be near your fiancé," Mother preached. "As our daughter, your life is mapped out for you."

"We need to focus on Father right now."

"Dario is your future husband."

"I don't love him." Arranged marriages were outdated to my generation.

She lifted my chin. "Gigi, you need to be in his arms for comfort. You have to show a

united front."

"I'm not going over there. Besides, he's probably talking about who's responsible for this hit."

Suddenly, butterflies swarmed in my stomach. I looked up and there he was. Dario didn't have one-tenth of his looks.

Axel was here.

I wanted to run to him. Have him hold me in his arms, but I knew that would look suspicious, and not only because we weren't in a relationship. I was the daughter of the mob boss, and Alex was the enforcer. It was all kinds of wrong.

"Oh, there's Axel," Mother said.

Sweat formed on my palms, and my stomach knotted.

Axel walked over and bent to cup Mother's hands, his attention fixed on her. "What happened?"

That was the million-dollar question.

His eyes flickered from my mother to me. My mouth opened and closed. I wanted so badly to touch him, to be in his arms. He reached out and grabbed my hand.

I closed my eyes as a tear rolled down my cheek. "I don't know. We were all eating and laughing. Suddenly, a man called out Laurent's name and shots were fired."

"Axel, find out what happened," my mother demanded.

He responded, "I will."

"This can't be seen as a weakness for our family." Mother narrowed her eyes at Axel.

His stare was intense. "You don't have to worry, Mrs. Carrington. I'll take care of this personally."

I felt like I couldn't breathe. Nothing made sense without my father.

"Gigi, how are you?" Axel asked gently.

My gaze fixed on him. "I'm not handling it very well."

"Mrs. Carrington."

We all looked at Doctor Zappa as he approached us. My heart beat fast and I tried to steady my breathing, leaning into my mother.

"Is my father okay?"

All the family waited in anticipation.

The doctor shook his head and lowered his eyes. "I'm sorry, Mrs. Carrington. We tried everything we could, but one bullet hit his heart."

She froze. "What do you mean?"

I gripped her hand tight and shoved him back. "Where's my father?"

"We can speak privately." He gestured toward the hallway leading to his office.

"Get back there. Right now," I demanded. "You can still save him."

"I'm sorry. We did everything we could, but there was too much blood loss," he said.

I shook my head. "No, I don't believe you."

He slid his hands in his pockets, then sighed.

The doctor was wrong. "Do you know who my father is?"

"Miss Carrington. My team—"

"Do you?" I cut him off.

Seconds ticked by before he responded. "We tried everything." Doctor Zappa raked his eyes from my mother, then toward me.

Before I realized what I was doing, I swiped my hand across his face. "Get back there and save him or I swear to God, you will find out what the Carringtons can do."

The room went silent.

"Gigi, stop it." A look of embarrassment crossed Mother's face as she pinned me with a glare.

My head whipped around to avoid her eyes. She'd pay him off and have a new wing opened up at the hospital to make my outburst go away.

"Doctor, we understand. You did everything you could. Please excuse my daughter's behavior," Mother pleaded, walking away with him.

I jumped in front of her. "Are you crazy?"

"We're in public, so please be respectful," she murmured.

"Your husband is dead," I argued, close to dropping into a ball on the floor and crying in pain.

"Honey, these are the best doctors in the world."

"This is a serious matter, don't you think?" I probed.

"Gigi, I did not mean it that way. It's not okay for you to threaten people."

I pointed at the doctor. "My father is still alive. Do your job. Go back and help him," I screamed, shoving him in the arm.

The waiting room full of people hung on his next words. "Miss Carrington, there's nothing else we could do. Again, I'm sorry for your loss."

"Thank you," Mother whispered.

My shoulders dropped in agony. "Can I see his body?"

The doctor looked at my mother, then at me.

"There's no need for you to see him. Remember your father the way he was." Mother rubbed my back.

"I want to see him."

"I'm his wife. I say leave it alone," Mother remarked, folding her arms.

"No."

My head whipped back as she slapped me. "Are you out of your mind?" I gasped, covering my cheek.

The entire room went silent.

"Rest is what you need. You'll be driven home by Axel," my mother told me, wiping her nose with the Kleenex.

"You're unbelievable!" I snatched my arm out of her hold.

"I'll take her," Axel said in a raspy voice.

"I don't need your help," I snapped, stomping out of the hospital.

I pointedly ignored Dario and his parents. Seeing Fulgenzio near the entrance, I marched over and demanded to leave.

Fulgenzio blinked in confusion, his eyebrows bunched together. "Miss Carrington, we need to wait for—"

"I'm giving you an order. Follow it, or I'll fire you," I hissed, slamming my hand on the window.

I felt his presence behind me before he reached to open the passenger side door. Breathing became difficult. I shook my hands, rubbing each wrist, and closed my eyes, opening them after a few minutes.

Axel leaned around me and pulled the door open further.

I looked over my shoulder.

His eyes stayed on me. "I'm taking you home."

I nodded and climbed inside.

Axel shut the door, coming around to the driver's side.

Fulgenzio greeted him briefly, they shook hands, and he walked into the hospital.

Axel got in the driver's side and shut the door.

I tugged on my seat belt. "What about Turin?"

He put the key in the ignition, ignoring my question. "Tell me exactly what you remember."

Nervousness clouded my mind. "Everything happened so fast. One minute, people were laughing and excited. Next minute, the whole place was blazing with gunshots."

He pinched the bridge of his nose. "I'll find out what happened."

I cleared my throat. "Where are you taking me?"

"Home," he replied, avoiding my eyes.

When Fulgenzio drove me around, we talked, or he listened to me gripe about my parents. Whenever I was around Axel, his presence stunned me to where he rendered me mute.

My lip trembled. "I want to go with you."

"No."

"Axel, I'm not a child."

He pulled over to the side of the road, parked the car, and turned in his seat to face me. I blinked several times as I contemplated what to say. In my heart, I knew he thought I wasn't the right person to look into my father's death.

"Understand me clearly. You're engaged." His words stung.

"I'm not marrying him."

"You have to. It's the life you're meant to have." His eyes darted around the area.

"Fuck you, Axel!"

When I raised my hand to smack him, he grabbed it,

pulling me close to his chest. He stared at my lips, then my eyes. Was he going to kiss me? Caught in his intense gaze, I felt tempted to close the gap between us. I knew he knew what I wanted, and while my feelings were coming at a difficult time after receiving news of my father's death, I sought comfort from him. Our connection was unaffected by the passing cars and the flashing lights of the second guard car behind us.

"Axel."

My phone vibrated, but I ignored the call. Whether it was my mother or Ginerva, this was the first time I'd been alone with Axel in a long time.

Chapter 6

Axel

I couldn't deny my attraction to her, but I would no longer be objective the moment we went there. I would become possessive of her.

"*Splendida donna*," I mumbled under my breath in thick Italian.

My parents raised me to speak both my native Italian and English. I spent time in America and made friends, plus some enemies. When Laurent had Gigi go alone to Joaquin and Sofia's party, I was able to catch up with Joaquin. He was a friend before and after my parents died. We'd worked together on some deals that needed a special touch.

Once my parents died, I pushed everyone away and became hollow and bitter. The *policia* didn't work hard enough to discover why someone wanted to kill my parents, and I'd struggled to find the answers alone.

So I raised myself not to get close to people, and I respected Laurent when he didn't kill me after I was caught snooping around his business. He brought me in and molded me to work alongside him, to be his eyes and ears when he couldn't see the enemy coming.

I could sense my actions confused Gigi. She was a gorgeous woman and always brought out the beast in me, to where I started talking in my native tongue.

"I'm taking you home. Extra men will be on guard to keep watch. It's the only way to keep you safe until we find out everything."

I turned around, putting the car in drive to head home.

"Either you take me with you, or I'll sneak out. I have my ways, Axel," she sassed.

"Do you talk to your fiancé like this?" The word fiancé made her wince, and I wanted to take it back, but she pushed my buttons.

"He's not my fiancé. You know I don't love him."

"Gigi, you know we can't be together." I focused on the men behind us to avoid being distracted. Turin and I would need to rehash with Rosa what she saw tonight.

"Why? I see how you look at me. It's not a one-way attraction."

Laurent had my loyalty, but falling in love with a woman would never happen. I lacked any meaningful emotions beyond my job as an enforcer. A relationship would demand too much of me. I couldn't imagine being vulnerable, showing someone I cared, and then losing it all.

"I work for your father. The entire family and Carrington organization would have me killed if I touched you."

"If you're too chickenshit to give into your feelings, that's on you. You're older than me, and yet you act like a child. I guess I expected more from you."

I parked the car as we arrived at the family estate. "My only job is to protect you and find out what happened to your father. That's it."

Gigi didn't respond. She shoved the door open and jumped out before I could catch her.

I slammed my hand against the steering wheel. "Fuck!"

I wanted to chase after her, but I needed to focus. It wasn't long before the car behind me honked to see what I was planning to do next, but I couldn't focus on anything but Gigi's angry outburst.

I ran a hand through my hair. "Fuck! Fuck!"

My phone rang, and I removed it from my jacket. "Yeah."

"Where are you?" Turin asked.

"I just dropped Gigi at home." I glanced around the massive yard. Laurent and Rosa updated the place recently to include a small pond near the guard gate.

"Are we meeting?"

"Gather all the men at headquarters and find out where Lamberto is. He never showed up at the hospital." We couldn't go back to the crime scene. It would still be fresh. Police on our payroll should give up some information.

"I'm on it," Turin replied.

I looked toward the house, my eyes trailing to the third level of the sprawling estate. A light came on in her room that faced the front of the house. My distraction was cut short when car lights flashed behind me.

Mrs. Carrington briefly talked to Fulgenzio, and I took that as the moment to leave and meet Turin and the team.

Thirty minutes later, I pulled up to the Carrington

office building. I jumped out, raced inside, and headed toward the executive suite. Laurent had some legit businesses, and one was real estate. It wouldn't be too obvious with us meeting here at night because his team often worked long hours.

My eyes were drawn to the conference room once I left the elevator. Several of his men were gathered around Lazaro and Sandro, who were seated. Anyone who looked away from me told me something. I had a strong sense that this was an inside job.

When I saw Dario sitting at the table, I paused. "What are you doing here?"

The question brought a smirk to his lips. "I thought it was important that I sat in on this meeting." He leaned back in his chair like he needed to ensure I knew how to do my job.

"Mrs. Carrington told you to come." I never needed guidance on how to do my job when I received an assignment.

"Laurent meant a lot to me. He was like a father. Gigi is worried. Now I want to make sure we find the people who did this," Dario remarked.

I studied him as I listened to his words. Something told me it was all for show. I cleared my throat and pushed my hands into my pockets to control the urge to hurt him. I couldn't react in haste.

"Tell me what happened. What did you see, Dario?"

"Not much. I was talking to my father and Gigi when everything went crazy, I covered Gigi."

His words played over in my head. "Why wasn't he protected? I left my men with him," I challenged to see if anyone would come forward.

"That's a good question, Axel. Since you're an

enforcer, you're in charge. Why weren't your men trained up? I know everything that's going on. Once I take over, we're going to do some reshuffling," Dario said, trying to intimidate me in front of my men.

Laurent explained a while back that Dario and Gigi's relationship was purely business. Yes, he loved his daughter, but she needed to marry into another family to continue their legacy.

"The Carrington and Ramini family are coming together as one," Dario preached.

Suddenly, the door opened. Lamberto entered the room with his guards and took a seat .

"You're late." I was the only one that could get away with questioning him.

Lamberto was the Underboss. If I discovered he was behind the shooting, there would be hell to pay.

"I just came from the hospital. Rosa is distraught, and Gigi is crying. It was awful. We need to find out who did this for Laurent's legacy. I will step into his shoes until Dario marries Gigi," Lamberto assured the guys.

I shot daggers at him. That was the second lie he'd told tonight. I'd dropped Gigi off at home. On top of the gun shortage, he was lying about being at the hospital.

Dario caught my eye, and a crooked smirk appeared on his face.

"All right. We need to figure out who the shooter is and why he struck tonight at your engagement dinner," I started the conversation.

"I have a few contacts to check phone records," Turin said, leaning forward.

I looked at Lamberto. "Alvar told me you put in the request for only thirty packages."

Lamberto froze. "What are you talking about?"

I held his gaze. "Explain to me why there was a shortage of guns. On the same night Laurent was shot."

"Are you accusing me of something?" He cocked his head arrogantly as he challenged me.

"Don't hide now that Laurent isn't here to overlook your movements," I prodded, pushing his buttons.

"I'm not hiding!" he said thunderously.

"Why did you send me on a dummy mission the night Laurent was shot and killed?"

"I don't know what you're talking about," Lamberto blustered.

"I think you do. Lazaro and Sandro said you sent them over to wait for us to get there."

"They aren't in a position to know if something is wrong with a shipment," he spat.

"You told me there were supposed to be fifty guns. Something's not adding up, Lamberto."

A tense silence enveloped the room. "An accusation like that will get your tongue cut out," Lamberto barked.

"As enforcer, Laurent put me in charge to protect the family and the legacy. If you know anything, if you're behind any of this, I suggest you confess now because when I get through with whoever took the hit—"

"I know. They won't even be able to recognize his body," Lamberto recited, rubbing his forehead. He bit his lips nervously before changing the subject. "The funeral will need to be sped up to avoid Rosa and Gigi having to suffer."

"Gigi wants to see his body." Despite what I wanted, she was his daughter.

"I can speak for my fiancée, and she doesn't need to see it. That will only bring her nightmares," Dario stated.

I clenched my fists.

"I decide what she can and cannot do," Dario declared, staring at me.

"She's Laurent's daughter, and until you marry, she can make her own decisions," I argued.

"Gentlemen, this is up to Rosa as the mother and wife. She will decide," Lamberto remarked.

"I know she wants to have it taken care of quickly," Dario said.

"She's setting up a meeting with the lawyer soon. The family is still in shock, but we have to continue with business," Lamberto reminded everyone.

"We need answers about what happened. It's gonna be all over the media tomorrow. And our enemies will think we can be touched," Dario insisted.

"Dario will take his place immediately after the wedding, and it will be like nothing ever happened," Lamberto said.

Everyone stood and shook hands. Lamberto and Dario stood in the corner near the window, grinning as they talked quietly. He didn't look too upset for a guy whose fiancée was devastated by the death of his future father-in-law.

Turin and I made eye contact. If either of us found out they'd had anything to do with Laurent's death, they would discover what hell was like.

* * *

A few days later, I sat opposite Rosa, Gigi, and Aurora in the back of the limo procession, heading to the funeral. Mrs. Carrington had a closed casket and asked for the body to be immediately delivered to the funeral home.

Gigi hadn't talked to anyone since her father died.

She'd locked herself in her room, and even Aurora had a hard time getting her to come out and eat. Ginerva came to visit, but she turned her away.

Dario rode in the car with his parents, and Lamberto was in the other limo as the police escorted us through the streets of Italy. The Carrington family was loved by some and hated by many. After the funeral, I had a meeting with Casella's family. They were worried now that Laurent was gone. Things could get sticky if Dario didn't take his position. Plus, the family lawyer was meeting at the house tomorrow to go through Laurent's will.

Mrs. Carrington was drinking more than usual and putting even more pressure on Gigi to marry right after the funeral. If it were up to me, she'd move to America, leave everything behind her, and live her life. The limo stopped in front of the church, where the family had been longtime members since before Gigi was born.

"Gigi, please be respectful when we get out of the car, for your father's sake," Rosa said.

Gigi's head whipped around. "I'm not the one who ordered cameras to be at the funeral."

"Your father is known all over the world. It would be foolish not to broadcast it," Rosa defended.

I stopped Gigi as she reached for the door handle. "Let me."

I helped her out, and she adjusted her shades. Dario approached and bent to kiss her on the cheek, but she moved away. Embarrassed, he reached for her hand, but she sauntered around him. Rosa whispered something in his ear, and he nodded.

After Aurora got out of the car, I shut the door and strolled to the steps, catching up to Gigi. "You can't run off."

"He's pathetic," Gigi mumbled, watching her and Dario's mother hug.

"He'll be the leader of the family."

"I don't care." Gigi started to walk inside.

I extended a hand, cupping her shoulder. "Think of your father."

Although she wore shades, I knew her gaze was on me as I spoke about her father.

"Miss Carrington, what do you have to say about your father's death?" A reporter pointed a camera in her face.

"Get that camera out of my face!" Gigi snapped.

I pushed him back and ushered Gigi into the church. Rosa had the church put up a picture of Laurent from when he was younger, and the podium held a backdrop of the family. I escorted Gigi to the front row reserved for family before positioning myself in the corner of the church with a visual of the entrance and exit.

"What took you so long?" Gigi hissed at her mother.

"I needed to do damage control with the reporter from your little outburst," Rosa spat.

"Never should have invited them," Gigi argued.

"Gigi, I'm trying to do the best I can." Rosa blew out a breath and wiped her cheek with the handkerchief.

"Papa wouldn't want all this." Gigi waved her hand at the large crowd filling the church.

I had to agree with her because it seemed more like a TV event than a funeral. As enforcer, it wasn't my place to question her mother, but she appeared to do things to satisfy her own needs.

Forty minutes later, Gigi didn't want to see her father go into the ground, so I had Fulgenzio drive us home.

"Can we go to the beach for a minute?" Gigi asked.

I looked at her, then at Fulgenzio, and nodded. He

drove to the ferry and paid. Hopefully, the time away would help her grieve.

"Laurent talked about taking you to the beach when you were younger."

"Growing up in Rome, he made it a point to give me somewhat of a normal childhood, even with all the guards. Marina Grande was our special place we visited together." Gigi sniffed, remaining motionless for a moment.

I slid my hand into my pocket and removed my hand-kerchief, passing it to her.

"Thank you." Gigi wiped her nose and hugged her arms around herself.

"It's going to take time, but the pain will ease."

"I must look like a fool to you," she commented faintly.

I cupped her chin and turned her head in my direction. "You look like a woman who lost her father."

She opened and closed her mouth, placing her hand on my leg.

I released her chin. "Have you eaten?"

Gigi sat up straight and looked out of the window. "I'm not hungry."

I recognized her grief. She wanted to be alone and avoid people. My mouth thinned with displeasure. "You have to eat something."

"I don't love Dario," she blurted.

I sighed, planting my hands on the seat. "I know."

She swiveled quickly. "Then you'll help me convince my mother."

My expression stilled and grew serious. "Gigi—"

"Axel, please." She pressed her hand against mine.

I lifted her hand to kiss her palm as the ferry arrived

at the port. "You eat something after the beach, and I'll think about how we can convince your mother."

She grinned and climbed out of the car. Fulgenzio stood by the car with the captain. Gigi slipped off her heels, and I carried them while we walked down to the water. There were only a few people out during the afternoon, so we'd have enough privacy. She let my hand go and removed her shades, walking further into the water.

"Gigi," I warned in a gentle tone.

"Don't worry, Axel. I'm fine." She ran down the beach and paddled in the water.

I watched as she picked up a rock before throwing it further out. Suddenly, she dragged her dress off and dove into the water in her bra and panties. My head whirled to check if anyone had seen her, but we were alone.

"Come get in the water, Axel!" Gigi requested matter-of-factly.

"You shouldn't be in there."

She smirked, throwing her head back in the water. "My dad taught me to swim."

"He told me." I stood in the sand near the water's edge.

"Do you care about me, Axel?" she asked huskily.

"Of course, I care about your family." I valued Laurent and his family's support, but I knew her question went deeper.

"I know you're loyal to our family, but do you care about me?" She pointed at herself.

I gazed into her eyes. "We have to get going."

Gigi played in the water, "It's fine. You don't have to answer. Maybe I *should* marry Dario."

My thoughts went to a cold and dark place. "Fuck Dario."

"He's already talked about how he can't wait to be my first." Gigi searched my face.

I was surprised at her announcement. "You're a virgin?"

She nodded. Reaching behind her, she unhooked her bra and tossed it away.

"What are you doing?"

"Living life. My father is no longer here, and my mother doesn't care about me. I may as well enjoy my last days of freedom before I become Dario's wife." A wicked laugh erupted from her mouth.

She shouldn't be out here naked. "Get out of the water, Gigi."

"Come and get me."

She was the Don's daughter. Acting on our attraction would be perilous.

Chapter 7

Gigi

My intention when we came to the beach wasn't to hurt myself; hell, I thought I could sneak off with no one finding me, but Axel had increased the number of guards to protect my mother and me.

When the funeral was over, I explained we needed some space from everyone. Our family and friends pretended to care about us when all they wanted was money. As soon as the lawyer read the will, we wouldn't see them or their fake sympathies.

As a child, my father took me to the beach at least once a month, maybe more if I was good. Being Laurent's daughter was a curse, but also a blessing when Axel came around. Either the man was honorable or an idiot, but he never made a pass at me, no matter how many times I flirted with him. I guess I grew on him after I tried to sneak out one night, and he caught me when he arrived late to talk to my father. We argued, then talked, and I got to know him as more than the enforcer of our family...

"What are you doing?" Axel demanded.

Holding my heels and purse, I looked behind me. "Umm, nothing."

Axel's steady gaze bore into mine in silence. His broad shoulders were intimidating, and something in me wanted to submit. A strange expression flashed across his face. "Does your father know you're sneaking out?"

"He's out with my mother," I lied.

"Funny, I just called him and he answered."

"Well, they're not here." There was an open challenge on would break eye contact.

"How old are you?"

The same tired question his guards used to put me in my place like I was a child. As an adult, I could come and go as I pleased without a curfew.

"Old enough." I huffed, placing a hand on my hip.

"If that's true, you wouldn't be sneaking out."

Today was supposed to be me kicking it with my friends after a long day in class, but he wanted to play judge and jury for my father.

When I stepped around him, he grabbed my elbow and pulled me into his chest.

"I'm not a child. Move out of my way."

His mouth spread in a faint smile. "I don't take orders from you."

His accent made my stomach flutter. My breath caught in my throat as my eyes locked on his lips.

"How old are you now?" He caught the attention I paid to his lips.

"Eighteen," I answered in a whisper.

Axel shook his head, releasing me. "A baby."

His smile sent a spark up my spine. "How old are you?" I wasn't worried if he was a year or two older than me.

"Thirty."

"Oh." He was way older than I thought.

Axel quirked his brow.

"How long have you worked for my family? I can't imagine my father had just anyone come to our home."

"Since I was nineteen."

I learned at a young age that my father was powerful, but he never took me around his men besides the guards assigned to my mother and me. A few times, I'd had a crush on some of them, and when he noticed, they were reassigned and never heard from again.

"Why am I just now seeing you?" I wanted to know everything about him. Ginerva called me nosy, but I'd picked up a few things as the daughter of a kingpin.

"Because your father kept you away from his business."

I wanted to keep him here longer talking to me. "I know what he does as the Boss of the cartel."

"Keep that to yourself." He turned to leave.

I caught him with a hand on his shoulder. "Are you going to rat me out?" I quickly removed my hand and broke into a grin.

He smirked. "What would I get out of ratting you out to your father?"

"You must be high up in the family if you're here." I wanted to run my hand through his beard. His smile was magnetic.

"I take care of business for your father."

As expected, he didn't give an exact answer, and I commended him because you never knew who was listening.

"What about your parents?" I probed. This stranger

made me feel comfortable enough to want to do a deep dive into his life.

A cloud fell over his face. "They were killed when I was younger."

"Sorry to hear that." The mood shifted, and our flirty banter now felt awkward.

"You should get inside." He gestured toward the house, and a light came on downstairs.

"Shit, that's my father," I hissed, taking a deep breath and scanning the yard to see where I could hide.

"Thought you said your parents weren't home." He tilted his head and stared at me.

"Okay, I lied, but can you distract them until I get back in the house?" I begged, placing my hands together in prayer.

Axel folded his arms. "Now, why would I do that?" His eyes grew openly amused.

"Because I'll be your best friend." I smiled, sticking my hand out for a shake.

After he grinned, my heart skipped a beat. The door opened, and I raced to the side of the house, my back pressed against the wall and my eyes closed tight.

I heard my father speak. "Axel."

"Mr. Carrington," he answered.

"Did you take care of that problem?"

I wondered what problems Axel had "taken care of."

There was a pause, and Axel's gaze drifted toward me. "I did."

"Good. You didn't leave any evidence from the bomb, did you?"

At my father's words, I almost gasped in shock. The look on Axel's face was intense.

"Is something wrong?" Father asked.

Axel turned to face him. "Everything went according to plan, Mr. Carrington."

That was four years ago when Axel and I became familiar with each other. Right after, my father cracked down on me going out. I ended up with Axel as my guard, even though he was the enforcer for the family. Father put him in place to watch over me because I ditched all the other guards he tried to put on me.

Axel hated whenever I went shopping, especially with Ginerva. So again, we were back in each other's orbit based on my father. But I was no longer that young girl sneaking out of the house. Despite my love for the man, I wondered whether he loved me too, regardless of how forbidden it seemed to the outside world.

"Axel!" I yelled.

"What?"

"Put me down!" I fussed, wiggling in his arms.

Smack!

"Axel," I whined, rubbing my butt.

He carried me up the stairs to the car. The moment I'd removed my bra and refused to get out of the water, he'd jumped in and carried me out.

"Obviously, you wanted my attention," Axel growled, rubbing the sting away.

"Please put me down," I pleaded sweetly.

He let me slide down his body and it was clear he was aroused. I felt his thickness pressing against my stomach.

"Somebody needs to get that under control." I pointed at his pants.

"Shut up and get in the car." He was unmoved by my humor.

I started to remove the jacket he'd draped over my shoulders, but he shook his head. He held my dress, which I'd refused to put back on. "You're going to get sick. Keep the jacket on."

"What if I want you to take care of me?" My mouth lifted in invitation.

"We have a nurse on call."

I rolled my eyes. The ferry started back to the mainland, and Fulgenzio unlocked the car door. I slid in and grabbed my purse, removing my phone. I checked the time and noticed I had a few missed calls. The burial should've been over, so hopefully, I could go home to peace and quiet.

"I'm going to America," I announced, crossing my legs. I'd slipped my dress back on and removed Axel's jacket.

"Good idea."

I combed my hand through my hair. "Do you even care?"

Axel stopped and inhaled a breath. "Gigi, you know I care."

"Then kiss me." I turned to face him.

He closed his eyes, biting his bottom lip. "We can't."

The two words I always got from him. *We can't.*

"Then I guess Dario will get his wish."

"Is that supposed to make me jealous?" He chuckled as he rubbed his beard.

"I might be young, but I'm not stupid, Axel."

My phone rang, and I put it to my ear.

"Where are you?" Dario growled.

He was taking his role as my future husband too seriously and consistently tried to boss me around, but I wasn't like those weak females he was used to dating.

"Out." I glanced at Axel. Either I took the chance and

tested Axel while I was on the phone, or I cursed Dario out even more.

"With whom? I shouldn't hear from your mother that my fiancée is missing," Dario argued. He was more worrisome than my mother.

"I'm not missing. My guards are with me," I taunted as I stared at Axel.

"I expect you to check in with me," Dario said.

Axel stared at his phone, trying to ignore our call.

"Dario, I buried my father today. I'm sorry if I forgot to cover all the steps of being a fiancée."

Axel had said he wouldn't date me, and I needed a distraction from the pain.

Dario released a breath. "You're right. We had to bury your father and my mentor. I understand you need time for yourself, but you could still be a target."

He was right. I needed to stop being reckless. "I apologize," I said, and for a split second, I felt bad for going back and forth with him.

"Your mother has arranged dinner for our family at your home," Dario confirmed.

"I'll be there soon."

"I love you."

I cringed at his words. A part of me didn't know if I should believe him or not because of the way we'd been fighting.

"I know," I responded, ending the call.

"Make sure next time you take his calls away from me," Axel muttered.

I wanted to say something back, but it was torture being in the middle of my father's rules—that no one could date me who worked for him—and Axel's nonchalant behavior. I wondered if he genuinely cared or if he liked to toy with me because I was young.

"Dario's at the house." Suddenly, I felt like I had cheated on him, which was stupid since we weren't together.

"Good, he can help you during this time." Axel stretched his long legs and bumped into mine.

I studied his side profile, his strong chin and the line of his nose. I could almost hear his whispers as he kissed my neck and cheek.

"Do you have any leads about who did the shooting?"

Axel took a second to look at me. "I have Turin looking into some things."

The car approached the gate of our compound. Fulgenzio checked in with the guards before they opened for him, and he drove the spiral driveway to our home.

My mother loved this place and wanted me to keep it for my future children. I didn't have the heart to tell her I would be living in America for good when I got the chance. Now my father was gone, I had no reason to return to this place. She could sell it, and I'd be happy to find another home in Italy as my second place when I visited. Our extended family was spread out all over Italy and America.

I turned to Axel as Fulgenzio jumped out of the car and opened the door for me. "I want to be there when you get the information."

"Gigi, for the last time, you are not getting involved. It's too dangerous," Axel replied, standing on the other side of the car.

The front door opened, and my mother's brows dipped in confusion. I lowered my head, ready for the bashing to begin.

"What happened to your dress and hair?" Rosa questioned, tugging on the end of my dress. Her face filled with bitterness before she looked away.

"I went to the beach." I moved away.

She glanced from me to Axel, then Fulgenzio. "You ask to be alone, and this is what you come back looking like? A homeless person?"

"I'm going to my room."

She blocked me with her hand on my chest as I went to walk away. "No, I have guests, and you will come and sit."

"I don't want to sit and listen to a bunch of people tell me how much they loved my father when they probably had something to do with his death," I barked.

My mother's palm cracked across my face. "Gigi, baby, I'm sorry!" She reached to grasp my hand.

I yanked my hand out of her hold. "I'm going to my room." I hated Axel seeing me punished like a child.

I stepped inside and sprinted up the stairs to my bedroom. Aurora came out of my bathroom, and I lunged into her arms and cried.

"I hate her," I sobbed, burying my head in her chest while she rubbed my back.

Aurora kissed my forehead. "Shush, it's going to be okay, Gigi."

I shook my head and stepped back. "She never wanted me, Aurora, just the name of Carrington."

"Honey, you know better than to think like that." Aurora put her arm around my shoulder, squeezing me tight as we sauntered into my room.

I dropped my purse and phone on the bed and removed my dress. I remembered I needed to get my shoes, which were in the car. Stepping into my closet, I grabbed a pair of leggings and a T-shirt to prepare for a bath.

"I'm leaving for America after the reading of my father's will." My relationship with my mother couldn't be repaired after today.

Aurora looked sad. "When was this decided?"

My mother entered my room without knocking. "Can you knock before entering my room?"

"No one tells me where to go in my own home," she retorted, keenly aware I hated her now that all we had in this world was each other.

Her guests could wait while I changed my clothes. I didn't care how long it took. "Father

would have respected my privacy."

Mother turned to Aurora. "I have guests coming for dinner. Can you please go downstairs? I like to be prepared."

"Aurora is helping me," I replied.

Mother glared at me as she spoke to Aurora. "Aurora, can you make sure dinner is ready?"

I was surprised she hadn't fired Aurora now that my father was gone. She'd always complained about my father and me spoiling her. I didn't want Aurora to lose her job, even though I planned to leave tonight.

I wrinkled my nose and shook my head. "No, she stays."

Our gazes clashed.

"Aurora," Mother warned.

Aurora nodded her head and left.

"Go ahead and say what you have to say."

"What has gotten into you today?" Rosa snatched my wrist.

"Nothing besides my father being killed, my mother

slapping me, and being forced to marry a man I can't stand." I counted each situation on my fingers.

"Give me some respect. I'm still your mother, Gigi."

"Dario is using us for our money. He's probably planning to lock me away." I tugged my hand from her grasp and spun around to grab clean panties from my dresser.

Mother watched me move around the room and plop down on the bed. "Why must you act this way?" she asked, sitting by the headboard.

I gestured at myself. "Me?"

"Everything I do for you gets thrown back in my face." Rosa had a way of playing victim and villain at the same time.

"It's hard to believe."

She moved closer to me. "Who is getting in your head?"

"No one." I swallowed hard and squared my shoulders.

"Why do you believe all these lies? I've worked hard for this family," she said, placing her hand on my knee.

"Did you love my father?" It was a question I'd pondered for a long time.

"What kind of question is that? Of course, I loved your father. We were married years before you were born."

I'd held so much within me for years, and now I was battling a situation I knew couldn't be undone. "Feels like... It doesn't... You know it doesn't matter anymore."

"Say what you want to say." Mother clamped her jaw tight and watched me.

"I don't want to marry him," I made the plea with my eyes low and sorrowful. The thought of throwing me away for money seemed like a death sentence. Although I didn't think my mother had deep compassion for me, I kept trying to reach her.

"Gigi, we are not having this conversation again," she groaned.

"There you go again, not having my back." I threw my hands in the air.

"You're being a spoiled little brat." She pointed a finger in my face.

"I'm old enough to make my own decisions."

"The wedding is moving ahead." Her dark eyes were fixed on mine.

"I don't want to have an arranged marriage like you."

"Don't you dare talk about your father and me. I loved your father. Yes, it was set up by our families in the beginning, but he was a charmer and made me feel like the luckiest woman in the world." Raw hurt glittered in her eyes.

"There must have been something you wanted out of life or someone you desired more than anything, who took your breath away with just one glance." I was practically begging not to be pushed into a cruel marriage.

"We grew to love each other," she said, a satisfied light in her eyes.

"I don't doubt you cared about Dad, but you were never there for me the way a mom should be."

"In what sense? I fed you, clothed you, and sent you to the best schools!" she shouted, lacking any sensitivity to my pain.

"Seems like you want to pawn me off to another man to take care of me. I'm supposed to just go along with it? Give up my dreams and goals for America? What about my school?" I scoffed.

"You are being dramatic, Gigi," she mocked.

"What about my friends?"

"You can have all those things, Gigi."

"Not if I'm supposed to be some dutiful wife without a brain or a voice." My words were playful, but the meaning was not.

Over the last few years, I'd seen the same Stepford wife amongst their friends too often. Throughout history, women had allowed men to cheat on them, beat them, and force them into having children they never truly cared about, getting nothing apart from spending money and beginning the next generation of cartels. I wanted more for myself than the title of a trophy wife.

"Is that what you think of me?" she quizzed.

"No," I mumbled.

She rubbed my cheek. "Please understand, you can continue with your school. I'll make sure of it with Dario."

"What if I promise to date a few people you've always wanted me to date?" I bargained.

"Dario is expecting you. No more talk. Ramini and Carrington will become one big family and bring immense fortunes to you. Future grandkids. Think about how happy he'll make you."

If my father was alive, he would tell us both to stop talking, go to our neutral corners, and relax. "What if I'm in love with someone else?"

"No more talking. Come downstairs now." Mother was clearly over my tantrum.

"All right." I gave up.

"We're having a few people who were close to your father for dinner. Be respectful. Dario and his parents are here." Her annoyance at my detachment from the conversation showed on her face.

"I'm not hungry."

"Do this for me, all right?" A small smile appeared briefly.

"Okay," I answered.

She kissed me on the forehead before walking out of my room.

A frustrated breath blew from my lips as I sat back on the bed, gazing up at the ceiling. "Daddy, if you can hear me, please tell me what to do." My tears escaped before I could grab a napkin. "Should I go through with this wedding? What about my dreams of moving to America?"

I got up, locked the door, strolled to my dresser, and picked up the family photo of me with my parents at a party they'd thrown for me. I was around ten or eleven, and I'd asked for a princess-themed party. My father had spared no expense.

Fighting back more tears, I put it back on the dresser and sauntered into the bathroom to look at the crease lines underneath my eyes. I would need more makeup to cover my swollen eyes.

I pinned up my hair and got into the shower, turning it to the hottest temperature.

Chapter 8

Axel

Gigi looked annoyed by everyone at the table tonight. She barely touched her food, and as soon as her in-laws approached and hugged her, I could tell she'd completely checked out of the conversations. Almost defeated.

Her father put me in charge to keep her safe, but he never told me how to guard her heart against pain. All the "sorry for your loss" and statements of support seemed to cause her whole world to crash down around her.

She sat next to Dario, and I sat across from him. Mrs. Carrington was at the head of the table where her husband used to sit. Tomorrow, we had the reading of the will. Then Lamberto wanted to meet to discuss our potential movements on the people who killed Laurent.

Dario stood with a smug grin on his face. "Everyone, I want to make an announcement,"

Dario disgusted me. He'd had everything handed to him. Never worked a day in his life. Gigi was spoiled, but they were totally different in how they conducted themselves. I had no respect for Dario.

"In light of the fatal shooting of Laurent, and after approval from Mrs. Carrington, and with my mother's blessing..." Dario smirked, shooting a cynical glare my way.

I shifted in my seat, ready to bust my gun over his head if he disrespected Gigi.

Why do I care if he disrespects Gigi?

I shook the thought out of my head.

"... instead of the planned six months to get married, we moved it up to one month," Dario finished, captivating the room with his statement. He sat down with a tight grin on his face. His father patted him on the back, and his mother hugged him.

"*What?*" Gigi hissed.

"I thought you'd be happy about the date moving up." Rosa sat composed.

Darion nodded. "Especially with how hurt and distraught you've been since your father's passing—"

"His murder," Gigi snapped.

"Gigi, stop it," Rosa muttered as a war of emotions spilled over the table.

Gigi shook her head. "No, this is crazy."

"I know I should have talked to you beforehand, but I spoke with your mother, and she thought it was best." Dario thought he could control Gigi with an abrupt announcement.

"You agree with this?" Gigi asked, her gaze unwavering on her mother.

"A wedding is a beautiful thing," Rosa declared, too concerned with appearances.

"Without talking to me first," Gigi accused.

"Gigi, we think it is for the best," Dario said.

"I can't believe you. What about our discussion in my

room?"

"Dear, we can talk about that later." Her mother grabbed her drink and smiled at Dario.

Gigi tossed her napkin on the table, jumped out of her seat, and ran from the dining room. Dario did the same as I stood to go after her.

"I got her," I said with mixed feelings.

"That's my future wife. I can handle her."

My head swirled. "You still have a month before that happens."

We exchanged a long, hard stare, silently challenging the other to break eye contact first.

"Dario, sit. Don't worry about Gigi. Axel will handle it. He speaks her language." Rosa rolled her eyes, gulping the rest of her wine.

Dario sat back down as I made my way out of the dining room. I noticed the front door was open. She would inevitably end up in her favorite place when she was angry with her parents.

I walked around the side of the house to the backyard, down the ravine to the gazebo facing the lake. I slid my hands into my pockets and watched her for a few moments as she sat and stared up at the moon.

"You can't keep running off," I finally murmured.

Gigi shrugged. "Do you want me to marry him?"

"That's not up to me," I replied coolly when I wanted to say, "Fuck, no." If I could kill him without causing a mob war, I would.

Gigi sighed in irritation. "That's not what I asked you. Do you want me to marry him?" She turned her head to look at me.

The question was a stab in the heart. I took a step up the stairs, facing her with my back against the pole. The moon shined down on the lake, and the night air was crisp. "How many times have I explained? You know the rules of the cartel."

Pain flickered across her face. "I don't care about the rules."

"Gigi, this is my life. I owe everything to your father." Any falter on my part would have a ripple effect on the cartel.

"Axel, you act like I'm not a part of this world. I know the risk."

"I'm not good for you," I answered truthfully.

I couldn't lose another person because of my connections to the mob lifestyle. Dario wouldn't be my first choice, but at least he was in a position to take over the cartel and keep her secure, away from the damage I might bring to her from my unstable living. Turin had commented many times about how I lived on the edge, not caring if I died because I had no one to grieve for me.

"I'm living this cartel life. I lost my father because of his choices. With him gone, we can make new rules." Gigi always banked on simple solutions.

A strange surge of affection rose inside me, frightening me. "Do you know what I always promised your father?"

"No," she responded, returning her gaze to the lake. Being here brought peace for her to clear her mind.

"That no matter if he were here or not, I'd protect you. And that includes from myself." The thought tore at my heart.

"Do you think I'm some naïve little girl with a crush? I love you, and I know you love me."

My heart pounded at her words. "We're not having this conversation."

She pulled her legs up to her chest. "Remember what you did after your parents died?"

I clenched my fists. "Beat the shit out of somebody."

She chuckled. "That's what I feel like doing right now."

My mouth twitched. "That's what you have me for."

"So if I give an order to kick someone's ass, you'd go do it for me?" Gigi looked around as if someone was lurking.

Darkness had always lived within me. "Is that what you want?"

Our eyes fixed on each other. My soul was like a mirror to her eyes.

"I can't ask you to do that. My mother will ignore me from this point forward."

"What makes you think that?"

"She has money involved with this sham marriage."

"Rosa is many things, but I know she loves you." Rosa and I never had more than a surface relationship. Laurent never complained about his wife in my presence, but I knew from overhearing their arguments that she was demanding.

"I can't believe she's forcing me to marry him in a month. This can't be my life." She brushed her hand across the furniture.

"None of us can see how our lives will end up."

"Dario is not my choice. I want a choice in my life decisions. If you weren't working for my family, would we have had a chance?"

"Don't ask that question." I bent over and lifted her chin, and she smiled at me.

It was then I heard a throat clear. I looked over my shoulder and saw Dario with a smug look on his face.

Gigi narrowed her eyes, and I stood back to give her space.

"What's going on here?" he asked.

Gigi jumped up and wiped off her legs. "Nothing. I needed some fresh air."

He walked toward her, keeping his eyes trained on me. "My mother wants to talk about wedding plans, and I like to have my bride next to me."

Dario took her by the hand, and a long brittle silence stretched between us.

"I need to meet up with Turin," I finally said.

Gigi watched me as she spoke. "Guess I'll start my first night as a dutiful bride-to-be."

"Just be quiet, nod, and agree to everything," Dario jested, pulling her close to his side.

I wanted to pull off each of his fingernails one by one. Another man touching her was not acceptable. But I knew that giving in to my feelings would destroy both of our lives.

To monitor them, I stayed a few feet behind. There was a moment when I didn't know if she was acting or if he said something funny to make her laugh. In the past, she laughed at me when she tried to teach me about celebrity gossip or those *Housewives* shows.

They walked hand in hand back into the house. A voice whispered in my head, warning me to leave her alone for good.

My phone rang, and I took it out to see Turin's name. "What do you have?"

"You aren't going to believe this, even when I show you."

"Send it to my phone, and I'll meet you at the bar."

I looked back at the house for a second, staring up at

Gigi's room as the curtains closed. Letting Dario take on the responsibility of Gigi was for the best, while I focused on finding out who killed her father. She and her mother would probably fight about the wedding for the rest of the night.

* * *

Turin passed me a cigar, and the server smiled at him as she left him a glass of Don Julio.

I grabbed the bottle of water. To keep my mind clear, I avoided sex and alcohol whenever I needed to focus. "Tell me."

"They know Alvar's wife is gone."

"What do you mean?"

Turin gestured across his throat. "Dead. Orson's people have pinpointed it at us."

"Someone set us up. Probably thought we got close and found out too much, so they made a bigger play to put it on the Carrington Cartel."

Turin nodded. "Right after Laurent was killed, Alvar's wife was found in his home with a slit throat."

Alarm bells went off. "Casella hit?"

"Not sure. Why would they take out their own?"

"To cause confusion. We've secretly been at war for years."

Cautious was the state of play between all three factions—the Carrington, Ramini, and Casella families. If one could test the other without making a sound, they would.

Turin sat in the chair with a pensive glare. "But they need us more than we need them."

"Doesn't matter. Power makes anyone take the first

shot." I puffed on the cigar and focused on the other couples in the bar.

"Casella would be an idiot to go against us."

What Turin said was true, but if word was back on Alvar, we needed to be prepared for anything.

"Might think we're weak because of Laurent. I would." Old play, to hit while the Don is gone and a new replacement is yet to be named.

"How's Gigi?"

My head turned at her name being mentioned. "Why?"

He downed the rest of his drink, slamming the empty glass on the table. "She's your weakness."

I scoffed. "I don't have weaknesses."

"You're defensive at the mention of her name."

"Because she just lost her father."

"He was a father figure to you as well. Have you processed that he's gone?"

I glared at Turin for trying to be my therapist. "I'm fine," I answered, blowing out more smoke.

I was used to death. It surrounded me constantly and losing my parents taught me that life was short and you couldn't get attached.

Born and raised in Rome, Italy, I was the only child of Antonella and Gaspare Bresciani. My mother stayed at home while my father worked in accounting—or so I thought. It was accounting, but he was doing the numbers for the Carrington family.

Our lifestyle came with many perks, but it ultimately killed my family. People wondered why I came to trust Laurent, and it was because he never wavered in his loyalty. I had recurring visions of our last evening as a family. My parents went out for dinner and left me alone. A few hours later, I got a call about their death.

Turin's demeanor shifted. "We need you to be a hundred percent now that Alvar and his wife are dead."

The hothead in me knew I shouldn't have killed him. I had a short temper. "That means we can't verify the information with Lamberto and Dario."

Turin chuckled. "Correct. You were rash in your response."

"Maybe we don't need him."

Turin waved his glass at the bartender. "What do you mean?"

An idea formed in my head. "Can you get all the records from the past twelve months?"

His eyes flashed with recognition at my request. "Possibly, if I can get into the office computer."

"That might be a problem if Lamberto and Dario are around."

Turin reminded me, "They won't always be around when the wedding comes up."

A vicious guilt stabbed at my chest. "True."

"So you think if Lamberto has done this before by faking the numbers, we might have something?" Turin picked up his fresh drink from the bar.

"Not sure, but Lamberto is too quiet for me, and the way he sent Lazaro and Sandro on that dummy mission..." Again I was pissed about the last-minute run I'd had to make.

"The same night Laurent gets clipped." Turin and I were on the same page.

Inner torment gnawed at me. "Can we go to war with our own people?"

"We might not have a choice, especially if Dario takes over," Turin responded.

A few girls came over, and Turin grinned.

"Saw you two and thought you could use some company," the blonde in a short red dress and red lipstick stated. The low V-neck of her dress exposed her breasts.

"I'm not interested," I replied, and her friend looked surprised.

"Sorry, ladies, my brother's in a mood," Turin smirked.

I snorted as I stood, removed some money from my wallet, and left it for the bottle girl.

Turin frowned. "Where are you going?"

"I need to see Orson." I buttoned my jacket.

"Tonight?" Turin pushed the brunette off his lap.

"Just a quick catch-up." I turned and marched out of the bar, tossing the cigar to the ground.

"Not by yourself." Turin caught up to me at the front entrance.

I unlocked the doors, hopped inside, and turned the window down. "Leave your car here," I directed, sliding the key in the ignition.

Turin climbed as I pulled into traffic. "Promise you won't kill him?"

I looked in the rearview mirror as we stopped at a red light and noticed a car on my bumper. "Check the glove compartment."

"What for?"

"I think I'm being followed."

"Who would be stupid enough to follow you?" Turin removed a Glock and turned to look out the back window.

I lifted the console to take out my pistol. "Good question. We're going to find out right now."

The light turned green, and I sped away from the crowded streets. I came around Via Condotti, and the car stayed right behind us. Turin slid the gun up, ready to shoot, as I stomped on the brakes. The car behind me also hit the brakes, stopping an inch from my bumper.

I pushed the car door open, gun in hand. Turin threw open the passenger door, and we started shooting as they reversed. I gritted my teeth and watched the car leave down another alleyway.

"We need to get out of here," Turin stated.

"If Lamberto is behind this, I'm killing him," I promised as we jumped back in the car and headed to Casella's.

We arrived at Orson's brothel thirty minutes later. I paused in the car, watching the men standing outside. It was late, and Orson had the place surrounded by his men and some police he'd paid off for coverage.

"Are we going in?" Turin asked.

"If we do, I need to know you're prepared not to leave." I glanced at him.

"Brothers, no matter what," he answered.

"Let's go." I secured my gun and stepped out of the car.

The men turned their heads as I slammed the door, their glares hard as I approached.

"What can we do for you?" the guard questioned.

"Need to see Orson."

"He's not here," the stocky guard replied, bracing his hands on his hips. I guess that was his way of trying to intimidate me.

"Tell him Axel is outside, and we send our regards about Alvar."

His upper lip twitched at my comment. Then he looked at the other man and nodded to let us go through.

The music blasted as we entered the club. Orson constructed the place with a bar in the corner, a few couches spread out, and a TV in the opposite corner playing porn. Orson made his money any way he wanted off the backs of naïve women.

A woman stood at the bar wearing a black corset, fishnet stockings, and a thong. She grinned and blew me a kiss as we approached.

"Where's Orson?" I asked.

She placed the tip of her finger in her mouth. "In his office. Can I help you with something?" She planted her hand on my chest.

I grasped her hand and turned her, placing my gun on her back. "If you want to make it out of here tonight, take me to him and be quiet." I rubbed my nose against her ear.

"Please don't kill me."

I stroked her hair. "Shush... show us to his office."

She nodded and led us through the crowd of people drinking and making out.

"What's your name?"

"Andrea," she murmured.

"Don't worry, Andrea, you're doing fine."

We moved along a hallway, hearing moans from each room we passed. Andrea pointed at a door, and I moved her behind me before knocking.

"I'm busy!"

I knocked again.

"Ugh, fuck!" he groaned.

I raised my leg and kicked the door open.

A woman screamed, and Orson jumped, trying to reach for his gun, but I leveled my weapon at him. Orson was only five foot six and in his late fifties, but he looked older because all he did was drink, smoke, and sleep with girls barely in their twenties.

I pointed at the chair. "Take a seat, Orson."

"Leave." Turin motioned at the woman.

"Come on, Axel, this is a bad move," Orson remarked bitterly.

Turin shut the door and locked it after she left.

"Have a seat," I directed again, standing beside his desk.

Orson lit a cigarette and blew out smoke. "What do you want?"

"Did you kill Laurent?"

A glimpse of a smile flashed before he answered. "No."

It was senseless to lie to me. "I don't believe you."

Back in the early days of the Casella reign, Orson had a lot of people scared and wanted to be a faction, but his greed became too much. It wasn't well known, but some of his right-hand men dipped into hard drugs and screwed him over. Once Laurent made people aware of who ran all of Italy and how Orson couldn't take land that didn't belong to him, jealousy became the biggest issue, plus a rumor spread that Orson tried to sleep with Rosa.

"I have no reason to lie." Orson coughed and took a sip of his drink.

"Did you ever hear from Alvar?" I taunted.

"I know you had something to do with him going missing." Orson stared at me.

I chuckled. "I had nothing to do with that."

"All I can tell you is that your home may not be so clean," Orson said.

"If you know something, it would be in your best interest to tell me."

"Axel, I know you think you're untouchable, but don't threaten me," Orson grumbled.

"As the Boss of the Casella family, we know you're in a position of influence," Turin said, switching to persuasive tactics. He had the patience I lacked and charmed people into opening up before I made a move.

"I don't know anything," he responded.

Orson's eyes darted from Turin to me, and I could tell he was covering for someone.

"I gave you a chance." I turned to leave while Orson yelled behind our backs. This game required more self-control from me than anyone else. Once I learned who killed Laurent, I'd proceed to what happened to my parents.

Chapter 9

Gigi

Our family attorney, Cyrus Pappalardo, was two-thirds done reading my father's will. His office was large scale and *grande* with old Italian paintings, furniture, and Italian pride. From what my mother said, he'd been around before I was born. Both families had been in each other's life since my christening. His daughter was also a lawyer and visited our home during the holidays. It was interesting how he tried to make it seem like I didn't know my father was into illegal business, but I knew everything about my dad. The man he was in the public eye never came home to my mother and me.

Cyrus cleared his throat, took a gulp of water, and read on. Axel stood off in the corner, while my mother and I sat at the end of the table, with Dario beside me. At first, I was shocked when we walked in and he was there. Then my mother explained that he wanted to be there for support.

"What was that last part, Cryus?" Mother brought me out of my daze.

I looked from the scowl on her face to Dario's dark eyes.

Cyrus repeated his words. "His last will and testament state Gigi is to be the new boss."

"There must be some mistake," Mother snidely remarked.

"Gigi is not running anything," Dario barked.

Cyrus held the papers up, pointing the pen to the circled section. "Mrs. Carrington, it's here in plain black and white."

My mouth was dry. I picked up the glass of water and gulped it down. "I don't understand."

"Laurent left you fifty million in a trust. He left your mother the house, cars, and a monthly stipend until her death."

"A stipend! I've worked too hard to be on a budget," Mother argued. Her usual poise and dignity were absent as she jumped out of her seat.

Cyrus's face was bleak. "I promise it's not a small budget."

"When did he put her in charge?" Dario demanded. "It was always going to be me."

Dario pissed me off with his condescending tone. "Dario, I can speak for myself,"

I spat, straightening in my seat.

"About five years ago, he came to me to change his will," Cyrus replied. "Gigi has to get married to run the family business, or it will be split among the other cartels."

Mother replied, "That can't happen. Dario is going to run the business soon as they get married."

Cyrus fixed his glasses. "Until she hits twenty-five, Mrs. Carrington will control her trust fund."

I slammed my hand on the table. "But that makes no sense. I won't control my life. Either my mother runs me until I'm twenty-five or I get married and have a husband control me."

"Do not embarrass me here," Dario whispered in my ear.

I jerked away from him. "You embarrass yourself." I turned my gaze to Cyrus. "Please continue?"

"As the only child, Gigi will be the new boss once she marries. That is worth a billion dollars.," Cyrus reminded.

"So, as her husband, I will be in charge?" Dario prodded.

Cyrus glanced at the document again. "He specifically stated Gigi."

"She's preparing to become my wife. I will not have her in that type of business," Dario objected.

"That's up to Gigi. I'm only the messenger," Cyrus said.

"I'm an adult. I shouldn't have to jump through these hoops," I grumbled.

"Please understand your father loved you, Gigi, and wanted the best," Cyrus reiterated.

"Can I think about it?" I questioned.

"You're not taking over anything," Dario stated.

I stood and grabbed my purse, leaving the office as Axel, Dario, and my mother rushed to catch up. The elevator doors opened, and Dario and Axel stood on either side of me, with my mother in front. I had knots in my stomach thinking about what I had to do. I wanted to move my hand an inch and touch Axel.

The doors closed, and I caught Axel's reflection staring back at me. I dropped my shoulders and shifted on my feet as I accidentally bumped into him.

The elevator dinged and Mother stormed off with Dario behind her. Axel waited for me to leave, and we headed for the car. I started to open the car door when someone grabbed my arm, and I whirled to see an angry Dario.

"Laurent was probably drunk when he made those changes. You're not taking over."

"This is not your business. It's my family," I said.

"My family will be your family, or did you forget? Get it through your head." Dario poked me in the forehead.

I looked at my mother, and she turned away. Axel started toward us, and I held my hand up to stop him.

"Gigi, didn't you say traveling and school are more important?" Mother asked.

I had a sinking feeling. "It is."

Rosa took a deep breath. "Then sign over leadership to Dario."

"That makes sense," Dario agreed.

It seemed pointless to fight them both. Maybe it was the best way for me to get out of everything. "What about the marriage?" I lacked trust when it came to Dario and his intentions. He had no morals. All he wanted was to break me down into someone else rather than who I was.

"We can talk about divorce when we've been married for ten years," Dario answered.

"This family doesn't believe in divorce," Mother answered.

My phone rang, and I released a breath. "Hello."

"Gigi, this is Cyrus."

At the mention of his name, I turned and walked a few steps away. "Yes?"

"Who are you talking to?" Dario snapped, trying to snatch my phone.

"Hey!" Axel stepped in between Dario and me.

"Axel, this is between Gigi and Dario," Mother intervened. "They need to get on the same page."

"I'm sorry, are you busy?" Cyrus queried.

I took a deep breath. "No, but I wanted to tell you I'm taking over the business."

A loud gasp could be heard behind me.

Dario's forehead creased and his eyes narrowed.

Cyrus broke into our stare-off. "And you understand the stipulations?"

A smirk creased my lips. "I do."

"All right. I'll have the papers drawn up," Cyrus responded.

I gulped. "Thank you."

"Also, your father bought a home in America and put it in your name. He knew it was your dream."

My face lit up. "Seriously?"

"So if you want the information—"

"Yes, please send me the details."

"Good. You'll do just fine, Gigi," Cyrus replied.

"He trusted me, and I'm willing to keep his legacy alive." I smirked at Dario as I ended the call, sticking the phone in my pocket.

"They'll never listen to you," Dario pointed out.

I shrugged. "Then they'll be my enemy."

Dario stomped to his car and my smile dropped. I was terrified about what I'd agreed to.

The car started and Fulgenzio turned into traffic. Mother and I sat across from each other in the back seat.

"You are not doing this, Gigi."

"Based on the will, I am."

She grabbed my elbow and pulled me face-to-face with her.

"I suggest you listen to me. You are to be married and focused on a family."

Out of the corner of my eye, I could see Axel observing our conversation.

"If you want to continue to get Father's money, this is the only way."

"Are you threatening me?" Rosa snapped.

"I want you to be on my side for once!" I shoved her hand away.

"I'm always on your side!"

A mother and daughter should have an unbreakable bond, but Rosa made it almost impossible with her lack of compassion and support. Her entire life was about picking at me—how I should sit, dress, look, and act.

I inhaled a breath, staring out the window and wondering how much longer we'd fight as enemies.

* * *

A week later, I was still in a state of shock. Tonight, I was going out with Ginerva to relax and get Dario and my mother off my mind. They'd been in my ear about doing the right thing and letting Dario take control. Now we'd buried my father, I had to go back to school, try to figure out how to get out of a wedding, and run a billion-dollar cartel ring.

We'd finished dinner, and I changed into a black leather bodice dress which showed a little cleavage and strappy heels. My hair flowed down my back in waves with golden highlights. Axel saw me step out of the house and did a double take. I knew he'd be watching me all night, and I wanted to give him a show.

When we pulled up at the venue, I rolled on the nude

lipstick, placed it in my clutch, and reached a hand out of the car into Axel's. The movement forced me close to his chest, and he slid his hand down to my waist.

An intense sensation coursed through my veins.

"I know what you're doing."

I angled my head and grinned. "What am I doing?"

"Playing games."

"For whom?"

"You'll get yourself in trouble." Axel tapped me on the thigh.

"That's the plan." I seductively strolled away, holding Ginerva's hand while Axel directed us inside to our reserved VIP section at La Cabala. They held stunning views and had the best food and bar in the world. People waved and greeted us as we moved through the crowd.

The guard stepped aside to allow us to sit. It was just past midnight, champagne was flowing, and dance music from Drake to Dua Lipa thrummed through the club.

"So happy to be out for once." I picked up the bottle and glass.

"How did you get out of the house without crazy security?" Ginerva took the glass from me and I poured another one.

"Axel has sharpshooters everywhere, and he only allowed me to come because I said I was going to sneak out." I laughed.

"What about your mother?" Ginerva snapped her fingers and tapped her feet to the beat.

"A long story, but she's out somewhere."

"How are you two holding up?"

A bitter agony popped into my head. "Honestly, my father was the glue that kept us together."

"Hello, ladies! Would you like complimentary shots

on the house?" Bottle service approached with tequila and lime shots.

"I plan on getting wasted tonight." I grabbed the glass off the tray.

"Drunk Gigi is the best." Ginerva laughed.

"Here's to new memories!" I held the shot up and took it straight, chasing it with lime.

"That was strong." Ginerva patted her chest.

"I want to dance." I snapped my fingers.

"Well, before you do, you might want to look over there." Ginerva gestured at the front entrance of our booth.

Dario stood there with his men.

He had a way of making my day even worse. "Fuck! Not in the mood for him."

"What happened at the reading?" Ginerva asked.

"Let's dance first." I took another shot and jumped up, pulling her with me to the dance floor.

Dario looked at me, and I rolled my eyes. Axel stood with Fulgenzio and Turin at the bar as we danced. I rolled my hips and raised my hands in the air.

Ginerva got in front of me and snapped her fingers. "Go, Gigi!" she encouraged and bounced to the beat of Lizzo.

For once, I felt like a normal girl, and I let all my inhibitions go, blocking out all my problems. I smiled as strong hands planted on my waist and masculine cologne wafted through the air.

"I can't wait to marry you," Dario whispered in my ear.

I jerked as I realized who was behind me. I turned to free myself from his hold, looking around the club to find Axel, but he wasn't next to Turin.

"Don't touch me!" I shouted, pushing his hands away.

"We are in public. Do not embarrass me," Dario seethed.

"We're not married yet."

He raised his hand, but was held up in a chokehold by Axel.

"What the fuck!" Dario shouted.

"Axel!" I screamed.

Dario's men jumped in, and Fulgenzio pulled his gun out. Tonight was about Ginerva and me having fun, and now a brawl was breaking out.

"Keep your filthy hands off her," Axel growled.

"Oh, shit," Ginerva muttered.

"Axel, I'm fine," I pleaded.

A hint of hurt appeared in his eyes.

"Are you sleeping with him?" Dario barked.

"Shut up!" Again, he made it about Axel and me sleeping together when nothing was further from the truth.

"You expect to continue working as the enforcer after this? You can kiss your life goodbye," Dario threatened.

Axel yanked his arm, and Dario cried out in pain. I worried Axel would kill him in front of everyone and go to jail. Both men had a lot at stake if something went wrong.

Suddenly I felt sick to my stomach. I wanted to go home and forget the night ever happened. "Axel, please let him go."

He looked at me.

The hurt lingered in my stomach. "I'm fine. He didn't hurt me."

"As soon as we get married, you're cutting ties with this family," Dario promised.

My brow dipped in annoyance. "I don't take orders from you."

Axel released him, and Dario straightened up. Axel grasped my hand and pulled me off the dance floor and through the hallway.

"What was that back there?" I questioned.

He pushed me up against the wall and then his mouth was on mine.

I groaned and wrapped my hands around his neck. "Axel..." I moaned as his warm hands gripped my waist. And then he stepped back abruptly. I looked from left to right to see if Dario was near. "You kissed me..."

He ran a hand down his face, letting out a frustrated breath. "I apologize. I wasn't thinking."

A part of me wanted to continue kissing, but I was worried Dario or one of his men would see us.

I closed my eyes and touched my lips. "No, you can't kiss me like that and pretend it meant nothing."

"You're getting married," he reminded me.

"Yeah, but he didn't say to whom," I jested, placing my hands on his chest.

He shook his head. "It would never work."

"Why do you keep fighting what we both want?" I stepped into his space.

"Because this will end badly for both of us." Axel rested his hands on my hips.

I ran a finger across his bottom lip. "That's if you don't fight for what you want."

"And what do you want?"

I looked into his eyes. "You."

Axel was the guy parents warned you to stay away from, but I knew the real man behind the killer. He wouldn't admit it to himself, but he was sensitive and compassionate toward me and the people he cared about. Dario hadn't once tried to talk and get to know the real me outside of our parents pushing us together.

He groaned. "I'm not good for you."

"Why do you keep saying that? Do I look like a little girl to you?" I grabbed his chin to face me.

"Did you forget you're my new boss and I'm older than you?"

"So, that only means we can have more time together and my parents are an example of a couple with an age difference."

"It would put you in a bad position with the other families."

"Fuck them."

"Gigi." Axel's mind was made up.

I turned my head to see Ginerva, and I stepped back from Axel. "Um, we were just talking."

"Dario left already. You don't have to hide." Ginerva softly smiled on her approach.

Secrets between best friends had a limit. Ginerva knew how I felt about Axel and encouraged me to date other people as a distraction. At one time, I talked to other guys, but nothing transpired because they all lacked passion.

"I need to get you both home," Axel announced and started to walk out of the hallway.

"Not ready to leave," I informed him.

"Did you forget about business?" Axel asked.

I swallowed down the despair and forced a reply. "I need to coordinate my school schedule."

"Shit. I forgot." Axel pushed a hand through his hair.

"I can handle both."

He chuckled. "This is crazy. Laurent put you in charge."

"So you don't believe I can run things like Dario said?"

He glared at me. "Never compare me to him."

"Just take me home." I stomped away.

* * *

"I think he has something to do with my father's killing." Ginerva and I were in the kitchen in our pajamas. Even though our night was cut short, I was happy that Axel finally let go and made a move. My mind still swirled from the kiss and Dario's actions at the club.

Ginerva grabbed the sandwich I made for her and took a bite.

"Promise me, Ginerva."

She swallowed before she spoke. "Anything."

"If something happens to me, you'll make sure to get the truth out."

"Gigi, don't talk like that." Ginerva pouted.

Dario had a plan, and I needed to find out what he was up to and put a stop to it before it created trouble for my friends and family. "Only way to get through this marriage is to find a loophole."

Ginerva had a big heart and wanted the best for me. "Give up the business and run away like you wanted."

"And let my father's legacy go up in smoke?" He would be so disappointed in me.

"Then you have to marry Dario." Ginerva took another bite.

I wrapped up the bread and put the knife in the sink. "My life can't be this complicated."

She picked up the bowl of chips and popped some in her mouth. Axel went home for the night and most of the staff were asleep. My mother hadn't called, so I wondered if she'd spend the night out. If I found out she had a new man within a month of my father's death, I'd lose my shit on her and move out.

"Maybe Dario isn't that bad." Ginerva looked away hastily, taking a sip of her drink.

I sat on top of the counter and kicked my legs back and forth. "He's worse and I won't take him as a husband."

I grabbed some chips and crunched on them before I hopped down and headed for my bedroom. The will stipulated that I needed to get married, but it never specified Dario. If I had my choice, Axel would take his place as my husband and business partner in the cartel.

Ginerva grabbed her things and followed me. Aurora passed by us on her way to bed. We waved and said good night. Ginerva closed the door behind us, and I turned on the TV to find a movie for us to watch.

"Something funny or scary tonight?" Ginerva kicked her feet up on the bed.

"Anything to avoid my life."

Ginerva rubbed my back, and I pulled the covers over my knees, listening to her complain about the latest issues with her parents.

Chapter 10

Axel

Two days ago, I kissed her. Now I stood beside her at the table before all of our men. My chest was tight with pride, but I was nervous about how the men would challenge her today. Women in charge were rare in the mafia world, and Gigi was so young. When Cyrus read out Laurent's wishes, I was as shocked as everyone else. It would be dangerous for her to step into this position. By the hard expressions on the face of every man in the room, she wouldn't get out of this alive.

"As you all know, I called this meeting because I was named as the replacement in my father's will." Gigi had her hair pulled into a low bun and her curvy frame was shown to perfection in a black pantsuit. I hated that the other men in the room got to be near her and see what I saw.

Dario continued to glare at me following the incident at the club. We hadn't said two words, and I was sure he knew I had feelings for Gigi.

"Wait a minute. You're in charge and not Dario?" Lamberto asked.

Gigi cleared her throat. "Yes, that's true."

"We're still getting married, and I'm going to take over," Dario interrupted, a warning in his voice.

"Actually, Dario, that's *not* true," Gigi said.

The room erupted in confused conversation.

"Gigi, we talked about everything already," Dario said, becoming increasingly uneasy.

"We did, and I've decided," Gigi answered.

"You can't make a decision without your mother or me," Dario reminded her.

All eyes bounced from her to Dario.

"Sorry to inform you so late, but I already had it drawn up with Cyrus," Gigi responded.

I was perplexed by the time frame since I knew her schedule.

"Does your mother know?" Dario probed.

Gigi looked at her watch. "She will, right about... now."

Her phone rang on the table and she picked it up. "I'm getting married, but not to Dario."

"Bitc—" Dario caught himself as I moved toward him.

Gigi held me back. "It's okay, Axel. His pride is hurt. Anyway, gentlemen... We have a lot

to talk about. I know taking orders from me will take time, but I learn quickly. Plus, I'll have the help of my husband to guide me if I stumble."

"Bringing in an outsider is not how things are done, Gigi," Lamberto said.

For all of his faults, I had to agree with him.

"He's not an outsider. Axel and I are getting married," Gigi announced.

Every mouth in the room dropped in surprise.

"You stupid bitch!" Dario leaped over the table.

I shoved Gigi behind me and pulled out my gun.

"Dario, I wanted to avoid any problems, but if you call me out again..."

"This isn't over," Dario barked as Lazardo held him back.

"I need to talk to you," I whispered in her ear.

"Can it wait?" She licked her lower lip.

I got distracted for a moment. "No, now." I gestured for her to step into the hallway. We walked out of the room, and I closed the door behind us.

Anger crept in at being left out of the plan. "Is this your plan? To lie to everybody?"

"Do you want Dario to be my husband? To force himself on me, possibly beat me in order to get my father's business."

"I would never let that happen." For her to think I would allow such a thing was disrespectful. Women weren't taken to my bed by force, and I would never let that happen to her or any woman.

She waved toward the door. "I believe he's responsible for my father's death."

"He wouldn't do something that stupid."

"Then help me prove it." Gigi was furious and couldn't see the implications of her actions.

"A fake marriage?"

"Who says it has to be fake?" The rebellion in her peeked out. Gigi had a way of getting under my skin, and I tried my best to reject her at every turn.

I sighed. "Gigi—"

She grabbed my face and put her lips against mine.

I instinctively wrapped my arms around her and

pulled her closer. "You're dangerous," I mumbled, sucking on her bottom lip.

"Dangerous, but smart."

"What makes you think I want to get married?"

"Look me in the eye and tell me you would rather I marry Dario and I'll leave you alone forever," she muttered.

I thought about not having her in my life. Her slightest touch did something to me that no other woman could.

The door swung open, and we broke apart.

"The guys want answers," Turin remarked.

I nodded. "On our way."

Gigi squeezed my hand. "I'll handle my mother."

"If Dario was involved, I'll find out," I promised.

"And I'll be the woman who takes his last breath away." Gigi sauntered back into the conference room.

"The other bosses won't like this," Lamberto announced upon our reentry.

"That's understandable, but I assure you, it's a done deal. As of right now, I will keep things as they are, but make no mistake. I am my father's daughter. I won't allow betrayal and dishonesty to go blind," Gigi responded.

My mouth twitched with a smile.

"Lamberto, this will not stand," Dario argued.

Lamberto looked at Dario, defeated.

"Dario, I'd like for you to address all concerns to me from now on," Gigi directed.

My dick hardened as she "Bossed" him.

"Gigi, we all know you as Laurent's daughter, so you have to give us time to get used to this new look," Lamberto said.

Gigi sat down with crossed legs and folded arms,

looking at each man in the room. "Lamberto, I doubt you were told this when you joined the cartel, so I'd like you all to understand. I give respect when respect is given to me. Carrington Cartel is my family name, and Carrington blood runs through my veins. No one can deny that truth."

* * *

One year ago.

"What did you get me?" Gigi stuck her hand out and wiggled it at me.

"Nothing big, but I thought of you when I saw it in the store." I removed my hands from behind my back and placed the long, thin box in her hand.

She smiled, unwrapping the gift, and something in her eyes sparkled. "So you listen to me when I talk."

Tonight she was going out with Ginerva for her twenty-first birthday and I promised Laurent I'd make sure protection was tripled.

"A gold necklace with a symbol of the world."

"I know you want to travel when you're finished with school." Something she'd said during our many nightly conversations when she sneaked off to the gazebo.

Gigi bit her bottom lip. "Can you put it on, please?" She held the box up.

Lifting it out, I turned her around, pulled her hair to the side, and locked it around her neck.

"Thank you, Axel."

"You're welcome."

She stood on her tippy-toes and kissed me on the check. "The best birthday present."

"Your father got you a new car. My gift doesn't compare."

"Your gift is more valuable because you listened to me."

I released the magazine clip and removed my goggles, staring at the remains of my target sheet.

The meeting with Gigi had everything jumbled in my mind and I needed to think and get clarity on what she wanted me to do. A fake marriage could only backfire on her and possibly cause us both to be killed.

I watched her with the instructor as she planted her feet before giggling loudly. I didn't know what was so funny, but I had to break up this little moment.

"You broke up with your fiancé, proposed to me, and now you're flirting?"

The guy stepped back and Gigi moved the gun around without thinking.

I took it out of her hand. "You need more practice."

"Sorry, but I wasn't flirting," Gigi said.

"Yeah, right. Tell me anything to distract from the meeting."

She watched me lift the gun and release the clip. "My plan can work."

"Gigi, it would put us both in danger." Her life was dangerous, and her new role would only make it more so, possibly changing her for the worse.

Gigi expected me to always have the answers, but I'd lost my trust with Laurent's death. If she got a hint that I had doubts about her safety, she might not take the role and then marry Dario.

She stepped forward, pressing her breasts up against me. "When has danger scared you?"

I ran a hand over her hair, looking up to see the instructor staring at us. "Can I help you?"

He motioned in surrender and walked off.

Gigi giggled. "You're already behaving like a jealous husband."

"That's not a good thing." I shook my head. "I have to show you the warehouse."

"Where my father's business is based?"

I rubbed the necklace around her neck. "Yeah."

She covered my hand with her palm. "I never take it off."

We held hands. "Twenty-first birthday."

"A gift I sleep with at night."

"Do your parents know where it came from?" Not once did I think to ask if they knew I'd bought her gifts. When kids grew up in this business, each family would gift money. I'd given her jewelry.

She shook her head. "No. I don't plan on ever telling her."

"After we return from the farm, I think you should talk with Rosa."

"She's going to try to talk me out of the wedding to you, and I refuse."

"Gigi, I live alone in a condo. Are you willing to give up a massive estate for my place?"

She paused for a moment. "No."

"I didn't think so." My eyes roamed over her figure. Money was never a problem for me. I had plenty, but living in a massive home when it was only me didn't sound appealing.

"My father bought me a home in America. I want us to move."

I groaned, released my hold on her, and stepped back in frustration.

Her lids lowered, flickering her thick black lashes. "Why not?"

"My life is here."

"Can we talk about this later? I need to know every aspect of the business before Dario tries something."

"I don't want you digging into anything that has Dario coming after you," I said as we walked back to the car.

"Too late. I know he's behind my father's death."

"What do you remember about that night?"

Her phone rang, and she turned it off. "I haven't talked to my mother, and she's been blowing up my phone."

"Does she know about your marriage idea?"

"No, but I don't need her permission."

I unlocked the car door and helped her into the passenger side of my Lamborghini.

Fulgenzio motioned he was ready and started his car to escort us away.

When I reached the driver's door, I climbed in and slid the key into the ignition. "We'll swing by the farm first. What are you doing about school?"

"I can see about moving online if things get hectic, but I like the in-person experience. If we move to America, I could find a university."

"You have it all planned out."

She grinned, patting my knee.

* * *

The cartel's main facility for guns was housed on over thirty-four acres of land that Laurent held in his family for many years. It was reached by a winding road and only certain people got to come up here to work. Casella's primary goal had always been to get ownership over this land, and if Dario was behind anything, or wanted to marry Gigi to get control, it made sense. This place was a gold mine, and I rarely came here unless Laurent needed me to handle business personally. The Tuscany property housed about five bedrooms, with a wine cellar with a basement.

"Looks like a normal home," Gigi commented, shutting the door.

"That's the idea."

I took her hand, escorting her inside. A few men stood around the property with guns for security. The door opened, and Turin stuck his hand out for a shake.

"Turin, how long have you known about this place?" Gigi asked.

"Since I started working for your father," he answered.

"Weapons are housed here only?"

Turin and I looked at each other.

"Drugs come in and out sometimes," I responded.

Gigi continued to walk through the home. "This is the main house."

"We have people sleeping here twenty-four seven. Plus guards outside," I explained.

"Dario knows about this place?"

"He does."

Lamberto and Dario knew many Carrington family secrets; she could change up some of the setup, but it mostly was managed by them. Laurent allowed Lamberto to have a lot of freedom while he focused on his other businesses. Gigi would need to understand what came with trying to take things back.

"I don't want him to have access," Gigi voiced.

"Lamberto is the Underboss. He sets up the drop-off schedules," Turin informed her.

"Then I want you to take over that position." Gigi countered.

"Gigi, Turin can't do that."

"Why not? I'm the Boss of the cartel and I want him to monitor the shipments," Gigi demanded.

"We can discuss it more later."

She turned toward the window, looking out at our men loading up trucks. "Can we see the product?"

"Sure." Turin directed us to follow him to the shed at the back of the property. Guns were being loaded into crates as we walked through.

"Do you trust them?" Gigi waved at the men packing up the crates.

"They've been here from the beginning with Laurent," I replied.

"So tell me why that one over there is whispering to his friend." Gigi pointed at Gasto and Diego in the back of the assembly line. "Turin, bring them here."

Turin looked at Gigi, then at me for approval, and I nodded.

"What are you going to do?"

"Give me your gun." She extended her hand.

Killing our men in front of the crew wouldn't bring loyalty. "Gigi." I shot her a look.

She wiggled her hand at me. "Axel, give me your gun."

I removed it from my holster and checked the bullets, making sure the safety was on.

"Miss Carrington," Gasto said, wiping the sweat from his brow.

"You know who I am?" Gigi asked.

He hesitated briefly. "Um, ye-yes," he stuttered.

"Good, because I'll never forget your face from my father's dinner." Gigi raised her gun and pointed at his head.

"Gigi!" I warned gruffly.

She raised her hand to stop me. I knew she was hurting from her father's death. Hell, I still had nightmares, but to make a statement like this in front of her men without major proof would not look good for the other families.

"Gasto, tell me why I shouldn't kill you," Gigi demanded.

"Ma'am, I don't know what you're talking about," Gasto pleaded.

"When they brought my father out on the stretcher, I remember you and Dario talking."

My brow cocked up at that statement. She never told me this information from that night.

"Gigi, give me the gun." I covered her hand with mine and took the gun. I looked at Turin. "Take him," I said.

Turin directed Gasto to the basement.

"Where are you taking him?" Gigi asked.

"Nowhere you need to worry about. I need to get you out of here."

"Axel, I'm not a little girl. I understand what that means, and if you keep me away from how things work, I can get someone else to help me." Gigi folded her arms over her chest.

I pulled her arms apart. "Don't threaten me, Gigi."

"Then you'll be honest with me?"

"As much as I can."

"Fine. I'll let you think about my proposal. I don't want to go home just yet."

I sighed, grasped her hand, and led her out of the barn.

She looked deep in thought, staring at the landscape, as we drove down the road. "I care for you, Axel."

I glanced at her before turning at the curve in the road.

"If I invited you to dinner, would you go?"

I chuckled at the question.

"What's funny?" She turned to face me in her seat.

"I know how to ask a woman out."

"Then ask me." Her eyes sparkled at the curl of my top lip.

I looked at her and licked my lips, then lifted her hand and kissed the back of her palm. "Dinner between friends."

"For now." She turned to face forward, and I thought about what I just agreed to do with no hesitation.

Laurent might have thought I stepped over the line with his daughter today. I couldn't help but feel regret if she ended up hurt by my actions. A fake marriage could complicate her life more than she knew. "Dinner is the only thing I can offer."

I hadn't dated since I turned eighteen and before my parents' death. When I became locked in with the cartel, the only thing I had time for with women was sex, and often with two or three women at a time. Many times, they bored me easily and didn't understand we weren't in a relationship, so I cut them off and found a replacement until even that didn't fill the loneliness. To this day, I could recall only a few specific women who'd satisfied me enough to get through the night. If Gigi went with Dario, at least she'd know the traditional route of marriage when the husband had a mistress.

She sat back, typing on her phone as I drove, turning on the radio. Today came as a surprise in a good way; the car ride and being alone with her put me at peace. I might sleep through the night without an issue for once.

Chapter 11

Rosa

"**W**here the hell have you been?" Dario snapped as soon as I answered his call.

I took it off speakerphone and glanced over my shoulder to make sure no one was eavesdropping on the call. "Lower your tone," I hissed.

"That bitch made me look like a fool!" Dario shouted.

When I got the paperwork about the family business being taken over, I knew it would cause problems. "I know." I stood from the bed, walked into the adjoining room of the hotel, and paced.

"I'm trying to give you time, but my patience has run out."

"She knows nothing about running a gun and drug cartel," I insisted.

Dario was pissed. "Then you need to force her to marry me."

I gripped the phone tighter. "If you give me time, I can be convincing."

His voice held disdain. "Seems like you're more

concerned with the trust fund and keeping the details of Laurent's death to yourself."

I froze at the statement. "Are you threatening me?"

"Figure it out. It's too late to change the wedding plans. The deal will be off and your shit will unravel."

Men often thought I was some idiot they could manipulate, but underneath the beauty was brains and anyone could be taken for a ride and set up. Dario was foolish if he thought I'd drop to my knees and do his bidding without a backup plan.

"Then let me figure it out. This is your mess," I argued.

"You better fix it. She's your daughter, and you ensured we'd have no problems."

"Gigi is different. You knew this."

"I promise you. If I go down, you're going down with me."

I winced at his words, then remembered who I was. His lack of manhood was showing. "Fuck you, Dario. You don't get to tell me what to do or threaten me."

"It's your fault that the little witch is running the business."

I paced back and forth in front of the TV. Gigi would never disobey me. "She still has to marry you."

"Have you not been listening to me?" Dario demanded.

"What are you talking about?" A headache formed, and I rubbed my temple.

"She's fucking marrying Axel."

I gasped. "What the hell do you mean she's marrying Axel?"

"She came to the meeting, told everyone she was running the show, and that she was marrying Axel."

There was no way Gigi and Axel were a couple. I shook my head. "Dario, I think you misunderstood."

"She called off our wedding. Do you know how much time I have put in with her? And he waltzes in and takes what's mine."

"Calm down. I need to think. She's my daughter. I have to figure out what's going on."

He growled. "I'm the idiot who listened to you and my parents."

"I got a message from Cyrus. Everything was finalized, and now you are telling me she's marrying Axel? That makes no sense. He's too old for her."

"Have you looked in the mirror? Laurent was older than you by ten or fifteen years. What the fuck does it matter?"

"It was different for me. Gigi is naïve and impressionable."

"My father will care about this. The deal will be off for Lamberto. He stuck his neck out for us and this is how you repay him. I'm supposed to be the Boss of the family."

"It doesn't matter what Gigi thinks. I'm still in control of her trust. I'll get her back on board. Your wedding will go ahead."

"My trust is very thin in your hands."

"Let me do things my way. I understand her. She is my child, after all. I gave birth to her. I know how she thinks."

"We're past that."

"She wants someone to listen to her and go along with her ideas. I can get her back on board. This could still work. I didn't set all this up to have her destroy everything."

"All our plans will be shattered because you can't control her." Dario groaned.

"Nothing has changed, just shifted, and it's all supposed to be mine."

"Then you need to get it together and figure out how to get her under control because all this does is set us back. You're the one who wanted him gone, and now she takes over and I get nothing out of this deal."

"I'll admit I underestimated her. I shouldn't have left her alone."

"You have one day to get her back on board or we'll have bigger problems." Before I could respond, Dario ended the call.

I tapped my forehead, closed my eyes, and tried to focus on how to get things back on track. After a few relaxing breaths, I looked toward the bedroom door, then dialed Gigi's number.

"Hello," she answered.

"Where are you?"

"I'm out for dinner."

"With who?"

"Ginerva."

I knew Gigi, and she hesitated before she answered, which made me suspicious.

"What's going on?" she asked.

"Dario called and threatened not to marry you," I lied.

"The marriage to Dario was your idea. I never loved him."

"Are you calling the wedding off?"

"No, I care about someone."

Minutes passed as I tried to hold my composure. "Who?"

Gigi tried to brush me off. "We can talk when I see you at home."

"He's hurt, and you need to get him back. Dario loves you, Gigi."

"Sorry, Mom, but I don't want to marry him and you can't make me."

Cyrus fucked up all of my plans and now Gigi thought she could cut me off? She'd regret going against me. "If you want any part of your trust fund, you'll rethink your answer."

"The bank still controls my trust fund and needs both of our signatures."

I started to crumble, but held it together and counted to three. "Listen to me carefully, Gigi. I've worked hard for you, and if you back out of this marriage, I swear to God—"

"Mother, I love you, but I am no longer a child. I'm a grown woman."

Anytime she wanted to get her way, she'd throw up her age, but I didn't care. Money and power controlled this business. "The Ramini family will not be disrespected."

"I will bury the Ramini family."

"Do you hear yourself, Gigi?" I rubbed my temple.

"Who's side are you on? Your daughter's or the cartels?"

"Gigi, it's not like that." The door opened and my guest walked out with nothing but a towel around his waist. "I can't talk about this right now." If we panicked now, the plan would go up in smoke. "Who are you with? I can come to you."

"I'm heading into a meeting. I'll have to check back with you."

"You said you were at dinner with Ginerva."

"I have to go," Gigi muttered.

Everything I'd worked for was falling apart.

"Hey, why do you look annoyed?" Edmundo kissed the back of my neck, wrapping his arms around my waist.

"Gigi called off the wedding to Dario."

He froze. "Why?"

I turned in his arms, letting out a lackluster breath. Another round in bed would help, but time wasn't on my side. "She wants to be in charge of the business." I caressed his chin.

He slid his hands down to my butt, burying his face against my neck.

"Is there anything you can do with Cyrus?" Edmundo asked as he released me and sauntered to the bar, grabbing a glass and pouring a drink.

"I can try."

Bitterness spilled in his voice. "Try harder."

"At the end of the day, she's my daughter, Edmundo."

"And he's my son."

"He already threatened me. I suggest you curb your words."

He placed the glass on the table. "Come here, *mi amore*." Edmundo extended his hand.

"Where's your wife?"

"I told you about bringing her up." Edmundo grasped my hair in a tight fist.

"Ah..." I winced.

He captured my lips. "Be quiet, Rosa."

"Let me go, Edmundo," I demanded in a shrill voice.

He grinned. "You get feisty and sweet all in the same breath."

"Let me go or I'll scream."

"Get her on board." He let me go, and I stumbled back.

"I will get Gigi back on board, but you need to control Dario. Because if my daughter stays in charge, I can have her remove him and put a new underboss in his position.

He chuckled. "Carrington Cartel is not powerful right now. I would think carefully about your foolish idea."

"Then get off my case."

"You have until the end of the month."

"That's not enough time. She's planning on marrying —" I paused in fear before I spilled Axel's name. Axel was my trump card and if I spilled right now, Edmundo would take him out, removing Gigi completely. No matter how it looked, I loved my daughter.

I turned and sauntered into the bedroom, taking a moment to comprehend what had happened. I bent to retrieve my purse, jacket, and shades. Edmundo and Dario's trust was fading fast, and I needed them fully on my side.

"I need to go."

"We are not finished with this conversation."

"Didn't your wife call you an hour ago?" I cocked my head to the side.

"So you play the bitter mistress role now."

The words flowed, and power burned in my chest. "Mistress, yes. Bitter, no."

"How do you think your daughter will feel about her mother cheating and possibly setting her father up to die?" He dropped the towel and grabbed his boxers and pants.

"Go be with your wife, Edmundo. She needs you more than me."

"Jealousy looks good on you, Rosa."

I scoffed. "Dario is your problem."

"Then Gigi will be my problem if she goes through with cutting my son out."

My back was to him. "Believe me, Edmundo, you don't want to play these games with me."

"So we understand each other, *mi amore*." He grinned.

"We agree. I'll get Gigi back to the table and you'll calm Dario."

He stuck his hand out for a shake. "Not that I don't believe you, but I need this done as soon as possible."

"Clearly." We were both full of shit, but we each had information that could get the other killed. Right now, we had each to trust each other.

I looked from his hand up to his face without shaking. I left the hotel room, furious I didn't have the upper hand. Curious about Gigi's whereabouts, I messaged Fulgenzio.

Me: *Is my daughter with you?*

Fulgenzio: *She's with Axel.*

Me: *Where are they?*

Fulgenzio: *Not sure. We met at the shooting range.*

Me: *I told you she should be protected twenty-four seven.*

Fulgenzio: *Axel stated she was fine with just him.*

Me: *If something happens to my daughter, you're dead.*

I ignored him trying to call me and threw my phone on the seat after unlocking and entering my car. I closed my eyes and tried to figure out my next steps.

* * *

"Ginerva, you're close with my daughter. I know you want what's best for her." I poured Ginerva a glass of wine.

"Yes, Mrs. Carrington."

Her usual demeanor around me was lacking. Hopefully, my smile put her at ease. "Then you must know she's been acting pretty crazy lately about the wedding."

Ginerva gulped the wine and held out her glass for another. "She hasn't talked about the wedding."

"You have to understand that as a mother and only parent, it's hard to see her go down the wrong path."

"Not sure what you're asking me, Mrs. Carrington."

I leaned across the aisle and stared into her eyes. "Her idea to drop Dario and marry someone else."

"Gigi doesn't love Dario," Ginerva announced.

I hated the word love. That would come in time. Security was more important. "Love is overrated." I waved my hand, motioning for her to continue drinking.

Ginerva looked perplexed. "But?"

"No but, Ginerva. It's time for Gigi to grow up and learn that she has to do what's best for the family."

"The family wants her to marry someone she doesn't even like," Ginerva replied.

This back-and-forth was causing me a migraine. "She knows Dario from when they were younger, so it makes sense to put them together."

"I don't know."

I covered both her hands with mine and squeezed, a loving smile on my face. "Please help me convince her she's making a mistake with Axel."

"Axel?" Her eyes grew wide in shock.

"You didn't know?"

Ginerva fumbled. "I mean..."

"Tell me, you can trust me."

"She's always had a crush on him."

That revelation surprised me. "Really?" Men weren't allowed near Gigi or me unless it was a guard and they'd been with us for years.

"Maybe I shouldn't be talking about this with you, Mrs. Carrington."

"Ginerva, stop stressing. I'm her mother, the only person you should talk to about her feelings."

"He likes her. Well, I think he does."

My plan might crumble if their feelings were mutual. "Interesting."

My phone startled us and I raised my finger for her to hold on.

I put on my best smile. "Well, isn't this lovely to hear from you?"

"Sorry, I've been busy," Lamberto responded dryly.

Ginerva focused on her phone, and I turned my back to her. "Where are you?"

Lamberto answered, "At the farm."

I glanced over my shoulder at Ginerva, and she smiled as she finished her wine. I picked up the bottle and poured more into her glass. "Ginerva, I need to take this. Give me a second." I walked out of the kitchen.

"Dario and Edmundo have called me," Lamberto expressed.

"What did they say?"

"Not good things, I'm afraid."

"You're not listening, are you?"

"Rosa, you've always been a good talker."

"Good at a lot of things." I turned to look in the kitchen.

Lamberto sighed over the phone. "Gigi is not stable."

"I heard." Our butler walked past me, holding a few items in his hand, and I gestured for him to leave me alone.

"Then get her to put Dario in charge."

I harshly whispered, "Won't be easy. Apparently, she's in love with Axel."

"Who told you that?"

I looked out of the window near my front door, responding hurriedly, "Dario. And Ginerva just confirmed."

"Axel's working with Gigi?"

"Not sure, but we need to keep an eye on him." Axel could be a problem, and that made my skin crawl.

"What if he knows?"

I shook my head. "All of our bases are covered."

"This can get messy."

"I made the call and I regret nothing."

"You say that now, but when she gets deeper into the business and finds missing money and decisions that aren't approved by Laurent—"

"Keep your voice down." I covered the phone with my hand.

"Alvar is dead, and Orson wants answers," Lamberto explained.

Another headache started. All I craved was a harder drink from the wet bar tucked into the alcove. I could take away my home from me because of all this bullshit. The original works of art Laurent purchased for me, the custom banisters and Italian floor tiles that cost a hundred thousand to be installed. "Then handle it. It's not my problem."

Lamberto ignored my comment. "Obviously Axel is behind his death."

"Do you have proof?"

"He was to meet Alvar during the night of the shooting."

Ginerva walked into the hallway.

"Are you leaving, Ginerva? I planned to cook dinner and we could talk more."

"Unfortunately, my parents want to meet up for dinner," Ginerva responded.

"Tell them we should get together for dinner one day soon." I hugged her goodbye.

I watched her leave and close the door behind her.

"Handle Orson and I'll figure out Gigi." I clicked the end button and sauntered back into the kitchen. I prepared some noodles for a stir-fry and mixed them with chicken and veggies.

. Gigi impressed me today and showed she wasn't as naïve as I thought.

"Axel might be a problem." I sank down on top of the stools and ate my dinner. Families would fall if my dreams didn't happen, and I'd have no problem pulling strings within my family in America if it brought Gigi back to my side. Might be time for a reunion. I'd keep that in my back pocket in case Axel tried to come for me.

Chapter 12

Gigi

Axel allowed me to enter first, and I scanned the living room, marveling at the artwork on his walls. His place was decorated in warm colors, and had an enormous fireplace, a black leather couch, and pictures of his family on the mantel.

Axel grinned. "You can have a seat on the couch."

"What are you going to order?"

"I can order or I can cook."

I rested on his couch. "You cook?"

"Yes, I can cook, Gigi." He removed his jacket and placed it in the closet.

Axel's place was cute, with wooden floors, brick walls, high ceilings and bookcases. "I want a tour of your place."

He rolled up his sleeves, extended his hand, and escorted me down the hallway, where I noticed more artwork on the walls.

"You love art," I observed

"Yeah, something I picked up from my father."

"Surprised you like something other than being an enforcer."

He chortled, releasing my hand when we made it into the kitchen. "First, you help me cook."

"If this is a date, shouldn't I be on the receiving end?"

He paused with a wide grin.

"Not that type of receiving. Well, not yet anyway," I kidded.

He opened the fridge and grabbed spinach, tomatoes, and frozen fish. The minute I told Ginerva about my date, she'd be asking if I slept with him.

"Do you want something to drink?"

"Wine, if you have it." The view of him from the back elicited sinful thoughts.

"Wine for the Mafia Boss." He placed the glass in front of me and studied the amber liquid in his glass.

"Have you at least thought about what I said?"

"Tonight, no business talk."

I took a large swig of my wine. "Marriage is a big deal."

"Which is why I said in the first place not to go down this path with Dario or me."

I removed my jacket and picked up the knife to slice the tomatoes. "Truth or Dare?"

He drained his drink, then poured another. "What?"

"Truth or Dare. It's a game."

"Too old to play games, Gigi."

I put the knife down, turning to face him. "If you tell me the truth, I'll drop the fake marriage idea. If you take the dare, you have to take it seriously."

He shook his head as he refilled my wine glass. "You never learn."

"Pick one."

"Truth."

"How did I know you'd choose the truth?" I laughed, took the glass out of his hand, and sipped it all down.

"Do you think with your parents' death, and my father's recent death, that you're afraid to give yourself room to love someone fully?"

Axel stood with a stern look on his face. Finally, he moved to the stove, turned it on, and poured his ingredients together. "My parents are off-limits."

I slammed my glass down. "But mine aren't?"

He looked at me. "We're not doing this, Gigi."

"Why? Give me a good reason. All those nights of you coming to sit with me at the gazebo. Was that just 'babysitting?'" I emphasized with air quotes.

"Enough!"

"You want me and you're scared."

"Childish." He turned his back to me.

I grabbed his arm and turned him to face me. "I might be twenty-two, but you're the one acting like a child."

He glared.

"Dario might be an asshole, but at least he doesn't pretend and hide his feelings." I knew my words would sting.

"He's probably better for you," he murmured.

"If you truly believe that, then I should go and prepare for my wedding."

We had a standoff as he towered over me, but I wasn't intimidated by him anymore.

He clenched his fists. "What do you want me to say?"

"Anything. Hell, you were there when I got my car, and taught me how to drive. You were there when I found out about Dario and me, and every time I sneaked out because of a fight with my parents. You always talk to me like a real person." I teared up.

"It will get messy."

"Feelings are messy." I slid closer to him. "I have feelings for you, Axel, and no matter how much you try to push me away, you're in here." I lifted his hand and placed it over my heart.

Axel released a breath, ran his hand up to my neck, and gently gripped it from behind. His other moved to my waist as our lips crashed together in an intense kiss.

"The minute someone hurts you, I'll kill them," he stated, rubbing his thumb across my lips.

"Is that your way of confirming that you like me a lot?"

The fire alarm went off, and we pulled away to maneuver the burnt food into the sink.

"Guess we're ordering out now," I teased.

* * *

I finished my third glass of wine, dropped the pizza crust, and wiped my hands.

As soon as we cleaned up the mess from the burned food, Axel went out to grab a pizza. I suggested we get it delivered, but he explained he didn't want people to know where he lived. It was easy for me to relate to his line of thinking, so I stayed behind and roamed around his place.

"Exhausted." I collapsed under the blanket.

Axel massaged my feet as he sat at the other end of the couch. "It's late."

"What time is it?"

He glanced at his watch. "Almost one a.m. You can sleep in the guest room."

"Thanks. I have a meeting after class tomorrow."

"How are you going to run a gun business and college?"

"Always get myself into situations."

"Then Laurent bails you out." He chuckled.

"Either my father or you. I guess I am spoiled." He released my feet, and I climbed over his lap.

"What are you doing?"

"Just talking." I unbuttoned his shirt slowly.

"Not happening, angel." He grabbed me around the waist, lifted me up, and walked us to the guest room, where he placed me on top of the bed.

"Wait. Can you stay with me until I fall asleep?" When I reached for his hand, he lay down behind me, his arms around my waist.

"I refuse to spoil you." He kissed the back of my neck.

I turned and outlined his tattoo on his chest with my fingers. "Tell me about this tattoo."

"It's my parents."

"When's the last time you went to their grave?"

His gaze was fixed on the ceiling. "Recently."

"I think about my dad every day."

"Still fresh for you, the way he died."

"Deep in my soul, I know something is fishy with Dario."

"If that's true, let me handle him."

"When's the last time you brought a woman home?"

"I told you I've never brought anyone here."

"Never?"

"You are the first."

I observed him. "The first girl to be in your guest room."

"You think I'm some man whore?"

"Yes."

It was wonderful to see his guard come down with me when he laughed. "I've devoted all of my time to work."

"Have you ever thought about retiring?"

"This is my life, angel."

"What about kids?"

"No one should want me as a father."

"Why? You've shown me how loyal and special you are."

He climbed off the bed. "Go to sleep." He kissed me on the forehead.

I pouted. "Good night, Axel."

He paused at the door. "Good night, angel."

* * *

Two years ago.

I wrapped the towel around my waist and stepped out of the bathroom, accidentally bumping into Axel. My hands fell to his arms, while he caught me around the wrist before the towel and I fell to the floor.

"Sorry," he replied gruffly.

"What are you doing here so late?"

"Business."

"Is my dad still in his office?" I looked over my shoulder.

"Yeah." His eyes trailed down my body.

"I guess I should get dressed." As I walked around him and brushed against his shoulder, I ran my hand through my wet hair.

"You should."

"Morning." I stretched and sat up in the bed in only my panties and the shirt he gave me to sleep in for the night.

"I need to get you home," he said.

"What time is it?"

"Early."

"Thank you for last night."

He stared as I rose out of bed, picking up my dress and heels.

"You're welcome." He pushed my hair behind my ear.

An hour later, I stepped out of his car and bent, looking at him with his shades on, and smiled. "You still owe me that Truth or Dare."

"Get to class, angel."

"I like it when you call me angel." Turning, I sauntered into the house and shut the door behind me. I leaned against it, sighing dreamily.

"Someone looks like they had a good time last night." Mother stood with a cup of coffee in her hand.

"Mother, good morning." I stepped away from the door and headed toward the stairs.

"I hope you used protection," she remarked.

I paused at her comment, whirling around. "All we did was talk."

"You expect me to believe that, little girl?"

"If I want to sleep with him, it's my choice."

"So you'll whore yourself out! I'm so glad your father isn't here. He'd be ashamed."

"Funny, that's how you got that ring on your finger."

My head whipped back as she slapped me. "Understand something, little girl. I am the parent. I could take all of this away like *that*." She snapped her fingers.

"Then do it! I refuse to live my life in a bubble for you and cartel rules." I threw my hands in the air.

"That marriage is not happening. Over my dead body will I allow Axel to become your husband."

"Not up to you."

"We'll see about that." She sipped on her coffee and stared at me.

I left her alone and went to get ready for my day. I only had one class and then I'd work with Lamberto to get all the files on running the business.

Chapter 13

Axel

Gigi had plans to go to the office later, and I had Turin set up recording a few days after the initial meeting to announce her. I knew we had a snake in the family, but I couldn't pinpoint if it was one or two people working together.

"For now, I'll pretend." I removed my jacket and laid it on the chair as my phone rang

"Who's that?" Turin stood next to me in the slaughterhouse.

Our little problem squirmed in the seat, his mouth muffled.

"Gigi." I padded to the back room with the two-way mirror. "Hello."

"I thought I told you about swarming all these guards at my school."

"What are you talking about?"

"My professor is going to kill me with all these guys around me."

"I can talk to him."

"No, sir. I'd rather not have that happen, and he ends up missing."

"Did you talk with them about moving to online classes?"

She sighed. "I did and they're not happy, but I want to try."

Turin talked to Lazaro, tying the problem's hands to the chair.

"Are you listening to me, Axel?"

"Yes, you want to handle the meeting later today."

"Will that be a problem?"

"Should it become a problem, I will let you know."

"I can tell you're distracted."

"Turin and I are dealing with a problem."

"Why didn't you tell me?"

"Because it's my job to get rid of problems before they come to you."

"Only way they will respect me, Axel, is because of you."

How did this become my fault?

"Never mind. I'll talk to you later."

"Gigi, did you get the notes from today?" A deep voice on the other end of the line asked.

"Who is that?"

Gigi ignored me. "Hey, Jacque. Can I finish this call first?"

"Sure, sorry about that," Jacque replied.

"Sorry, what did you say?" Gigi responded to me.

"Tell Jacque to take his own notes," I grumbled.

Gigi giggled. "Never knew you would be jealous."

"I've never lied about being possessive over what's mine."

"When did I become yours?"

I chuckled at her question. "Not having this conversation with you."

"Fine, act like an asshole." Gigi ended the end call.

The door opened, and Turin popped his head in to check. "We need to hurry."

I marched out behind him and tossed the phone on the table. "Open your eyes," I demanded, smacking him across the face.

He screamed and tried to pull himself off the chair.

"We know you were in on Laurent's death."

He shook his head.

"Tell me the truth and I might let you live."

"I promise you, Axel, I don't know anything."

"That's too bad. You want to die at my hands?"

"Lazaro, please..." he begged.

I cut my eyes at him. "Lazaro can't help you, Franco."

He cried as snot and blood spilled down his cheeks.

Turin put in the work of getting the video footage and found Franco was the driver of the car that night. Lazaro and he went way back to childhood, and he thought I would spare him.

I squatted in front of him with the pliers and cut off two of his toes.

"Please! Argh... Ugh." He started to pass out.

"Give me the hammer."

"We need some information," Lazaro commented.

I shook my head. "He's not going to talk."

I hit both of his knees Tord his eyes rolled in the back of his head, his bloody mouth causing him to choke.

I shot him in the head and chest.

"What now?" Lazaro inquired.

"Keep looking."

* * *

"I'll call you about the tutoring thing," a guy I assumed was the one from earlier remarked and I watched him hug her, then walk toward his car.

I left Turin with Lazaro to clean up the mess and went to Gigi's school to surprise her with a ride home. I watched Gigi get in the car with Fulgenzio and drive off. Placing the cigar in the tray, I opened the door and jogged over to her little friend. Before he could slam the door shut, I yanked it wide open and snatched him out.

"Hey, man!" he shouted.

"Shut the fuck up."

"Who are you?"

I pulled the gun from behind my back.

He held hands in prayer. "Wait... Wait!"

"What's your name?"

"Huh?"

"Name!" I yelled.

"J-Jacque," he stuttered.

I smirked. "Stay away from Gigi."

"She's just a friend."

"She doesn't have friends," I drawled arrogantly.

"Okay, sorry."

"Next time she tries to talk to you, ignore her."

"But—"

I slammed the gun across his face.

"Sorry. I promise to stay away."

"Good. As her husband, I'd hate to kill you," I lied.

His eyes widened in shock.

After handling that issue, I jumped back in the car and drove to the office. Gigi was addressing the men for the second time in her capacity as Boss, and I wouldn't wait to fuck somebody up if they tried her again.

I talked to security as I passed through the double doors of the office building and onto the elevator. "Is she here?"

The doors opened to reveal Turin with a scowl on his face. "She is, but you need to see something."

"Can it wait?"

"Has to do with the cameras," Turin whispered.

I glanced at him with a hiked brow. We stepped into an office and shut the door behind us.

Turin handed me his phone. "Watch."

"She's fucking playing us. I know this marriage is bullshit," Dario said.

"What do you want me to do about it? I'm not in control," Lamberto replied.

"We need to get evidence and push it off on him. Maybe if she sees he's behind Laurent's killing, she will come crawling back to me," Dario answered.

"When this first came up, I thought it would be easy to get rid of Laurent."

"I didn't realize he would change his will on us," Dario mentioned.

"The plan was properly set to make everything easier on us. This is beyond what we need to do. Laurent should have been an easy target. You become the Boss and I get half of the business," Lamberto admitted.

"Gigi is too stupid to be the Boss. Maybe go after Casella. We set it up where Casella is behind now," Dario announced.

"Gigi wants to meet and go over shipments. If she notices numbers moved around, I'm beyond fucked, which is why we need to figure out how we can get rid of Axel."

"I'm better for her. We shouldn't be seen together for a little while."

"What are you saying?" Lamberto asked.

"I'm saying that it's too hot right now. Let her think she's in charge, and if she fucks up, it's on her. Then we vote her out," Dario answered.

"I need to talk with Orson," Lamberto said.

"Fine. Get what you can out of him. We're back in charge again."

"Gigi and Axel really a couple?"

"I don't know. I hate his smug look. Gigi was a virgin. I don't care if she let him fuck her. The little bitch was only going to be allowed to have my babies. Entire marriage would be for show and I have my women on the side."

"Women like her are pure. You have to mold them to be the perfect wife and put them in their place if they step out of line," Lamberto suggested.

Their conversation disgusted me and I wanted to kill them both where they stood. Gigi had no clue about the deception wrapped around her life.

Turin took the phone out of my hands and I sat back in my seat to think.

"He's going to make a move on her," Turin said grimly.

"I think she's right."

"About what?"

"Us getting married."

Turin nodded. "That puts more legit backing of her within the family if she has a husband."

"Dario has to be taken out."

"Too powerful. His family would join forces with Casella if we did."

My mind raced with how I would kill them all. "We

have a tail on them both, correct?" I headed out the door and down the hallway to the conference room.

"I'll beef it up."

I made it to the door and stood outside, staring at Gigi while she talked at the head of the table. "Keep them on watch while I figure out the play."

The door opened, and one of the guys came out. I headed inside and went to stand in the back of the room to face Dario and Lamberto.

"As I said, I saw the layout of the farm and started looking at our numbers," Gigi continued.

"Laurent trusted me to handle the orders, Gigi." Lamberto said, sipping on his water.

"He's no longer here, Lamberto, and we were all still grieving, but I want to spread in another direction."

Lamberto and Dario glanced at each other.

"Spread?" Lamberto repeated.

"The De Luca and Fuertes Cartels are friendly. We've done business in the past."

"The Casella family won't like this, let alone my family," Dario argued.

"Casella has been taking advantage for a long time. We need to find new sources."

A whispered conversation ensued.

"Gentleman, I can triple our income with this move," Gigi insisted, clasping her hands in front of her.

"No," Dario answered swiftly.

"Your permission is not needed. I'm only bringing this up as a courtesy."

When she was in her hoss mode, I wanted to grab her and suck on her full lips.

"Gigi, I have to agree with Dario about moving away from Casella Cartel," Lamberto said.

"You said it yourself, Casella doesn't like us. If we go in a different direction, they'll have to reassess their prices because we'll find someone to outbid them," Gigi explained.

"The three families have worked together for years. You can't come in and change things up like you're changing your fucking panties," Dario joked.

Everyone laughed.

I surged to my feet and Gigi motioned for me to stop.

"Dario, what you and everyone else fails to understand is that I make the calls."

"You'll start a war," Dario seethed through his teeth.

Gigi leaned her elbows on the table. "War is what I'm after."

I took Gigi to pick up her clothes from her place two hours after the meeting, and she insisted we go out together. Initially, I said no because I disliked being around people, but she said she'd stop talking to me if I didn't go. When I asked Gigi if that was what her mother and father did on a daily basis, she replied that her mother was worse because she talked more and wrecked the entire house if no one listened.

"You look like a killer." Gigi placed the menu on the table.

The men had checked the place out before we came inside, and I ensured the server put us in the back corner with my back to the wall so I could see when someone came through the door.

"I am a killer."

"Tonight, can you just be my date?"

"Gigi, I'm here."

"Yes, but you don't seem to be in the mood."

She was right. I didn't know how to tell her I had

evidence and was ready to kill two people in the organization—one being her ex-fiancé.

"I'll always give you my attention."

"Thank you, but I wanted to talk to you about something."

"Go ahead."

"Hello, can I get you two anything?" The server arrived at our table.

Gigi ordered for both of us and the server left to get our drinks after placing water on the table.

"What did you think of my ideas today?"

"I understand you need to do what Laurent would want to continue his legacy."

"That's why I'm worried I might have made a mistake." She cupped her chin, leaning on the table.

"You're brilliant, Gigi. Never let anyone get in your head."

Her lips curled into a smile. "I want to travel to America. Can you set up a meeting with Antonio De Luca and Joaquin? I know you're close with them."

"That won't be a problem."

Our drinks were planted in front of us and silence filled the air between us for a minute.

"Who's Jacque?"

"Jacque?"

"Is he a problem?"

She leaned back in the chair with a cocky smile. "He's in my class."

Our server returned with the food.

"He sounded familiar with you," I said once she was gone.

"Are you jealous?"

"It would get messy between Dario and now me."

Her grin fell from her face. "Are you calling me a slut?"

"No. I need to make sure I only have one person I might need to kill."

Gigi blew out a long-held breath. "No killing unless it's mafia-related."

"That I can't promise."

"Please," she begged.

"Don't beg for him."

"Axel, it's not that serious."

"Everything with you is serious," I commented.

"I'll stay away from him."

"Good, but I already talked to him."

Her eyes widened. "Please tell me you didn't threaten him?"

"If you sit in front of me and beg for his life, we're going to have a problem."

"I'm ready to go."

"Eat." I grabbed my napkin and fork.

"No longer hungry."

I groaned and pulled out my wallet, waving for the server to put our food in bags to go. I walked Gigi to my car, dropped the food in the back seat, and drove back to her place.

Her mouth opened and closed. "Why are we here?"

"I have work to do."

She turned in her seat. "You're lying."

"Gigi, I told you, I will not play games."

"I know, but Jacque is harmless."

"To you, but I know what he's trying to do."

"I want to go back to your place."

"No."

She reached for me and I moved out of her hold.

"Axel, please." She leaned over and kissed the side of my neck, sucking on my ear.

I grabbed her thigh and gripped her head, pulling her lips to my mouth.

"Mmmmm," she moaned.

I bit her bottom lip, pulled away, and started the car, heading for my place. A part of me knew the next step I was about to take would force me to put my heart in her hands and that someone, even if it was fake, had the power to undo me. The thought of being vulnerable again pissed me off, but even with Gigi being young, she'd taught me I needed to live my life.

It didn't take me long to get us home. I tossed her bag over my shoulder and dragged her upstairs to my room.

"Shit!" I pushed her against the wall and gripped her smooth brown thighs in my hands, rubbing up and down her leg before removing her heels.

"Take it all off," she whispered.

I stared at her eyes, then her lips.

"Once we do this, there's no turning back. You'll be mine, Gigi. I won't compromise."

"Same." She palmed my dick.

I gripped her dress and ripped it down the middle so her breasts popped out. "Fuck, you are beautiful."

A small breathless whisper escaped her lips.

I grabbed her hands, locking them in mine, and planted them above her head as my tongue dipped between the seam of her lips.

Chapter 14

Gigi

My dreams were about to become reality and the very thought of disappointing Axel had the hairs on the back of my neck prickling. He had way more experience than me and probably liked to be in control in the bedroom. I wanted to show him that even though I was a virgin, I could be sexy.

He trailed open-mouthed kisses along the side of my neck and my back arched off the wall as his strong hands gripped my breasts. I watched as he moved down my body until he was hovering over my pussy.

"Axel!" I gasped as his warm breath covered my sacred place.

"Keep your eyes open," he demanded. He pulled my thong aside and his tongue flicked over my heated flesh.

I propped one leg on his shoulder for deeper penetration. "Fuck!" My chest heaved rapidly.

Without thinking, I spun around to face the wall with both hands planted as he continued his meal.

"Oh!" The slap of flesh on flesh made me jump.

"That's for acting like a brat." He smacked my ass again.

He moved, pressing his large body against my back and grinding his hips against my butt. "Take me, please."

"When I'm ready." He pulled me back and grasped my neck.

"Axel!" I cried out as he tweaked my nipple.

We made it to the bed, our eyes on each other as we removed the rest of our clothes.

He shook his head as I reached for my thong. "I'll do that."

I lay back and spread my legs. Axel crawled between my thighs and lashed the tip of my nipple with his tongue. His large body covered mine, and I wrapped my legs around his waist. He looked into my eyes and smiled with a spark of eroticism. A sense of urgency drove me and I slipped a hand down his chest to grasp his thick shaft.

"You need to get on birth control," he rasped.

I nodded because kids weren't in the plan at the moment. Too much was going on and trying to manage the business and school was enough.

"This marriage might be fake, but I protect what's mine." In one fluid motion, he pushed into me.

My head flew back, and I sank my nails into his arms. The pressure was too much. He buried his head in my neck and kissed my shoulder, softly rubbing along my body to distract me from the pain. Gradually, the burning sensation gave way to pleasure. He curled into my body, slowly moving in and out of me.

"Axel!" I cried out, squirming beneath him.

I gasped when he pulled back, bent my legs wider, and picked up his strokes.

"Gigi, baby," he moaned.

His grunts of pleasure aroused me and made me feel good. I arched off the bed, digging my heels into his back and matching his urgency. Our bodies slapped together in the quiet room, and my body soared higher and higher.

"Oh, yes."

Skin to skin, we became one.

"You ready to come, baby?"

"Yes!"

"I knew this would undo me and now I can't give you back," he muttered.

"Please! Axel! Fuck, you feel so good."

He pulled out abruptly and got behind me, holding onto my leg. "So fucking sweet and tight. Come for me, baby."

He pumped faster, rubbing my clit. I tossed my head back and moaned in ecstasy, grasping his hand when he pulled my face around to kiss me.

"Uh... I'm coming." I quivered in his arms.

* * *

My eyes popped open, inspecting the room, and saw it a little after three in the morning. I felt the urge to pee and tried to move out of Axel's tight hold, but he pulled me back.

"What are you doing?" he growled.

"I have to pee."

"Hurry back."

"I thought you would kick me out afterward." I stood in only his shirt I'd thrown on after we showered last night before falling asleep.

He grunted.

I came out of the bathroom and slid back into bed, laying my head on top of his chest.

He rubbed my back down to my butt. "Are you still sore?"

I reached beneath the sheet to caress his dick. "A little, but the bath helped."

Axel bent and kissed me on the lips. I straddled his lap, and he moved his hands under the shirt, lifting it over my head so my curls tumbled over my breasts.

His eyes burned over me. "I'm not good enough for you."

"I never needed you to be good, only to show me you care." I pressed a kiss to his lips and slid my arms around his neck, nipping his ear and rocking my hips back and forth. "What do you have to do in the morning?"

He cupped my cheeks and squeezed. "What do you have in mind?"

"Finalizing our agreement." My heart filled with anticipation of being a wife to him. Even if we didn't last long, I needed to make sure he knew I would be the best thing he'd ever have in his life once he left.

He pecked me on the lips, sliding inside me gently. He assisted me while I was on top and rubbed my nub until I shattered for him.

"Axel!" My body jerked, collapsing on top of him.

As my breathing calmed, he rubbed my back, kissing my forehead, and we drifted back to sleep.

Hours later, I reached for him and discovered an empty bed. I smiled at the soreness between my legs. Glancing around his bedroom, I noticed the large windows and a balcony beyond that I planned to explore later.

I pushed the covers to the side and climbed out of

bed, sauntering to the bathroom to clean up. Forty minutes later, freshly showered, I found Axel in his office on the phone. He waved for me to enter, and I sat on his desk and crossed my legs.

Axel placed a hand on my thigh while he talked. "Set up the flights and tell him it's an emergency." He finished his call and turned toward me.

I raised an eyebrow. "Flights? Where are you going?"

Axel leaned forward and kissed my knee. "I scheduled my jet to take us to America."

My eyes widened. "When are we going?"

"This is a work trip, Gigi. No shopping and hanging."

I pouted. "Alright, grandpa."

I jumped down off the desk and turned to leave, but he extended his arm, pulling me back into his lap.

"*Cara*, you aggravate me." He lightly bit me on the shoulder.

"I'm tired of you treating me like a child. It would be a matter of time before we went back to being distant if last night hadn't happened."

"I apologize. You're right."

"Thank you. I need to call Ginerva to see if she can meet for breakfast."

"We leave in two days."

I run a hand over his beard. "Will I see you tonight?" The look in his eyes captivated me.

"What do you think? I need you around me not only because you keep me sane, but you've given me you."

* * *

An hour later.

Ginerva scooted forward in the chair, put her phone

down, and waited for me to talk. It was strange for us to go days without talking, and I missed my best friend. Before I arrived, I ordered ahead with all of our favorites.

I offered her one of my crepes. "You look pretty."

"Thanks. So what's new with you?" She slipped her napkin on her lap and picked up her glass of water, downing it.

I forced the food down before I spoke, looking around to make sure no one was listening to our conversation. "A lot, and I apologize for being distant lately."

"Explain."

I cut into my crepes, tossing a piece into my mouth. "I slept with Axel."

Ginerva dropped her fork and choked on her food. "How was it?"

I closed my eyes and recalled our night together. "Amazing." I opened my eyes again with a smirk.

Ginerva put two fingers in the air. "Are you together now? I have so many questions. What about Dario?"

I leaned forward on the table and cupped my hands around my mouth to whisper, "Dario is not a factor in my life. Axel and I are together and getting married."

Her eyes grew bigger. "Maybe that's why your mother —" She stopped abruptly.

Her comment caught me by surprise. "My mother?"

Ginerva sighed, rubbing her temple. "I don't want to be in the middle, Gigi." She looked around nervously. She crossed her arms over her chest and lowered her head to avoid eye contact.

"You're not. You're my best friend, and I trust you."

She mumbled, "I had dinner with your mother the other night."

I frowned. "Dinner?" My mother hated having guests

unless she had something to gain from it. Most times it was to get money from my father.

She nodded. "At first, I didn't think anything of it because we've done it before, but she asked me a lot of questions."

My palms became damp. "About?"

Ginerva squared her shoulders. "You and Axel."

That caused an alarm bell to go off. "Explain everything."

"Mostly about your relationship and the wedding with Dario."

"She's snooping."

Up went her eyebrows. "You need to be careful."

"She's harmless."

A worried expression marred her face. "Maybe you're right, but she seemed pissed."

"Rosa is delusional. I was blind to it at first, but now I can see she's going around trying to sabotage what my father created."

"Just be careful."

"You should listen to your friend, Gigi," Dario said, appearing from nowhere.

The last thing I needed to interrupt my day was Dario. Ginerva looked between us as he slid a chair up to the table.

"Ginerva, do you mind if I speak with Gigi for a second?"

I grabbed her wrist as she stood. "No, we have nothing to talk about." My brow puckered threateningly.

Dario picked up the butter knife and cut into my food. "Gigi, we have plenty to talk about. I suggest Ginerva leaves if she wants to make it home safely." He tossed the food in his mouth and smirked.

Whenever I talked back, his first course of action was to threaten me.

"Gigi, it's fine. We can catch up later." Ginerva grabbed her bag and left the restaurant.

I watched her walk out to her car, then narrowed my eyes on Dario as I sat back in my seat.

"This idea to push Casella out will not work," Dario muttered.

"Okay." I pressed my fingers together on the table.

Disapproval gleamed in Dario's eyes. "Are you listening? I'm the only one keeping the men from revolting against you."

"Okay." Each nonchalant answer pushed his buttons.

Dario's icy gaze ran over my body. "Something is different about you."

I reached for my bag and coat. "What do you want, Dario? I'll never be with you."

"While you've continued to act like a bitch, I've secured the men's trust and if they believe you're taking them in the wrong direction... It won't be good for you."

"Of course, because you believe you have all the answers." I snorted.

"I know I do."

I pushed the chair back, sliding my arms into my coat. "Casella is behind my father's murder, and you want to keep working with him?"

"There's no evidence of that."

"Because of you!" I yelled, and the other guests glanced in our direction.

He grasped my hand as I spun to leave.

"Don't do anything stupid," he warned.

I yanked away and marched out of the restaurant.

Fulgenzio held the car door open, and I climbed in, waiting as he jogged around to the driver's side.

Me: *Ginerva, I promise to explain everything soon.*

Ginerva: *Are you all right?*

Me: *Axel and I are flying to America. When I get back, we can talk.*

Ginerva: *Please be safe.*

Me: *You too, and stay away from my mother.*

I closed out of that message thread and went to text Axel when Dario's name popped up.

Dario: *War with Casella will break Carrington Cartel.*

Me: *I see your threats continue.*

Dario: *I can forget everything if you come back and we get married.*

I smirked at his response.

Me: *I have a real man now.*

Dario: *Fuck you and Axel.*

Me: *He did, and I liked it.*

I blocked him and scrolled to Axel's name.

Me: *Hey, Dario crashed my date with Ginerva.*

Axel: *Did he touch you?*

I nibbled on my bottom lip nervously, wondering if I should answer that question. Axel was possessive as my bodyguard. Now we'd stepped over that line, he could kill Dario before we found out the truth.

Me: *No, just threatened me.*

Axel: *Don't lie to me.*

Me: *He didn't. He brought up the Casella deal.*

Axel: *Stay home until I get you.*

Me: *Okay.*

Chapter 15

Axel

New York, two days later.

I slipped a tip to room service and pushed the cart of food to the table, setting everything up. After we'd flown in, we came straight to the hotel, unpacked, and slept for hours. Gigi had plans to check out the property her father had set aside for her.

The door to the bathroom opened, and she emerged with a towel wrapped around her hair. "I didn't hear room service knock."

"The door was already open when I stepped out for the paper."

She sat down and grabbed the orange juice. "What's on the agenda for today?"

"I set up a meeting with Joaquin and Antonio. Tomorrow we can do whatever you want."

A grin curved her lips. "Maybe a show or something."

Second thoughts poked in my head with her vision of why we were here. "This isn't a vacation, baby."

I didn't miss the glare flash across her face.

Silence sprinkled the room. "Never said it was."

"Good, Antonio might want us to show favor."

She tipped her head. "Show favor how?"

"A few guns for free."

Gigi popped a strawberry in her mouth. "Is that what has happened in the past?"

"A few times."

"Then I'm fine with that arrangement."

I admired her awareness of the cartel business and was pleased she took her position seriously. "All right." I picked up my phone and sent a message.

"What time do we have to be at the meeting?"

"This afternoon."

A grin creased her face. "Can you go with me to see the house?"

"I need to get the shipment arranged."

"How about Lazaro or Turin handle the drop?"

Her prompt negotiation had me smiling. "You have something else on your mind?"

Gigi drummed her fingers on the table. "I know it's a fake marriage, but can we get a ring?"

"Already have the papers drafted and signed, Gigi."

"I know, but I'd like to get a ring. To make it official."

Her eagerness was cute, but something behind her eyes told a different story.

I stood and walked over to my briefcase and grabbed the paperwork stating we were husband and wife.

"Mr. Bresciani, I have the papers you ordered." Cyrus handed me a white envelope.

I flipped it over and removed the documents with a certificate of marriage on top. "No one knows you have these, correct?"

His breath quickened. "Only you and me."

"And after a year, she can take over her trust fund?"

"She could, unless someone has it reversed."

I tensed. "Do you think Rosa would protest?"

He lowered his eyes. "Mrs. Carrington approached me about changing it to Gigi's thirtieth birthday, but I refused."

"From now on, anything dealing with Gigi, you call me first."

"You sure it's fake between you two?"

"Yes. Remember to call me if anyone attempts anything else."

That night, I'd planned on talking to Gigi, but work had us both preoccupied, followed by a flight on top of Dario showing his ass.

"Axel. Axel!"

"Huh?"

Frustration bubbled in her face. "Where did you drift off to?"

I tapped my foot. "Thinking."

"About?"

"You."

She smiled. "What about me?"

"I had Cyrus draw up the marriage license."

"Did you sign it?" Heat flushed her cheeks.

Air stalled in my lungs. "I did."

Gigi held her hand out. "Let me see."

I slid it over.

Gigi searched through the papers. "Everything looks fine."

"We're married on paper, but not legally." My eyes roamed over her intently.

She shifted in her seat. "It says my trust fund can be released if I stay married for one year."

"Yeah, it's a loophole Cyrus never explained at the reading."

Her face showed softness. "Oh."

My eyes sharpened at her quietness.

"Dario and my mother can't know about this at all, or I'll be sitting in a dark room until the wedding day."

I reached over and lifted her face to look at me. "Cyrus said she tried to change it after we left."

Gigi's mouth tightened. "There's something evil about a mother who refuses at every turn to love a child."

"Underneath the hate, she loves you."

Gigi went back to eating her food. "Doubt we're talking about the same Rosa Carrington."

"Anyway, you can get your ring now," I teased.

She dropped the papers on the table. "Well, I kind of had a thought now."

"No more ideas." I rose from the chair.

She grabbed my hand and pulled me back down to the chair. "Wait! Hear me out."

"Go ahead." I shoved my hands in my pockets.

"Why do we have to fake it, when we can do a year and I can get my inheritance?"

"Gigi, you're not thinking clearly." I shook my head.

"More clearly than you. The other night, you told me I belonged to you. Unless that was a lie." Gigi leaned over the table with her lips a few inches from mine.

My nostrils flared. The glow of her skin entranced me. "Angel, you're mine, from your pink toes to your plump lips, curly hair and soft thighs. I can't sleep without you."

"So I propose we get married for real, and stay married for a year and I'll get my trust fund and give you—"

"I don't want your money."

She stepped back. "So, what do you want?"

"You think I'm doing all this for money?"

Gigi drew back and moved from the table. "If it's not money, then what? To clear your conscience over my father's death?"

"Angel, I'm going to pretend you didn't say that." I stopped and inhaled a deep breath before we got into a full-blown argument.

"Think about what I said. I need to change." She turned and went to the bedroom.

I huffed. A real marriage. The thought of her with someone else filled me with anger to the point of wanting to kill anyone that looked her way. Her on top of an empire and me behind her to watch her back and protect against any enemy.

The bedroom door opened again, and she strutted out in a gray pantsuit. Her makeup was subtle and her hair cascaded down to her back. "Are you ready? I already called the realtor."

"Give me a minute." I hopped up and went to change.

* * *

Dullness shrouded the room. When I made the call to come here, I'd provided little detail on the nature of the visit or who I would bring with me.

Both gentlemen sat silent and waited for me to begin, avoiding Gigi's glare. When they found out about Laurent, everything was halted on their end until a leader was appointed they could trust. Since Gigi came aboard, there was still hesitation on their part.

"Miss Carrington, my wife, Sofia, and I would like to extend our condolences on your loss." Joaquín said.

Antonio did what he does best and stayed silent.

"Thank you. I appreciated the flowers at the funeral," Gigi answered.

"Axel, it's been a minute since we've talked," Joaquín said.

"Work, plus changes in the family."

"Axel informed us you're the new cartel leader, Gigi," Antonio challenged.

"That's true."

"Tell us why you've come here."

I began to speak when Gigi remained silent.

Antonio held up a hand to stop me. "We want to hear from her."

"Mr. De Luca, you've known me as Laurent's daughter, a kid in your eyes, but tragically, things change."

"I agree," Antonio replied.

"Axel told me you are loyal to my father and have a longstanding business relationship."

"He's made us very rich," Joaquin answered.

"And I want to continue what he started."

"Women aren't usually in charge."

"I've learned, which is why I came to you both, because I need your backing and trust."

Antonio raised an eyebrow. "With whom?"

"My family and associates."

"Casella and Ramini family," I added.

"Explain," Joaquin probed.

"I believe they're behind my father's death and if they want me out, I'll be next. When I said I wanted to do business with you, it became apparent I would be on my own."

"You think it's an inside job?" Antonio asked.

"I have evidence."

Gigi whipped her head toward me. "What evidence?"

"Recording. I wanted to wait before I showed you."

"How long have you known?" she questioned.

"A few days."

"One thing I can tell you, Gigi, is that the men you love in this business make decisions that are best for you in their minds. Don't take it personally," Antonio explained.

"I know that now."

I reached in my pocket, removed the phone, and played the voice recording.

"That's Dario," Gigi said.

"Turin set up devices in the office."

"Wow," she responded.

"What do you need from us?" Joaquin queried.

"Come on board and we'll give you ten crates as a favor."

"That can lead to war. Orson Casella isn't my favorite, but we've been cordial," Antonio said.

"Understood, but Dario and Lamberto are trying to take over and push Gigi out." At this point, we need to call in all our favors.

Joaquin looked from me to Gigi.

"The fake marriage... is that true?" Joaquin asked.

"Yes, my mother and father arranged for me to be with Dario, but he's never been someone I wanted."

"How does Axel fit into your plans?" Antonio challenged.

I didn't like to put her on the spot, but we had to show our cards in order to get support.

"I love Axel, but my mother hates him. When Cyrus told me it didn't matter who I married, I talked with Axel and he felt the same."

"I'd like for you to come to dinner with my wife," Antonio said.

Gigi glanced at me, and I nodded.

She nodded. "We can arrange that while we're here in town."

"Twenty crates, plus kilos," Joaquin stated.

Gigi eyed him. "I can agree to those terms. You've given your full support to handling Ramini and Orson."

"Whatever you need," Antonio replied.

Gigi smiled in answer.

* * *

Once we finished our meeting, the realtor sent the address of where to meet her. Fulgenzio came with us, along with a few more men for protection, who drove behind us to the location. Gigi had an idea to go to the jewelry store before dinner with Antonio and his wife. I didn't need a ring, but she explained women can get catty about those things and she hated to look like an embarrassment on her first trip.

"That's her." Gigi pointed at the brunette standing on the porch after the gate closed behind us.

The property was miles out of the city in Upstate New York and sat on forty acres of land. After parking, I came around to help Gigi out.

"Ms. Carrington, so happy to finally meet you," the realtor said.

Gigi extended a hand. "You too, Lois. Please call me Gigi."

"Gigi it is, and this must be your husband." Lois reached her hand out for a shake.

"Axel," I responded.

"Welcome home to you both. Your father and his lawyer talked about you fondly."

Lois held up a phone to the door, and it unlocked automatically. We stepped inside and I heard doors close behind me.

"Check the perimeter, and see what we need to do for security," I instructed Fulgenzio. "I know Laurent bought the place a while ago, but in case we're not here all the time, I want eyes on the place."

The front entrance felt like a museum. It was white with a winding staircase and art on the walls. Gigi talked with Lois as they toured the living room. I went in the opposite direction, down the hall to the other rooms, finding a door at the end of the hall with a light on. I pushed forward and saw it was a bedroom with a few pictures on the wall.

"Hey." Gigi touched my shoulder.

"Yeah."

She leaned toward me. "Do you like the place?"

I spread my hands around her waist. "It's fine."

"Just fine?"

"What do you want me to say?" I pulled her into my chest.

"Anything besides fine."

Reluctantly, I let her go. "How about this place is amazing and I can't wait to eat your pussy in every room?"

"Is that all you think about? Sex?"

"Possibly."

She stretched her arms around my neck. I ran my hands down to her ass and cupped both cheeks.

"Mmmmm," Gigi moaned into my mouth.

I pulled her into the bedroom and shut the door behind us, nudging her to the bed on her back. The memory of her smell incited me into an animalistic lust. I quickly stripped her of her clothes, kissed up her thighs, and nuzzled my nose against her smooth silky, brown skin. She never denied me on our first night, and I hoped she wouldn't now since we weren't at my place.

I trailed a hand across her stomach, taking in the sight of her plump breasts. I dipped my head and devoured her caramel toned nipples, and she arched off the bed.

"Axel. Oh, baby," she groaned, rubbing a hand across my head.

I let her control the flow as she kissed me, sucking on my tongue. Slipping a finger in her panties, I circled in and out as she writhed beneath me.

"Did you lock the door?" she whispered.

I looked at her seductively. "No."

"Axel!" Her eyes popped open.

"Shush." My gaze was bold on her body.

"But what if—"

I covered her mouth with mine to shut her up. Unbuckling my belt, I lined myself up and slid inside her, caressing her cheek. We stared at each other for a moment, enjoying our connection.

"Damn, Gigi," I groaned when she met my strokes.

"Oh, God! Right there." Her eyes rolled and her face filled with lust, her voice almost unrecognizable.

I spread her wider, speeding up my strokes before we had guests interrupt.

"God, you're everything." I never spoke during sex, but Gigi wasn't like most women. She had no idea of the hold she had on me. She didn't know a year of marriage was all I could give her.

Gigi turned us over so she was on top. She braced her

hands on my chest and bounced up and down. "Make me come, baby."

There was a maddening hint of torture when I was inside of her I couldn't describe. "Fuck, you're the best of me."

"Tell me again."

I knew it was wrong because she was emotionally invested. "I can't imagine a world without you."

"Shit!" she gasped. "I can't hold it any longer."

I pumped harder and faster.

Then came a knock on the door.

"Go away!" I yelled.

Gigi laughed. "Be nice."

Aching for another round, I plunged back into her sweet entrance and circled my hips slowly. I buried my face in her neck. I never wanted to let her go.

Chapter 16

Gigi

I slid my bottom lip between my teeth as Axel pressed a thumb against my opening. I cleared my throat, flushed from our earlier lovemaking. Antonio had a car pick us up to bring us to his home for dinner with his wife, Sabrina. We'd met before briefly at a party, and now we would be doing business, we could get to know each other better.

"Gigi, you're in school, correct?" Sabrina asked.

I cleared my throat and nudged Axel's hand away. "Uh... huh."

"Newlyweds," Sabrina teased.

Axel chuckled at my embarrassment.

"Nothing to be ashamed of. Antonio never lets me go a day without touching me." Sabrina placed her hand over his, and he lifted it to his lips.

I changed the subject. "How did you and Antonio meet?"

They looked at each other. "His club."

"Was it love at first sight?"

"Yes," Antonio said as Sabrina responded simultaneously with, "No."

Axel chortled.

"We tell this story all the time, but he's going to make it seem like love at first sight," Sabrina replied.

"The moment she came into my orbit, she became mine," Antonio stated.

"I know you have kids now, but was it hard in the beginning juggling work and married life?" They seemed like a replica of Axel and me in that I wanted him from the first time I saw him, and he kept me at arm's length.

Sabrina looked at Antonio for a moment. "At first I played hard to get. He made it very clear I was his woman even before we even went out on a date."

Sabrina laughed, and Antonio winked at her.

"Reminds me of someone." I poked Axel in the shoulder.

"Love is a complicated thing, but I don't regret the struggles we had because he was everything I needed," Sabrina explained.

"Marriage is the number one priority, business second," Antonio expressed.

"How long are you two here in town?" Sabrina asked.

"Until tomorrow," I answered.

"You should come to lunch with Janice and me," Sabrina suggested.

"I haven't seen her since the party."

Sabrina chuckled. "She would love to get away from the kids."

"Axel, do you mind?"

"No, have fun."

"Great. You men can do business tomorrow, while we have lunch and maybe some shopping," Sabrina tittered.

"Pops, where's the other control?" Their eldest son

came into the room. He was the spitting image of his dad.

"AJ, how many times have I told you to keep your games together?" Sabrina fussed.

"Sorry, Mom," he murmured. He seemed like a sweet boy.

"Where's your brothers and sisters?" Antonio questioned.

AJ shrugged.

"I'd advise you to wait on children, so you're not dealing with these types of nonverbal answers," Sabrina hissed.

"Look in the toy room," Antonio replied.

"Are you going to speak to our guests, AJ?" Sabrina challenged.

"Hi." Their son darted out of the room and we burst into laughter.

"That's your son," Sabrina sighed.

Antonio reached for her, pulling her out of her seat and into his lap. "She's grumpy because she might be pregnant." Antonio ran a hand over her cheek.

Sabrina slapped him on the arm. "Stop telling people that. Not pregnant," Sabrina argued.

"Spoiled."

"Because of you."

They fussed back and forth.

* * *

Sabrina invited me out to her family's restaurant for lunch with her friend, Janice. Their other friend, Liz, was out of town with her husband, Bruno. They explained about the weekly hangout the girls organized without the husbands and kids.

Food filled the entire table, and we had a massive choice. Antonio told his staff to give us anything we wanted and was even going to close the place down for us, but Sabrina told him not to stress everybody. Still, the guards assigned to us remained laser-locked on our table.

As soon as we clinked glasses, I drank the entire wine. I looked at Sabrina and Janice as mentors because they were older and for their work as a boss.

"I remember meeting you at the party, Gigi," Janice remarked. "How is everything going?"

"Life has been crazy," I replied, refilling my glass.

"Sabrina told me about your father's death. We all live this life, but it hurts when someone close to you is taken away," Janice said softly.

"I've had so many condolences, I almost feel numb," I said sadly.

"We understand. You're young to be dealing with so much," Sabrina expressed.

I drained my drink. "Axel has been a great help."

"He's not bad to look at either." Janice hiked a brow.

I covered my face in embarrassment.

"You two have good taste. Antonio and Carlo are nice to look at."

"Momma always said if you open your legs, make sure it's something to brag about," Janice joked. "Those eyes captured me. One thing led to another, and I ended up having all his babies."

"Not babies anymore." Sabrina laughed.

"That's true. I remember a time when I only had to worry about changing a diaper. Now it's girlfriends and boyfriends calling." Janice gulped her champagne.

"Antonio never told me if you liked the guy who was

arranged to be your husband," Sabrina said, turning her gaze on me.

"He and I grew up around each other, but I never liked him in that way. He's always been a jerk."

"Probably the playboy type," Janice commented.

I nodded. "He's an asshole who wants me to be the little wife at home and give him sex. I know he wants my money."

"So he doesn't love you?" Sabrina queried.

"No. He told me it's all about him being in charge of the business. I refuse to give up my family's business and my body to him," I snarled.

"Good. You did the right thing," Janice replied.

"I'm not sure what I mean to Axel. I don't know if we'd be here if my father was still alive."

"Are you having a big wedding?" Janice asked.

"No. We're already married on paper, but I need to get my ring."

"Why not go to the courthouse before you head back and we'll have a little party before you fly home," Sabrina suggested.

"I can't. Axel's not the party type."

"On paper, without people you know as witnesses of your love, doesn't seem like something your father would want," Janice remarked.

"A dream wedding would be somewhere like Greece, but I have to get back to running a business."

"Maybe we could do a little something at Sabrina's house." Janice volunteered her best friend's home.

Sabrina spat out her drink. "How are you giving up my place for a wedding?"

"Oh, please. You love to throw parties," Janice teased.

"Shut up, Janice. But if you want a small, intimate

ceremony, Gigi, I'm sure we can pull something off," Sabrina announced.

"Thank you. Let me talk to Axel first."

* * *

Later that evening.

"We are gathered here to entwine two souls as one," the pastor announced.

I smiled at Axel before scanning the room. Sabrina, Janice and their husbands and kids were all witnessing as we tied the knot. My dream wedding would have been with my father walking me down the aisle in a church surrounded by family and friends who loved me.

I clasped Axel's hand and thought back to all those times he let me talk his ear off about my fucked-up life and the decisions that were placed upon me because I was the daughter of the most ruthless Mob Boss in Italy. This time, I had the choice and did what was best for me.

I repeated the words from the pastor. "I do."

"Axel Bresciani, do you take Gigi Carrington to be your wife, to have and to hold, in sickness and health?"

"I do." He pulled me into his chest as the pastor pronounced us husband and wife.

The room erupted in cheers and claps.

"Really mine."

I looked into his eyes. "All yours for real."

Love shined bright in his eyes.

"Time to really party," Janice joked.

We laughed.

"She'll party for anything, a wedding, a promotion. Hell, a new car," Carlo quipped.

Janice slapped him on the arm and everyone laughed

at the two of them as they went back and forth.

I wrapped my arms around Axel's neck and leaned into his chest, cupping his chin.

"Husband."

"Wife." He rubbed my cheek.

"Before you two party, let's go into my office," Antonio interrupted.

Sabrina pursed her lips at his request. "Business was taken care of yesterday, Antonio. We only have them for a small amount of time."

"*Bella*, let me finish up, and I'll get them back to you in a minute." Antonio kissed the tip of her nose, and she puckered up for another kiss.

"Here they go." Janice chortled.

I giggled and strode through the hallway into Antonio's office with Axel, while the rest went to gather around the dining room for dinner. Axel closed the door behind us. Antonio sat on the edge of his desk, shifting to pick up an envelope, and holding it out to me.

"Here's the agreement we spoke about, plus a few names of my best assets in Italy who can help on your return journey."

I removed the paperwork, skimming over it before handing it to Axel.

"I'm familiar with these names. Joaquin is fine with giving a portion of his percentage to cut ties with Casella?" Axel probed.

"Joaquin, more than anything, is about loyalty, and if Orson betrayed Laurent, it's only a matter of time before Fuertes would get stiffed," Antonio implied.

"Are you letting us handle it our way?" I needed to know before any decisions were made without my input. Men instantly tried to protect women—it was a natural state. But I was in power and wanted to make the moves that would have an impact.

"To an extent. I need assurance my name won't be implicated. As you know, I've cleared my name in high-profile issues, but any type of rumblings of war business—"

"Could hurt the De Luca Cartel. We understand."

"You know, you remind me of someone," Antonio mentioned.

"Who?"

"A former foe, Queen. Like you, she was dealt a blow with her father's death," Antonio remarked.

"I believe my father might have talked about her a time or two."

"She was impressive. A boss in her own right."

"But?"

"She became too invested in trying to kill me."

"What happened to her?" I questioned.

Antonio paused in thought. "Same thing that will happen to Dario."

I understood clearly what I had to do—kill Dario before he tried to kill me. I glanced at Axel. "We'll fly out and get to work."

"Tonight, we strategize, and when we get back, it's time to put our moves in place," Axel announced.

"All roads lead to the Carrington Cartel," I resolved, letting out a deep sigh.

Hours after a lively celebration, we went back to the hotel, showered, and lounged on the balcony.

Axel held me against his chest. "Did you enjoy the trip?"

My chest felt as if it would burst. "I have. I could stay here forever."

The tense lines on his face relaxed. "Is that right?"

"Anywhere with you is my home, but I'd like a fresh start."

"Have you made arrangements for school?"

I went silent.

"Gigi." He nudged me.

"No. I'm stuck on learning the business." I became uneasy at the thought of my path now that I didn't have my father—or my mother—in my corner.

"You know I can't live here forever with you."

I pulled away. "What do you mean?"

"Gigi, my life is in Italy."

That set alarm bells ringing. I cleared my throat. "Business will be wherever I want it to be."

He stared at me. "Not how it works with me."

My guard went up. "Explain."

"I travel, in and out, no matter the time."

"So if we had children, I'd basically be raising them alone."

His face showed confusion. "Children?"

"Tell me you want children, Axel?" My misgivings increased by the minute.

He gave me a narrowed glance. "I don't argue."

"Who says we're arguing?" I raised my voice.

"Your parents might have had a relationship like that, but I'll never raise my voice to you, and I expect the same in return." He clipped my chin, rose from the chair, and headed back into the suite.

I stayed out and gazed at the night sky. His demeanor had completely changed, and I wasn't sure if I should continue with the conversation while we're both upset or let things calm down and try to talk tomorrow. I would love children in the future, but not while I was in school.

Sabrina and Janice were prime examples of married women with kids who handled their responsibilities.

For Axel to blow me off like I was crazy to want kids was stupid. We hadn't talked about the big stuff, but I knew we loved each other. He'd see that being an enforcer for the rest of his life and having nothing to show for it beyond money couldn't bring happiness.

I got up, stepped into the suite and found him lying in bed watching American football. I climbed over his lap and placed a hand on his naked chest. "I don't want to fight."

"I don't either."

I chose my words carefully. "Can we call a truce for now?"

He turned to face me. "Laurent put me in a position to be who I wanted to be. Nothing will change that. My conscience is clear and I stand behind my decision to stay in the cartel."

"I get that."

"Then I will never have this conversation again. You may have the Carrington last name, but it means nothing to me as your husband. You might be the Boss of the cartel, but not me."

My only response to his words was a nod of agreement. He kissed me and shifted his attention back to the game. I climbed under the covers and dozed off with a lot on my mind to take back with me to Italy. We had plenty of opportunities to create whatever we wanted together. Children weren't an immediate priority, but I couldn't deny I wanted Axel's babies at some future point. I wanted children to love, especially with the way I grew up. I didn't want to continue the negative cycle and pressure placed upon me.

Chapter 17

Axel

Silence spread as soon as the metal door closed. Gigi's boots clanked against the floor. We'd been back from Italy for a week and stayed low, only coming out briefly to handle business at the farm.

I'd helped to assemble Gigi's resources for battle with Lamberto and Dario, but it was up to Gigi to command the room and get all the guys to respect her as the Don of the family.

My eyes raked over each man as they studied her. The only thing they wanted was to know she wouldn't lead them into something without a plan. There were two types of Bosses—those who led without crumbling and those who did. Dario left crumbs that would lead to his own demise.

Today, Antonio had arranged for us to meet with the team for backup to deal with Dario and Casella.

"Gael, pleasure to meet you." Gigi extended a hand.

"Nice to see you both," Gael responded.

"What did Joaquin have to promise you to assist?" I asked.

He chortled. "More than you can imagine. I had to leave my wife and kid, so it cost you a lot."

"I'll be more than happy to repay," Gigi replied.

Gael glanced at Axel. "You know he owes me."

"Your husband owes me for saving his life, plus he can afford it," Gael remarked.

Gigi frowned. "I don't understand."

"Axel isn't broke. I hope you don't think he's only operating off his money from the mafia," Gael said to annoy me. We'd bantered back and forth like brothers for years.

"She knows enough," I countered.

My heart raced as Gigi stared at me suspiciously.

"Investments and money from my parents," I said, easing her mind.

"Oh," Gigi responded.

"Tell me what this is all about and why I needed to be here," Gael grumbled.

Gigi leveled her gaze on every person in the room. "I requested for you all to be here today. This is life or death, but I would not ask for something I wasn't prepared to sacrifice myself for."

"Casella has hands in everything. What are you proposing?" a guy in the corner of the room asked.

"Orson Casella is behind my father's murder."

The room fell silent.

"What proof do you have?" another soldier demanded.

"Dario Ramini and Lamberto, my underboss, set it in motion," I responded.

There were grumblings and whispers.

"To state something like that without proof could

mean death for us all," one blurted out, brows knitted together.

"We have proof," I answered, dragging my eyes away.

Gael's gaze darkened.

"Axel and I are married. Dario is hell-bent on destroying my life because I chose someone else," Gigi explained.

"Antonio and Joaquin okayed this union?" Gael wondered.

I opened my mouth to reply when the windows shattered with the staccato of gunfire. I lunged for Gigi and pulled her down, covering her with my body.

"Stay down!" I patted along her arms and legs to check for any wounds.

"Are you hit?" she questioned, reaching to grasp my hand.

"Fine. Stay next to me." Pulling the weapon attached to my ankle, I handed it to her before pulling my gun.

Gunfire exploded around us as I lifted Gigi into my arms and backed out of the room toward the exit stairs.

Gigi screamed, and I tightened my grip on her, running and aiming my gun, when the door behind us burst open.

"It's me!" Gael yelled.

A few men entered behind him as bullets hit the walls. Sirens blared close by, and I spotted the door leading to the alley just as someone yanked it open.

I raised my gun and returned fire. The other person dropped to the ground.

"Shit!" Gigi's voice trembled as I lowered her to her feet.

"You're fine. We're almost out of here."

We stepped over the body, and I peeked into the hallway. "This way." I kept her behind me, with Gael at her back.

"How did they know we'd be here?" Gigi whispered.

I didn't reply, but my gut told me Dario was behind this.

A quick glance through the office windows showed nobody there. "Fulgenzio is probably in the back if he heard the gunshots," I muttered.

"Take the stairs. The elevator is sitting ducks," Gael spoke.

I ran a hand over my head and glanced out of the window to the streets, now slammed with police and ambulances.

"Fuck. We have to go through the back before the cops come."

"Follow me." Gael was loyal, and I knew he wouldn't sabotage or jeopardize our friendship.

We ran through the exit to the back alley. I was relieved when I saw Fulgenzio with the car, waving for us to climb inside. I got Gigi in safely and slammed the door behind Gael and me, punching the window in frustration.

"Calm down. We're okay," Gigi said, her eyes filling with tears.

"Fulgenzio, take the alley onto the freeway. We need to stay off the radar," I commanded. I pulled Gigi to me and pressed a kiss on her forehead.

Gael pulled his phone out and sent a text as Fulgenzio swerved onto the main road.

* * *

Hours later, we ended up at the farm. Gigi showered in the bathroom with the door open while I contemplated my next moves.

"Is she alright?" Turin asked at the end of the phone.

I watched her warily when her head fell into her hands. "No, she's shaken up."

"Do you need me to come out there?"

I chewed on my lower lip. "No. Find Dario and Lamberto."

"Did you lock down the farm?"

"Yeah." I rubbed my eyes.

"Whenever you give one-word answers, I know you're ready to kill someone."

I huff in amusement. "He made a bad choice today."

"Dario and Lamberto often do, but that doesn't mean you retaliate out of frustration without thought."

Turin was always giving me a reason to pause before reacting, but no one would be able to stop me once I got my hands on them. Not even God.

"Gael is here," I muttered.

"He's a good pick. Listen to him."

"Any news on Orson?"

Turin sighed. "Not yet, and it's pissing me off. Usual hangouts are dry."

"Make sure we get word soon. Be ready to kill everybody if no one comes clean."

His voice faded in and out. "Lamberto won't let you kill Dario."

"He'll have no choice once I kill his family."

"Think before you act."

The shower turned off. Gigi stepped out and wrapped herself in a large towel.

The nagging in the back of my mind refused to let me think straight. "Keep me updated."

"I pray you remember you have a soul," Turin said.

"My soul died with my parents." I clicked end and dropped the phone on the counter.

Gigi approached, and I pushed a few wet strands of hair out of her face.

She exhaled a heavy breath. "How are you feeling?"

"Worried about you," I answered.

Gigi stepped into my arms, and I buried my face in her neck, caressing her back as I held her close.

"I was proud of you today."

A sense of inadequacy swept over me. "Me? Why?"

Slowly, she picked up the dry towel on the counter and wiped the excess water off her

chest. "You protected me like you promised."

That surprised me. "I'll always protect you."

Looking away, she muttered, "Yes, but to see it in action made me love you more."

"We should eat."

She shook her head and stifled a smile. "There you go, changing the subject, when feelings are involved."

I took a seat on the couch near the window, watching Gigi continue to dry off and change into fresh clothes. Trucks arrived on schedule to take the next load out for a gun sale with the Irish Mob. I drew my fist up in frustration at the thought of all of my enemies being able to get that close.

"My father built up an incredible reputation. To see his life cut short isn't fair," Gigi murmured.

"Too bad he won't see how far you've come."

She slipped onto my lap. "Is that a bad or good thing?"

I kneaded her thigh gently. "You're a good thing, Gigi." I pointed to her heart. "Never think otherwise."

"Honestly, I felt like you thought I was a selfish, spoiled, naive girl."

I nipped her chin. "You were."

She gasped and slapped me on the chest. "I knew I shouldn't have married you. Maybe I can find someone to take your place."

I held her down as she started to get off my lap. "What I mean is that you showed growth and maturity, but I liked when you were selfish and spoiled because at least you owned who you were. Not like most women."

"We've never talked about your past girlfriends."

I measured how to answer her question. "Girlfriends don't work in my world."

Her eyes narrowed at my answer. "Ugh, you are an asshole."

"Yeah, but I'm your asshole." I smirked, kissing her lightly. "We need to go talk to Gael about our next moves."

My phone rang in the bedroom, and I extricated myself from Gigi to answer it.

"Where is she?" Dario demanded.

"In front of me. Why?" I asked as Gigi joined me.

"I heard what happened."

My lip curled. "How did you hear?"

"Some of my men called me. Plus, my father."

"Tell everyone she's fine with her husband."

He laughed. "You think that fake marriage means anything to me?"

"You can believe whatever you want. The marriage license proves we're married."

"Cyrus was paid off. That won't hold up in court."

"That's the excuse you're going to use? Just admit she wants nothing to do with you beyond work." If I let on that I knew he was behind everything, we'd spook him and Orson.

"The moment she sees you for the crazed animal you are, she'll crawl back to me."

"There's always a risk of that."

"Are you making moves outside of the cartel?" Dario asked, indicating he knew about New York.

My forehead creased in irritation. "Why do you ask?"

"Any time my family is in jeopardy, I need to know."

"The Ramini family has no sway with me."

"Carry on, Axel, and find yourself on an island alone." Dario's anger was punctuated by the dial tone.

I could only wonder what his next move would be.

Gigi took one look at me and anger lit her eyes. "Dario threatened me again?"

"Leave the worrying to me."

She cuddled up to me. "Our life will never be normal."

I kissed the top of her head. "Only we can make it normal."

She sighed. "I need to talk to my mom and check in on her."

"Make sure to leave out the shooting."

Gigi nodded, picked up my phone, and dialed her number. I climbed off the bed and went to check in with Gael and Fulgenzio, who were outside by the barn.

"That was a close call today." Gael stood with his arms crossed.

I kicked the rocks into the grass. "You're here for a short time, and I appreciate the backup. If you need to get back to your family, I understand."

"Never ran away from a fight."

"She's all I care about." I pointed at Gigi as she stood in the window on the phone.

"Wouldn't doubt that. My family comes first for me."

"A battle with three other families won't turn out well," I said as more trucks drove away without supplies of guns.

"Joaquin and Antonio knew what they were doing when they requested I come here to help," Gael reminded me.

"Liaise with my right hand, Turin, to catch you up on everything."

"Send me his number."

"Fulgenzio is going into town and can drop you off."

"If we strike now, they'll be caught off guard. Set up an exit plan," Gael suggested.

"I never run from a fight," I said, repeating his earlier words.

"Only cowards run. But we may need to lie low after the smoke clears. Bloodshed tends to reach the political spectrum in Italy."

"Gigi's talked about moving permanently to America."

"An option you should keep in your back pocket."

"Weakest move he made was killing Laurent."

"Men like him only think in the moment," Gael pointed out. "Laurent probably got close to the truth."

"I tested him earlier about how he heard what happened."

Gael smirked. "Dario deserves credit for being so bold."

"When I wrap my hands around his throat, I'll give him all the credit he deserves."

Chapter 18

Axel

A turbulent passion swirled around Gigi; it was like she held my heart in her palm. To please was my mission and goal tonight.

She stepped off the bed and sauntered toward me in only her lingerie. When I tried to speak, she covered my mouth with her finger. "Let me take your jacket." She slid her hand under my jacket and threw it on top of the dresser.

Gigi held her breath as my fingers teased the soft skin of her inner thigh. I tugged at her nipple and moved my free hand between her thighs.

"One thing you haven't let me explore is how to please you," she murmured, unbuckling my pants as she walked us back to the bed. She cupped my erection in her hand and stroked.

Sitting on the edge of the bed, Gigi kissed the head of my dick. She looked up at me, her eyes burning with desire and the need to please me.

"Fuck, you're beautiful like this." I snatched off my

shirt and kicked off my shoes. "Just take it easy, and don't use your teeth."

The flush of her cheeks showed she was inexperienced, but I loved to see her become more confident in the bedroom. A shiver ran up my spine when her warm mouth engulfed my dick, then suddenly eased back.

"Am I doing it right?"

"Yeah. Shit," I grunted

Gigi went further until she gagged and her lips swelled. A low groan left my lips when a few tears appeared in her eyes. Ready to be inside her, I grabbed the back of her head and gently pulled myself out of her mouth before claiming her swollen lips in a heated kiss. Hungry moans escaped her mouth as I nudged her back on the bed. I skimmed over her hips, pressing a kiss to both and nibbling her stomach.

"You smell so fucking good." I dipped a finger into her wetness, slowly flicking it across her nub.

"Baby," she choked.

I nipped at her soft skin. "Am I pleasing you right?"

"Yes. Oh, God." Gigi whimpered under my hold.

I pushed her thong down and slowly unrolled her stockings, planting kisses up each leg. Her stomach flexed with each touch as I tasted her. My tongue slowly circled her naval before I licked a trail to her breasts and gently bit each covered nipple.

I slid each bra strap from her shoulder, unhooked it, and tossed it aside. Picking up her wrist, I checked her pulse and smiled.

I kissed her deeply, leaving her weak and confused. "Just breathe, baby."

"Axel!" She gasped as I inserted a finger in her wet heat.

Moving down her body, I tossed her legs over my shoulder, keeping eye contact with the slow penetration of my tongue.

"Fuck," Gigi whispered as I snaked a hand up to tweak her nipple.

She jerked and tried to clap her legs around my head, the first hint of her orgasm coiling. I smacked her thigh, pushed her legs to her chest, and stuck my tongue in her asshole.

"Yes!" she cried as slick wetness coated her thighs.

Desperate to be inside her, I removed my pants, lined up my dick, and pushed forward, savoring the tightness of her pussy.

I let out a raw groan, pulling out and pushing back in three more times. My mouth grazed her earlobe before I kissed her on the lips. "Pretty pink pussy."

She smiled as she squeezed her inner muscles. I growled and interlocked our hands, hovering over her chest and drove harder and faster into her slick folds.

Releasing one hand, I caressed her sensitive, swollen nipples. "Goddamn," I grunted.

Her pussy throbbed around me. "Ah! Keep going."

"You sure, baby? You like this?" I shivered at the delight of her touch.

She nodded.

"No! Tell me with your words," I demanded, searching her eyes for understanding.

Her mouth dropped open, then closed.

"If you don't speak, I'm going to stop." I ran a thumb along her delicious wetness.

Her eyes popped open wide. "Yes, that's all I want."

"Let me hear you."

"All I want is you."

The shapely beauty of her naked body taunted me for more. "Every day I see you, I think of how good you feel."

"Uh, uh, shit," she whimpered

"I would drown with you." I told her my deepest thoughts. Sweat dripped down my body as I lowered to whisper in her ear. "I love you."

Tears pooled in her eyes, and I kissed each one away as we both came together. My dick twitched again. I closed my lips around hers, snaking my tongue inside her mouth to tangle with hers. Gigi wrapped her arms around my shoulders and we fell into a long make-out session, slowly rocking back and forth.

"I love you too," she purred.

* * *

"Any word yet?" I stood in the bathroom as I talked to Turin.

"We got something better."

My head pounded with anxiousness. "What?"

"Edmundo."

I looked over my shoulder to make sure Gigi was still asleep.

"We take a hit on him. That puts a bug in his ear."

Anticipation buzzed through my body. "Where is he?"

"I got him at a hotel."

A tense silence enveloped me. "Where are you?"

"Outside your house."

I grinned. "Keep the car running."

I marched back to the bedroom and checked the time. 3 a.m. I pulled on jeans and a black shirt and snatched up my jacket, wallet, and gun, then jogged out of the house to Turin's car. Fulgenzio was on high alert, and I lifted my chin in acknowledgment that I was leaving.

I climbed in the car. "How long has he been there?"

Turin glanced at me. "Four hours, maybe longer."

I checked the chamber on my gun. "Is someone sitting on him now?"

Turin held his phone out to show a photo of Edmundo going into a hotel room.

"He seemed like the type to be faithful."

"Men like him are only faithful to power. The minute his son was ready to take over as Boss, Edmundo set himself to get millions off these deals."

"Can't blame him."

"Are we going after Lamberto as well?"

I shook my head. "Not tonight. Depends on the conversation with Edmundo."

Turin inquired, "Did you tell Gigi?"

"No."

"Keeping things from her won't end well."

"Focus on the road."

It took an hour to reach the hotel where Turin had tracked Edmundo. Obtaining the room number, we stepped into the elevator. I watched the floors go up and breathed deeply to compose myself.

We stepped off the elevator and I followed Turin to a door, where he slipped a key into the lock quietly. We eased into the dark presidential suite with our guns drawn. The front room was empty, the TV off, and the blinds closed.

I opened the closet door and noticed a suitcase. I held it up, saw it was locked, and placed it back down. Wandering into the bedroom, I pressed my ear to the door. Turin made a motion with his hand and gun out, ready to go.

I slowly unlatched the door and opened it to see Edmundo in bed asleep with someone next to him. At Turin's nod, I moved to one side of the best while Turin moved to the other, his gun aimed at the sleeping man. I tapped Edmundo on the nose with the butt of the gun, and his eyes blinked open slowly.

"Huh... What the...?"

I place a finger to my lips to be quiet. Edmundo's eyes widened as they focused on me. He turned his head to see Turin.

"Axel," Turin whispered.

I watched as he drew back the covers from the other person to reveal Rosa Carrington.

"It's not what you think," Edmundo said, trying to get out of bed.

I gripped him by the shoulder and dragged him out.

"Edmundo, what is going on?" Rosa screamed.

"Keep quiet, Mrs. Carrington," Turin barked.

"Turin, have you lost your mind?" Rosa spat.

"How long has this been going on?" I queried.

Rosa pulled the covers up to her neck. "Edmundo, keep your mouth shut."

I nudged the gun to the side of his head. "Answer me."

"We've been having an affair for a while," Edmundo muttered under his breath.

"I told you to shut up. He's lying!" Rosa shrieked.

"Rosa!" Edmundo spat.

"Did Laurent know?" I rasped.

Rosa was clearly annoyed at us finding out. "What I do in my marriage is none of your business."

"Get dressed," I ordered, storming out of the room.

"No. You get out of here," Rosa replied.

I turned to face them. "Does Gigi know about your little affair?"

Rosa paled but ignored my question. "Why are you here?"

"Get dressed."

I marched into the living room, pacing back and forth. Minutes rolled by before they emerged from the bedroom with Turin.

"Sit." I gestured to the couch.

Rosa sat on the couch. "What we do as adults is none of your business."

"Where's Dario?" Turin questioned.

Edmundo hunched his shoulders.

I hit him across the face with the butt of my gun.

Edmundo yelped and covered his cheek.

"Have you lost your mind?" Rosa shrieked, standing in front of Edmundo.

"Laurent is dead because of his family and Casella."

Her eyes narrowed. "Nothing could be further from the truth. Laurent was friends with Edmundo and Orson."

"Then he'll tell me where Dario is hiding."

"My son is not hiding, and you're making a grave mistake." Edmundo grunted.

"Did Lamberto put you up to this?" Rosa demanded.

"Lamberto has no clue."

"So you follow your own rules like always." Rosa shifted and reached for the phone, putting it on speaker.

"Rosa, it's almost four in the morning," Lamberto grumbled.

"Axel has Edmundo at gunpoint," Rosa explained.

"Huh?" Lamberto mumbled.

"The real question is why are you here in a hotel room with Edmundo, a married man, and the Boss of another cartel?" I said coldly.

She shifted from one foot to the other. "Laurent and I had an understanding," Rosa revealed.

"Axel, what you are doing can't be undone," Lamberto stated.

"Then meet me at the office. We have a lot to discuss."

"Including you faking a marriage with my child," Rosa hissed.

"Gigi and I are married in every sense of the word."

"Under duress. I will have her committed to get her away from you."

"Rosa," Edmundo whispered.

"No, Edmundo. I'm sick and tired of her doing things behind my back."

"She's an adult. You haven't complained about the money in her trust fund," I pointed out.

"Another thing you have no clue about."

"Rosa, shut up!" Lamberto yelled.

I squatted down in front of Edmundo. "I'll ask you again. Where is Dario?"

"You don't have to answer that," Lamberto replied.

"If he wants to live—"

"Dario isn't responsible for your parents' deaths," Rosa snapped.

I froze. "Leave my parents out of this."

"You think avenging my husband will ease your guilt over not being able to save your parents," Rosa continued, undaunted.

"Rosa, leave it alone," Lamberto warned.

"He needs to know."

"Know what?" My voice was deadly calm.

"Your father was disloyal," Rosa stated.

Shock flew through me. "Liar!"

"It's not a lie, and you poisoning my daughter about Dario will only end in her leaving you," she seethed.

Ignoring her, I returned my attention to Edmundo. "I won't ask again."

"Axel!" Lamberto shouted.

Frustrated, I fired a warning shot.

Rosa screamed.

"Shit," Turin groaned.

I wrapped a hand around Edmundo's neck and squeezed. "Tell me what you know."

Edmundo looked from me to Rosa.

"Shut up, Edmundo," she said coldly.

"Why look at her? Rosa, is there something I should know?"

Her mouth tightened. "I can help you if you want answers about your parents."

"You're trying to save yourself."

"At this point, I would be a fool to not give you the truth."

"Go ahead."

"Laurent had your parents killed," Rosa confessed.

Edmundo's eyes ballooned in surprise.

I got in her face. "You're lying."

Rosa backed up. "Axel, I would never lie about something like that."

"Laurent and my father got along great, like brothers."

"Edmundo can explain, but he was stealing from my husband."

Edmundo lowered his head, covering his eyes in frustration.

"Keep going."

She darted her eyes around the room. "Only if you remove the gun."

"Not happening."

"He stole two million dollars. I overheard him in conversation with Lamberto and Edmundo," Rosa whispered.

"Shut the fuck up, Rosa," Edmundo barked.

Amusement glinted in her eyes. "You loved your father, but he was disloyal to the family."

"Stop with the lies. Rosa. You're just trying to cover for your affair."

"How do you think you got the money from the insurance policy? Laurent felt terrible about everything and gave you a job."

"Then who set the bomb?"

Rosa was momentarily speechless. "That I don't know."

"Dario isn't off the hook."

Tongue-tied, she sat in shock. "You need to keep this under wraps."

"Gigi has to deal with her parents' betrayals the same as I have." I turned and walked away.

Rosa wasn't off the hook, and Edmundo was worthless, like his son, allowing others to handle his business decisions. Even if their affair was based on love, the cartel wouldn't allow it to go on once everything was out in the open. It would look bad on all fronts.

Chapter 19

Gigi

Dario was off the radar, and that pissed me off and stressed me out. Axel hadn't come back to the farm, so I had Fulgenzio drive me back to his condo, ready to confront my husband for skipping out on me during the night.

Before I could insert the key, the door was yanked open. "Turin!"

"Hi, Gigi. He's in there, but he's in a mood," he replied in a low, husky tone.

"What do you mean?"

"He can explain everything, but it has to do with his parents and your mother."

My brows dipped low in confusion as I stepped through the door and removed my coat. "Okay. Are you going to the office?"

He checked his watch. "For a little bit. We have to run the surveillance from the shooting."

"Please make sure I have the information by the end of the day."

"Sure thing." Turin hugged me.

I sauntered into the living room and laid my coat on the couch, smelling cigar smoke through the air. I approached the kitchen and saw Axel with a glass in his hand and a cigar.

"Either you killed someone, or someone pissed you off," I joked, but he didn't laugh. I closed the space between us. "Hey, you all right?"

He blew out smoke. "Have you spoken with your mother?"

"No. I came back from the farm because you left in the middle of the night."

He grunted, drank the rest of his vodka, and poured another one.

I pointed at the glass. "How much have you had to drink?"

"Not enough."

"Seems like something is bothering you," I said in a soft voice, letting him know I wasn't the enemy.

"Something or someone." He gazed at me.

I planted a hand on his chest. "Did I do something to hurt you?"

"No."

"What's with the attitude and the distance?"

His laugh was harsh. "I can't have space?"

My mouth dropped open. "In what world does a married couple need space?" Maybe I was naïve, but we couldn't go to sleep angry at each other, not after the last few days of us getting closer.

"Gigi, I need a break."

"A break?" I scoffed.

He rubbed his forehead. "A few minutes to think."

"About what? Talk to me and I may be able to help."

"Rosa said your father killed my parents." His voice broke.

My heart beat faster. "And you believed her?"

"Who else can I trust to tell me the truth?"

"Me! Your wife."

"If you knew the things I've seen over the years, you would understand."

There was truth in his statement. I'd never be able to understand his life, but I would always listen and remind him of the great man he'd become. "Then talk to me about them."

"She said he stole two million dollars and your father found out."

I cupped his face. "He loved your father."

"I guess not enough."

"Rosa is a liar. You can't trust her."

"I caught—" He stopped abruptly.

"Caught what?"

"Nothing." He relaxed and put the glass on the table.

"Trust works both ways and I've given you my trust in this marriage, from my heart, body, mind, and soul. Let me help you."

"You know Dario and Lamberto are working together."

I nodded. "Yes, I saw the evidence."

"Last night, Turin called me to meet him."

"Okay, did you find Dario or Orson?"

He shook his head. "No, but it was still a surprise."

"Feels like you're keeping something from me. Same as my parents."

He regarded me with impassive coldness. "Never compare me to them."

Only a few hours ago, we'd given each other undeniable respect and admiration. "Speak then."

"Rosa was in bed with Edmundo."

I stared at him. "Edmundo Ramini?"

"Yes."

I laughed. "Axel, I think you've had too many glasses of vodka."

"It's true, Gigi."

I shook my head. "My mother may be a lot of things, but she isn't a cheater."

"Ask Turin."

"I can ask my mother. She wouldn't lie about something that big."

"I'm starting to think you only hear what you want rather than the truth, Gigi."

"Rosa is a bitch. I know her better than you, but she would never betray my father like that."

"I saw it with my own eyes! Edmundo and Rosa in bed at a hotel."

I dug into my pocket and removed my phone and sent a message to Turin.

Me: *Send me the picture of Edmundo.*

"Who are you texting?" His brows knitted together.

"Turin."

His eyes darkened dangerously. "Are you saying you don't trust me?"

I cocked my head to the side. "Even you have to know it would never happen. It's gossip, and my family doesn't need to be hounded."

"No, I'm trying to get you to understand. As the Don of the cartel, you can't leave room to fuck up, even if it's your family," he remarked.

My heart raced. Maybe I was in denial because why

would she do something like this and trample over the family name? Dad hadn't even been gone six months, and she'd already found someone who was not only married, but his son was supposed to be my husband.

Turin: *She's back home now.*

Me: *Thank you.*

I stared at the photo, and sure enough, she was in a shirt in a hotel room with Edmundo on the couch. My throat tightened with emotion. "Wow."

Axel pulled me closer and kissed my forehead. "I know you're pissed, but you need to wait before you confront her."

"She's disloyal. How can you say I should ignore what's in front of me?"

"Because Edmundo will lead us to Dario, and if Rosa can control Edmundo..."

I hated that Axel was right.

"My instinct is always to protect you, even from yourself."

"I can't believe my father would kill your parents," I whispered.

He paused, dropping his hands to the side. "The truth will come out."

"What does that mean for us?"

"As of right now, you trust me, and I trust you."

* * *

The moment I made the decision, I regretted it. It wasn't right, but I needed answers, and he was the only one who could give them to me. Axel and I had been distant the last few days after his huge bombshell. I was disgusted that my mom would lie on her back for someone else.

"Stay in the car, Fulgenzio." I reached for the door handle, pushing it open. Fulgenzio hadn't been happy when I demanded to be taken to a potential enemy's home.

"He's going to kill me if I don't go inside with you."

"Who's going to tell him?"

His mouth tightened and he shook his head.

"Besides, they won't do anything in broad daylight with cameras everywhere." I stepped out and shut the door, sauntering up to the front door and ringing the bell.

"Miss Carrington, we've missed you around here," the Ramini's housekeeper said.

"It's Mrs. Bresciani now, Celestina." I held up my left hand.

"You got married." Her eyebrows stretched high.

"I did. Is Mr. Ramini here?"

"Yes, in the backyard. Follow me." She stepped aside and closed the door behind me.

I hadn't been back to their home in months, possibly a year. Nothing had changed. Mrs. Ramini was a stickler for ensuring the place looked like a show home.

I thanked Celestina as she opened the back door. Edmundo was pacing back and forth while on the phone. I removed my purse and placed it on the table before taking a seat.

"Gigi, what a surprise." He finished the call and motioned for Celestina to leave us alone.

"Is it?" I clasped my hands together, crossed my legs and made direct eye contact.

He took a seat across from me. "Not an unpleasant surprise, but to what do we owe this visit?"

"Come on, Edmundo. Let's not kid ourselves."

His eyes narrowed. "Edmundo?"

"That's your name."

"A few weeks ago, I was going to be your father-in-law. Have you forgotten I'm cartel hierarchy?"

I lifted my shoulders. "Is that supposed to mean something? I'm the Don of the family and I go by Gigi."

He gritted his teeth. "Watch it."

"Or what? Tell me exactly how you will disrespect me? Because you've betrayed my father by sleeping with his wife," I hissed.

His eyes shifted as he gulped. "I don't know where you heard that ridiculous allegation, but it's not true."

"Were you talking to my mother before I interrupted?" I propped my arm on the back of the chair.

"Rosa and I are friends."

"I would respect you more if you were honest with me."

"He lied. We were only talking."

"Oh, talking? And who is he?"

"Listen to me. Dario is not happy about your broken engagement. There's still time to get back together and move forward as a united family."

"Unlike you, Edmundo, I respect my marriage."

He chuckled, and his eyes darkened. "You little bitch. You have no idea what to do with the power you have."

I was finally seeing the real Edmundo. "Tell me what to do with it then?"

He pressed his finger ton the table. "I should have trusted my instincts and told Dario to drop the idea of you and him."

"Something we can agree on."

"Yes, I slept with your mother and will continue to sleep with her."

The casual way he spoke about their affair disgusted me.

"Nothing to say? I guess the cat's got your tongue now. What can I say? Your mother's an attractive woman and she needed comfort. She felt abandoned by your father."

"Son of a bitch!" I slammed my hand on the table.

"Little princess can't handle the truth about her father."

"My father got you in the position you're in today and this is how you repay him?"

"Laurent was a bastard. He wanted to control everything and cut my family out."

"That's not true."

"If you take the blinders off, Gigi, you'll find your parents aren't perfect."

"Sounds like I should be saying this to Dario."

"Get out of my house. We have nothing else to discuss."

"We have plenty to discuss, considering someone tried to kill me."

"Not my burden."

"Where's your son?"

"Dario is out of town."

"Why are you lying for him?"

"He's preparing deals for the cartel."

"Without consulting me first?"

"Lamberto should have communicated. He's the underboss."

"I know you're behind the lie that my father killed Axel's parents."

Edmundo grinned.

Our stare-off continued until the door slid open.

"Gigi, I heard from Celestina you were here." Mrs. Ramini held her arms out for a hug.

I embraced her out of obligation, but nothing between us felt like genuine love anymore. "I came to talk with your husband."

"I'd love for you to stay for lunch."

"Sorry, I have another engagement."

"Gigi, we aren't mad that you and Dario can't work out your differences," Mrs. Ramini stated.

"Thank you."

She glanced at me, then at her husband. "I guess you two have something important to talk about. We can chat some other time."

"Yes, another time."

"Oh, tell your mother I said hello and not to forget our shopping trip," Mrs. Ramini remarked.

"She will love that, won't she, Edmundo?" A solid look of guilt appeared on his face.

Mrs. Ramini smiled and walked away.

Edmundo jumped out of his seat and charged at me.

I reached into my purse to grab my gun, and he gripped my arm. "Try anything and I'll scream," I seethed.

"Get the fuck out of my house. If you want to continue to have my support, you'll ignore what you've heard."

I dropped the frown and smirked, snatching my arm away.

"Fuck your support." I strode into the house and out the front to my awaiting car.

"Everything worked out?" Fulgenzio pushed the gas and drove out of the area.

"It will in time."

My phone rang and I pulled it out of my purse to see Axel's name. I looked at Fulgenzio. "Did you tell him?"

"Who?"

"Fulgenzio, you're my guard. I have to trust you."

His eyes cast down. "I'm sorry, Mrs. Bresciani. He's my boss."

"No, I'm your boss and friend. I can handle myself. Axel will freak out for no reason."

"Yes, ma'am."

I tossed the phone back in my purse and threw it on the seat.

Later that evening, I visited the farm to inspect how things were going and found Turin in the office. I walked in and shut the door behind me, scanning the office holding records of my father's business.

Turin studied my face. "Gigi, what are you doing here so late?"

"Axel doesn't know I'm here." I dropped my coat on the chair.

Turin looked behind me and saw Fulgenzio at the door for protection. The scowl on his face reminded me of Axel. "Where is he?"

"Working."

His expression stilled and grew serious. "Sit, please."

"Thank you." We'd never had a conversation without other people around, and I wanted to pick his brain. Not only about my father's business, but as a longtime friend of Axel.

"Running through the numbers."

"How are they looking?"

He scratched the back of his head. "Not great."

"Tell me the truth, Turin. Seems like everybody wants to control me."

"You know how this business runs. Laurent would tell you to focus on what you can see in front of you."

"He would want me to be two steps ahead and not foolish."

Turin sat back in his seat, lacing his hands behind his head. "What do you know so far?"

A faint smirk spread across my face in disgust at my comment. "Edmundo and my mother are having an affair."

He waited before he spoke. "Did you talk to her yet?"

I sat back in the chair in a huff. "No, but I plan on it."

Turin ran down the details. "Okay, well, you know Dario and Lamberto are working together."

"Yes. How do all the pieces come together?"

"That's the mystery. Orson is working with Edmundo somehow."

"But Ramini and Carrington have a long-standing deal. Casella is not to have more than what they negotiated in the truce."

Turin flipped the papers in his hands. "Money is being taken monthly."

I sat forward. "Where does it go?"

"Million-dollar question."

"I know Dario is behind the shooting and he's supposedly out of the country."

He lifted a folder and placed it in the drawer. "Did Edmundo tell you that?"

"Yeah, and something tells me he's lying."

Turin clasped his hands together. "Protecting his money."

"They've never had a loving father-and-son relationship beyond Dario wanting to be in his shadow."

"We'll catch Dario, but Lamberto needs to be handled."

"Trying to take him out too early would put me in a bad spot."

"All the families will have to agree on his removal."

I spread my hands wide. "Do you think... never mind."

"Tell me." Turin leaned back on his elbows.

"Do you think all the families gave permission to kill my father?"

The door slammed open and I swung around to see an angry Axel.

"Turin, give me the room," Axel said quietly.

"Axel, I can—"

He lifted a hand to cut me off.

Turin stood and approached Axel, whispering something in his ear before leaving the office.

Axel rolled up his sleeves and glared at me.

I stood slowly, my throat tight with nerves.

"What did you accomplish?" he asked in his thick accent.

I paused. "Accomplish?"

"Please don't repeat. You heard me."

His dominating attitude and boldness to challenge me proved I wouldn't run over him like I did with everybody else. I shouldn't be turned on, but it was kind of hot.

"Edmundo only confirmed the affair."

"Anything else?" He stalked toward me.

"Dario is out of town working on a deal." I mumbled the last part.

"Out of town. Right."

"Where were you?" I changed the subject.

"Busy." With long, purposeful steps, he moved in front of me.

I licked my lips, awaiting his next move. "With what?"

"I had to oversee a drop-off at the dock."

"Is that why you're mean and aggravated right now? Did something happen?"

His hand dragged over my cheek. "Everything is fine."

"Did Orson get a clue that we are moving away from them?"

"He didn't. I'll let him know, though."

I ran my hands over his shoulders and up his neck, standing on tiptoes to press my forehead against his. "I want to be there."

"No."

I poked him in the chest.

He looked down at my finger. "You went to see Edmundo and came here without telling me. You need to lie low."

"I'm not running."

"One thing Laurent always told me is to never get comfortable." His words were etched in my mind, and I knew what my next decisions would mean for me. I couldn't attempt a big shot at anyone without having a backup plan. None of those men took me seriously as a mob boss. I needed to stand firm in what I wanted, with or without Axel's approval.

"Edmundo is spooked now, so we need to be careful," he muttered.

"Are you still upset about my father?"

He released a breath. "I don't want to believe he's behind my pain, especially when he brought me into the fold. At some point, he probably figured I would find out."

"Do you believe Edmundo and my mom? Because it could've been an excuse to throw you off."

"Maybe, but I'll find out."

"Let's go home."

He kissed the top of my head. "No more going rogue."

"Can't promise you anything."

I repeated his words from the fake marriage. Our noses nuzzled, and I sank into his chest, closing my eyes. Our relationship would be different from my parents' and I wouldn't let anyone determine how it should be. Turin made some valid points, and I wanted to ensure my decisions were clear to the family. Rosa made it her mission to hurt me no matter what, but she wouldn't win at taking Axel away from me.

Chapter 20

Axel

I dried off, dropped the towel on the counter, and brushed my teeth. Earlier this morning, Turin called and said he wanted to meet and it was important for me to come alone. I'd crawled out of my warm bed with Gigi still asleep to get prepared for more bullshit.

"Morning, are you hungry?" Gigi wrapped her arms around me from behind.

I looked down at her hands. "I'll get some on the way."

Gigi released me, and I turned to face her. She lifted a hand to smooth my hair. "Who are you meeting?"

"Turin."

"Should I be there?" Gigi took my hand and interlocked our fingers.

I pulled back to watch her. "No."

"Axel, are you keeping something from me?"

I ignored her question and leaned down to kiss her.

"Where is your head at after the news of your mother?" I had issues I wanted to escape from, but I wanted to make sure she was handling the situation with her mother.

She placed her hands on my chest. "Trying to decide if I want to confront her."

My hands slipped down to her hips. "That's a decision you have to make alone."

She raised her lips for another kiss. "What if I want your opinion?"

"My feelings about your mother wouldn't be helpful." I patted her on the butt. "Talk to her."

"She betrayed me."

"She betrayed your father, not you."

Gigi's face dropped and she stepped back, walking out of the room.

I stopped her before she left. "What did I say wrong?"

"Nothing, Axel."

"You say it like you're pissed at me."

She paused, dropping her shoulders. "Wouldn't matter."

"I'm confused. Explain."

"You have no feelings, so you don't care."

Her words pissed me off, but now wasn't the time for me to get upset. "My feelings are you should do what you want."

I walked into the closet and picked out a suit and shirt for the day. I placed them on the bed and started to get dressed.

"Why can't you give me an inch of sensitivity and listen?"

"I've given you more than any other woman."

Her eyes grew into slits. She marched out of the bedroom and I finished getting dressed. Ten minutes later, I entered the living room of an empty condo.

"Gigi!"

Silence.

"She's pissing me off," I mumbled and walked down the hall to the guest bedroom. Wrapping a hand around the knob, I found it locked.

"Unlock the door."

Silence.

I hated to be ignored. "Gigi, unlock this door right now."

Silence.

"If I shoot it open, I'll have a lot of people scared."

Silence.

I grinned at her avoiding me. "I guess this is what I have to expect whenever we disagree."

Silence.

My phone rang. I figured it was Turin letting me know he was here. I grabbed my wallet, keys, and gun, and left the apartment.

* * *

Turin pulled up in front of the local bar he owned and put the car in park. "He's in there."

"How many people are with him?"

"About three guards."

"What else do you know?"

"I did some digging about the day Laurent was killed."

My head spun toward him.

Turin handed me his phone. "I should have told you the same night, but I wanted to triple-check."

"These are text messages." I glanced at him.

"Rosa and Dario."

That caught my attention.

"She made the call," Turin announced.

My eyebrows slumped in disgust. "Rosa planned it all."

Rosa: *I'm giving you the chance to own the world.*

Dario: *How do I know this isn't a setup?*

Rosa: *No reason to lie to you.*

Dario: *Gigi will hate you.*

Rosa: *Edmundo and Lamberto got onboard.*

Dario: *I want Don's position.*

Rosa: *Then kill Laurent.*

Dario: *If I made it, what insurance do I have that I won't get caught?*

Rosa: *Boss moves come with Boss decisions.*

"Shit." I continued to scroll through Rosa's messages from Lamberto and Edmundo. Rosa even talked with Orson a few times.

"No one is trustworthy," Turin explained.

"Fuck!" Air stalled in my lungs. I couldn't breathe. Turin was right, I needed to have control and moving too fast would disrupt things.

"See now why I wanted to wait?"

It made my skin crawl that Rosa had more hands involved. "If this gets out, Rosa's not the only one who gets hurt."

"Gigi will be devastated."

It felt like the walls were closing in. I absentmindedly cracked my knuckles. "Fuck. Fuck!"

"It's your call." Turin waited for my answer.

"I need to think." Fear was something I'd never dealt with, and now it assailed me. It made me second guess all my choices with Gigi. I'd never had to worry about keeping promises until I agreed to us going into marriage.

"First, we handle Orson. Then I need to talk to Rosa."

Turin cocked his head to the side. "Is that wise?"

"She's my wife's mother."

He smirked. "Your wife."

"Fuck you."

"Time to get to Orson."

I thought of how crushed Gigi would be by Rosa's involvement with Laurent's death. It could send her to a place I wouldn't be able to reach.

Turin removed his gun, checked it, and climbed out of the car. A few men came from the alley and I moved around to the back to enter through the exit. Loud cheers rained over the room. I slipped up to the side of the bar and looked around the crowd, spotting a few people sitting in a corner booth. Orson kissed one girl, while another poured him a drink. Orson laughed with one of his guys, then picked up the glass of bourbon and forced the rest into his girl's mouth.

"Have someone bring him to the bathroom," I demanded, then turned and went to the men's bathroom, waiting in a stall.

A few guys walked by as I waited. I heard a loud laugh and knew it was Orson. I pushed the stall open and heard Orson grumble as he took a piss with his head down. Slipping on my black gloves, I stalked up to him, gripped the back of his head, and slammed it down on the top of the stall.

He shrieked in pain and swung his head to look up at me.

"Shush..."

Orson tried to get up, and I knocked him back down. "A-Axel."

"You forced my hand, Orson."

His shoulders slumped. "I didn't do anything."

My mouth twisted in a threat. "I want the truth."

"Please, it wasn't me."

I slammed him into the stall again. Orson had fucked us over by deciding to not follow the rules Laurent had put in place. "What do you know about Rosa and Dario?"

Blood dripped down his face. "Rosa?"

"Rosa Carrington."

"We never talk."

"I know Rosa is behind Laurent's death."

Orson stiffened. "Laurent and I weren't friends, but we had an understanding."

I removed my gun and pushed it against his cheek. "What do you know?"

He raised his hands in the air. He was fucking disgusting.

I got a whiff of piss and became even more aggravated. "Tell me!"

"Rosa made a deal with Lamberto and Edmundo!" he shouted.

There's more to the story. "What did you get out of it?"

"If Laurent was taken out, Dario stepped in to broker a Casella and Ramini Cartel alliance."

"Who would control the zones?"

"If the plan goes through, Edmundo and Dario," Orson croaked out.

Carrington owned all the borders of Italy. We allowed Casella to get a portion through a truce, but they must have found a way to get rid of Laurent, and Edmundo had talked his son into running a bigger deal.

"Once again, Orson, you've disappointed me." I removed the safety and shoved it in his face.

"Please, Axel. We can help each other."

"Where's Dario?"

He stuttered. "I-I don't know."

"Wrong answer."

I pulled the trigger and Orson's dead body slid to the floor. I wiped the blood off my gloves and walked to the door, letting Turin inside.

"Cleanup crew is on the way," he said.

My hands itched to shoot him again. "He told me Rosa and Lamberto were on board with controlling all the borders."

"That would leave Gigi with nothing."

"They're trying to take over."

As we left the bathroom, the cleanup crew came in with their supplies to get rid of Orson's body.

"Time to deal with Edmundo."

"If we tip him off, that's a red flag and he might come after you," Turin pointed out.

After climbing into the car, I took my phone out and dialed Gigi's number. There was still tension between us from our argument earlier in the morning. Turin hit the gas and sped into oncoming traffic.

"She's not answering."

"Do you think she's still at the condo?"

"Let me check my cameras." I logged into the camera feed of my condo and watched each room; Gigi was not around. "She's not there."

"Check in with Fulgenzio."

Ending the feed, I dialed Fulgenzio.

"Sir, I'm with Mrs. Bresciani. Do you need to speak with her?"

I let out a relieved breath. "Where are you?"

Gigi knew I'd be irate if something happened to her, so skipping to hangout beyond school was an issue.

"At her usual lunch place with her friend," Fulgenzio answered.

"Keep her there. I'm on my way."

* * *

Turin kept the car running, and I hopped out and marched into the restaurant. Fulgenzio stood a few tables away. I glanced around him and saw Gigi, Ginerva, and two other people sitting at their table. Usually jealousy never peeked into my mind, but seeing my wife laughing with another man pissed me off.

I cleared my throat, cupped the back of Gigi's head, and bent down to kiss her on the lips. At first, she resisted and tried to move back, but I held her fast until she fully opened her mouth to my tongue.

"Why are you here?" Gigi quizzed.

"Who are your friends?" I pointed at the girl and the guy.

"These are classmates."

New people I never wanted to be around. "Come with me."

She halted my steps. "I'm in the middle of lunch."

"It won't take long."

"Axel," she sighed.

"Either we talk in private, or I can empty the entire restaurant." I held out my hand for her to take and pulled her into the hallway.

"You want to tell me why you interrupted my friends and me?"

I kissed her on the forehead and she flinched. "Get rid of your friend."

"Huh?"

I smiled at her discomfort. "The guy."

"Axel, you can't be serious."

"Have I ever joked?"

Alarm crept into her expression. "He's harmless."

"I told you already. I'm not in a playing mood. I know Ginerva and her family, but the new people will need to be vetted. And no guys."

"Jealousy. That's what this is right now."

"You ignored my call."

"It was on silent."

"Never have your phone on silent."

"Why are there so many rules? I want a normal life." Gigi threw her hands up.

A rebellious streak blazed inside me. "Too late for that. You're one of the most important people in Italy, even presidents and prime ministers."

She blew out a breath. "I needed to think after our fight."

"It was a disagreement, not a fight."

Gigi glared at me. "You always come back with semantics."

This was the complexity of being with me I wanted to avoid, no matter who I had in my bed—let alone as a husband. "How much longer are you going to be here?"

"Why?"

"We need some alone time."

"Is something wrong?"

"When we get home, I can explain."

"That sounds like more trouble," she huffed.

"I made a move and we need to discuss the consequences."

She looked apprehensive. "What move?"

"Say goodbye to your friends and meet me at the
house."

"Wait! Tell me what you found out."

I started to walk off. "Not here."

"Okay, let me wrap up with Ginerva and my friends."

"I'll come with you so I can meet your little friend." I
thought about all the ways I could alter her new friend's
face.

"Please don't embarrass me," she pleaded.

"He should be embarrassed to be out in public
looking for a death wish." I palmed her ass.

"Guys, sorry, I have a family emergency. I need to
leave," Gigi explained, and they all stood to give her
a hug.

"You can sit." I pointed at the guy.

His brows scrunched in confusion. "Excuse me?"

"Axel, please." Gigi grabbed my hand to calm me
down.

"What's your name?" I was still high on adrenaline
after taking care of Orson, and anyone could be the cause
of their own death if they pissed me off.

"Don't answer that," Gigi told her friend.

"He can speak for himself. From the way he laughed
at your joke, he's comfortable in your presence," I
snipped.

"Turin, can you help?" Gigi pleaded.

Turin stood off to the side with a hard expression.

"Turin can't save your little friend."

"Maybe you should go." Gigi tried to get the guy to
leave.

I placed my gun on the table. Everyone jumped back.

"Axel!" Gigi hissed.

"Hey, I only take a class with her," the guy stuttered.

"As of today, you'll transfer to another class. Better yet, another school," I demanded.

All eyes widened in shock.

"Are you insane? I'm sorry, everyone. Talk later." Gigi shifted around me and walked out the door.

I removed money from my wallet to place on the table and picked up my gun. "By the end of today, I expect you to no longer be in her school."

He agreed with a nod.

Turin and Fulgenzio were outside as Gigi sat in the back seat with the door open.

"That was embarrassing," Gigi snapped.

I leaned down, poking my head inside. "Go home. We'll talk."

"I'm not in the mood to talk."

"Then we can find something else to do."

I straightened and shut the door, waiting for Fulgenzio to start the ignition and pull off before stalking toward Turin's car.

Turin raised an eyebrow. "That could have been handled differently."

"When have I ever handled anything easy?"

He chuckled.

Gigi would learn soon enough. There were too many people out to end her, and the smallest slip up could be fatal if she let her guard down.

Chapter 21

Gigi

I used the tip of my tongue, making circular motions up and down his length as he jerked out the last of his cum. I was giddy. I was still new at giving him oral pleasure and he allowed me to take my time. A tremor heated my thighs and pussy. He helped me stand in the shower and turned me to face the wall. One hand rested on my hip and the other on my shoulder.

I planted my hands on the wall as he thrust forward. "Oh, God."

"Shit." He licked my neck and sucked on my ear.

His touch was divine ecstasy. A deep feeling of peace entered my being every time I was with him.

My head dropped forward. I closed my eyes, biting my lip as I stretched my legs out further. He leaned over my back and grasped my breasts, stroking me harder.

"My God. Don't stop, Axel."

"Good girl," he groaned when I rubbed his balls.

"Go faster, please." The quivering of my limbs weakened my knees.

He slapped my ass. "I give the orders," he growled,

smacking my ass again.

I trembled under his grip. Axel pulled out and cut the water off. He picked me up and carried me to the bedroom, putting me on top of the dresser. He kissed a path down my stomach, spread my legs, and gently sank his tongue into my warm center.

"I want you forever, baby," he panted.

"Show me how much," I challenged.

My words spurred him on and something dark came over his eyes. He hooked my leg over his shoulder, slipping a hand under my ass to stroke his finger close to my asshole.

"Oh... yes. Oh... keep going," I panted as his warm fingers closed around me.

"Take it, baby. Take what you own."

"God, Axel. I... too much!" My body exploded with heat and I quivered with pleasure.

Axel dipped his head and sucked on my nipple. "You had enough?"

I wanted to say yes, but he'd win, so I shook my head.

Suddenly, he lifted me off the dresser. I yelped. "Don't drop me!"

He cupped my head and kissed me deeply. "Hold on."

I thought we'd move to the bed, but nope, he flipped me upside down and held onto my waist.

I clung to his legs as he entered me again. "Sir, please."

My heart rushed faster, and noises of our skin smacking together made him more determined to push me to the edge.

Axel lifted me up from my waist and I reached my arm around to grip his neck. Before I could say another word, we landed on the bed. His manly scent covered me while his thrusts excited me, causing ripple effects.

"Are you ready to come now, angel?"

"Yes," I whimpered.

"Then come for me, angel."

All I could feel then was his tongue on my pussy as I came. He covered me on the bed, caressing my body as I quivered from my orgasm. I slowly opened my eyes as Axel rose to see him grabbing a cloth from the bathroom. He cleaned me up, and gently pulled the covers around us as I drifted into a deep sleep. I had no man to compare him to, but he made me feel like I was the only woman for him.

* * *

Rosa still continued to play the naïve role and pretended she was innocent of the issues within our family. My heart broke when she didn't own up to the bullshit involving Dario. I had thoughts of her lying in the ground instead of my dad. Maybe then it would make sense why she went behind my back.

Fulgenzio opened the door of the slaughterhouse.

I strolled in and saw a few of Dario's men tied up on the ground. "What did you find out?"

Turin, Axel, and his men stood around.

"Lamberto and Edmundo are hiding Dario."

I arched my brow. "Hiding?"

"After the confrontation with Lamberto, Edmundo set it up for him to escape," Turin said.

"Where are they?"

"That's what they're here for." Turin indicated the bound men.

I removed my shades and moved closer to look at the four men on the ground.

"Keep your distance," Axel warned.

I nodded in agreement. "Gentleman, do you know why you're here?"

They stared at me without speaking.

"Remove his gag." I pointed at the blond, lean-built soldier with blood running down his eye. "What's your name?"

He didn't respond.

I cracked my neck. "I can do this all day if you want?" I snapped my fingers and he turned to face me. "Is Dario your boss?"

"Fuck you." He spat on the floor.

I smiled. "Is that supposed to scare me?" I squatted down in front of him. "I'm Gigi." Making them feel comfortable was something I'd learned from my father and mother.

He grunted and looked away.

"Today is your last day to hurt, my friend. Men like you worship your boss and somehow become delusional enough to die for them. I can help you." It would be naïve to think them scared by my words alone. I had to show them I called the shots and held their lives in my hand. They would tell me the truth, but they wouldn't be leaving this room alive.

"You're Laurent's bitch daughter."

Axel approached, but I lifted my hand as I stood. "I can handle him."

He grinned.

"Handle me then, bitch," he hissed, trying to lunge at me.

I kicked him in the head. "Tell my men where Dario

is hiding!"

He scrambled to sit up. "Dario isn't hiding."

"Then where is he?"

"Where you least expect him to be." His statement gave me no clues, and I was tired of dealing with people who tried to mess with my head. "So you're ready to die for him?"

His eyes jolted up as Axel passed me the gun. I cocked it while he stood behind me with his hand on my hip.

"Aim for the head," he whispered.

I pulled the trigger, turned the gun toward the other men, and shot each one.

"Hey." Axel took the gun and cupped my face.

"I'm fine."

He kissed me on the forehead. "I'll clean this up."

"I need to run by the house."

Axel stood with me. "Okay. Take Fulgenzio."

"All right." I brushed a kiss against his lips and marched out to the awaiting car. The door shut, and Fulgenzio accelerated out of the area. I lay against the seat with my head down in thought.

I looked down at my phone as it buzzed.

Rosa: *Sweetheart, can we talk?*

I blew out a breath.

Me: *Yeah, call me.*

Rosa: *In person, Gigi.*

She always needed things her way.

Rosa: *Please.*

Me: *Okay. On my way.*

"Fulgenzio, can you go by my parents' home?"

"Yes, Mrs. Bresciani."

"Thanks. We won't be long. My mother needs to talk

to me."

The distance would help to clear my mind. I sat back, crossing my arms over my chest.

Axel texted to check up on me.

Husband: *Are you good?*

Me: *I will be soon.*

Husband: *What does that mean?*

Me: *About to have that conversation I've been avoiding.*

Husband: *What are you talking about?*

Me: *We can talk later.*

Husband: *I don't like you being vague with me.*

Me: *I promise I'm fine.*

I set my phone on vibrate and waited to arrive.

Once at my parents, I got Fulgenzio to give me a few minutes alone.

"I'll scream if I need your help," I told him.

I shoved my key in the lock when it swung open.

"Finally. I was worried you'd forgotten," Mother said, reaching out for a hug.

I followed her to the kitchen and saw she had lunch prepared for us. "Is Aurora here?" I removed my jacket, putting it on the back of the chair.

"No, I sent her to the store. I wanted alone time with you."

"Alone time? Since when?" I picked up the fork and took a mouthful of the scallops.

"Stop playing, Gigi. You've always been my priority," Mother responded.

"How many drinks have you had?"

She dropped her fork. "I am the mother, Gigi, and you are the child. Please stop trying to control my decisions."

That was the opening I needed. "Control *your* decisions? That's funny, because I've heard a lot about you lately."

"From whom? That husband of yours? Please, don't become one of those wives who turns her back on her family for a man," she scoffed.

"Family? You've done nothing but sabotage this family."

"How dare you speak to me that way!"

"Mother, please, come down off your high horse and be honest with me."

"Shut up!"

My brow hiked at her balled fists by her side. To get this upset meant some truth was in the air. If she thought I would let this go, she was mistaken.

"No, I won't shut up, Mother. I can't believe you had an affair with Edmundo Ramini."

She moved quickly, getting in my face. "That's a lie."

My muscles tensed. "Is it? Be honest."

"Baby, I love your father. We had many wonderful years." A change came across her face as she went into nurturing mode. Rosa couldn't fool me. I knew all sides of her personality.

I tried to calm my tone. "But you cheated."

She shook her head. "No, I've never cheated on him."

"I've tried so hard to gain your love."

"You have my love, but liking you lately is questionable by the company you keep." The real Rosa was back.

"Edmundo? Dario? Any of those names ring a bell?"

Her shoulders bunched up. "Both families are in business, so it's inevitable that people will see us out together."

"Turin and Axel found you in a hotel room with Edmundo."

She pointed her finger in my face. "That is disgusting! How dare you come in here and accuse me? You will regret how you've treated me," she growled.

"Why am I even here, Mother?"

"I wanted to clear the air between us and come to some sort of compromise. I'd like to build our relationship back to how it was before your father's death."

"You broke that trust."

"Everything I've done is for you."

I clapped my hands to emphasize my words. "Then. Tell. Me. The. Truth."

"Yes! I slept with Edmundo and I'll continue to see him."

"Make me sick to my stomach."

"Get over it and pray Dario takes you back. You're damaged goods now, but maybe we can convince him you were manipulated by Axel."

"I wanted Axel and pursued him. Dario and I will never be together."

"Axel is dangerous. You should want someone better for yourself."

"I want a mother who loves me."

She waved off my comment. If we would have had this conversation years ago, maybe we could have avoided this trauma.

Mother pointed the fork at my plate. "Eat your food."

"There's something else I need to speak to you about." I sat up straight.

"All these questions. My God, Gigi. Grow up."

"Did you work with Dario to take over the Carrington Cartel with Casella?"

Offended, she covered her chest with a hand. "I've never interfered in your father's business."

"I have it on tape." The idea of bribery stirred up in me.

My statement caught her off guard. "I... That can be doctored."

"At what point will you act your age and come clean?"

Her face twisted in anger. "You want the real truth?"

"For once, please."

"Axel is only using you for money."

"He has his own money," I corrected.

"From your father, of course, but he's after your trust fund."

"Then I gladly give it to him."

"Over my dead body."

"Well, hopefully you have protection because it's not looking good for you, Mother."

"What are you saying?" She blinked repeatedly; it finally seemed like I had her attention.

"I've tried to protect you, but Axel is on to you."

"On to me?"

"He told me you slept with Edmundo and worked with him to get Casella on board."

Mother grasped my chin. "Because he's trying to drive a wedge between us. Open your eyes!"

I removed her hand and put distance between us. "He loves me."

"The money is what he loves."

"Is it true Daddy killed his father?"

She shrugged.

"I need to know."

"If I told you, what would I get out of things?"

"That's all you care about? Money?"

"Yes."

"Wow."

She pressed her lips together, lifting her chin. "In time, you'll understand my choices."

I shook my head, annoyed by her response. "You're such a liar."

"I learned from your father. You think he was a saint? You're in for a rude awakening."

"He loved you."

"That man wasn't God, Gigi. Sorry I wasn't the perfect mother you wanted and needed, but I had to make adjustments and I'm owed for the time I put in with him."

"By trying to marry your daughter to a killer."

"You married Axel."

"Dario is behind Daddy's death."

She shook her head dramatically. "Dario would never hurt your father."

"Edmundo used you, and Dario is behind his death."

Rosa rolled her eyes and pushed her nose in the air. "That can't be any worse than the man you married."

"When you come to grips with who I love and where I am in life, I hope we can get back to a healthy relationship."

"You'll be waiting a long time." Rosa turned her back to me.

"Goodbye, Mother."

* * *

As soon as I got home, I stripped out of my clothes and threw up. If only my father was still here, he could tell me what to do.

I soaked in the tub with a glass of wine, candles, and the TV playing in the background. The disaster at lunch with my mother replayed over and over in my head as I tried to comprehend her actions. It was like she was a different person and not the mother I'd known all my life. How did you create a marriage, a life together, then have a child just to throw it all away for meaningless sex or money?

"So tired." I rested my head back.

The door squeaked open. "Fulgenzio told me you went to see your mother."

"Yeah." I took a deep breath, staring as he came closer.

"Anything you want to talk about?" He sat on the edge of the tub, caressing my cheek.

I rubbed my forehead. "So much. My head is spinning."

He shifted his weight. "We can talk, or if you need space, I can leave."

I grabbed his hand to stop him. "No, you're fine. I'm still in shock."

"Did she admit to anything?"

I released a long breath. "Sleeping with Edmundo. And she basically confirmed she worked with Dario to get Orson to cut a deal."

"Orson is conniving, but he's not a liar."

"I know."

"How long have you been in this tub?" Axel stuck his hand in the water; it was mildly hot.

He slid his hand across my shoulder, up to my neck. He titled my head back and leaned in to kiss me.

I moaned as his tongue swiped across my lips. "About an hour. As soon as I came back from her house."

Axel held my favorite soap sponge in his hand. He looked worn out. "I won't make excuses for her."

"She didn't make excuses beyond you being after my money, and I should go back to Dario."

Axel remarked, "That's never going to happen."

"I know. You've never asked me for money."

"Money never crossed my mind, but going back to Dario will never happen because he's going to be dead."

I smirked. "How was your day?" I put the wine glass on the floor, laying my head on his lap to face him.

He pinched my nose. "Worked some contacts to find Dario."

My hand slid up his chest. "What about Edmundo and Lamberto?"

"Lamberto isn't foolish like Dario. He knows hiding would make him look guilty."

I interlocked our hands, bringing them to my stomach. "Should I confront him?"

"Not yet. We got Orson, so they're scrambling. We can get him anytime." Axel leaned over to rub his nose against mine. His fingers lingered on my arm, and his breathing calmed.

"Wish I could go back."

"Life," he murmured.

"Harder than I thought."

We released each other and smiled.

"Maybe a little getaway will help you," Axel commented.

"The two of us."

Axel lifted my chin, eyeing me. "And a few men for protection."

"I'd love to hang with Sabrina and Janice again."

His hand caressed my breast. "In America." He

reached for the sponge, dipped it in the water, and ran it across my chest to my stomach.

"Your hands feel so good."

"What about this?" He sucked on my bottom lip.

"More." I grinned, trying to pull him in for a deeper kiss. The tub was big enough for us both to continue an evening of bliss after the craziness of the day.

Axel stood. "Finish your bath and come eat. I'm in for the night."

I stuck my hand out for a shake. "Promise."

He chortled and lifted it up, kissing my hand. "Yes, angel."

He tempted me with another kiss, which spurred me to want sex. Axel pulled back, and I groaned in aggravation.

"Temptress," he joked.

I finished up and brushed my teeth. I came out of the bathroom and marched into the kitchen to dinner on the table and candles lit.

My mood was peaceful. "Axel, I wasn't expecting all this."

He pulled out my chair. "You know I don't do feelings or emotions well, but I see you're hurt."

"You're hurting too. If my father really is behind your parents' death, what will happen to us?"

"We can talk about that another time."

"Are you avoiding the topic?"

"No, I want a quiet dinner with my wife."

His words warmed me. "Okay."

He poured us a glass of champagne. "To us."

I smiled. "To us."

Chapter 22

Gigi

I was on the phone with Ginerva, walking to my next class, when a guy bumped into me and I dropped it on the ground.

"Sorry!" He hurried off into the library behind me.

"Jackass!" I yelled back and bent down to pick it up.

Large hands with a familiar tattoo appeared in my line of vision. "Don't scream, or I'll kill Fulgenzio where he sits."

"Dario, what are you doing?" I hissed, looking up to see his signature smirk.

"Turn around and pretend you forgot something."

"No." I swallowed hard, challenging his order.

A gun appeared in his hand. "Turn around."

"Axel will kill you." I slowed my steps to halt his kidnapping attempt.

"He won't catch me."

"You don't know my husband."

Dario yanked the library door open, shoving me down the hallway and to the closet in the corner. "You think you've won?" he growled.

"I know your father is going to have a closed casket for you," I taunted.

I gasped as his palm connected with my cheek.

Dario's eyes narrowed. "Talk to me like that again and see what happens."

I pushed him back. "Get the fuck off me!"

"Axel's gotten in your head, but I'm running things now, sweetheart," Dario said without remorse.

"Ramini's family is washed up. I no longer care what happens to your family."

His lip curled with contempt. "My family goes down, so will yours."

I was tired of being underestimated. "Try it and see."

Dario removed his phone and clicked on a video of my mother on the ground. She was dead.

I covered my mouth in horror. "You killed her! Motherfucking bastard!"

"She owed me, same as your father," he seethed.

"Where is she?" I snatched the phone out of his hand to make sure I wasn't caught in some nightmare.

Dario's eyes glittered with satisfaction. "Dead in her home."

I shook my head in disbelief. "What about...?"

"Everyone is gone. The only way you survive is by committing to me. We stick to the original agreement and get married."

Savage anger burned in my chest. "That will never happen."

"Then you'll die like her."

"I'll never be with you."

"The Carrington name is no longer valuable, little one. I made sure of that."

"I'll die before I agree to marry you."

"Axel can't save you. Look at you. A pathetic and stupid little whore!" he snarled.

The door opened, and a professor stood there, his eyes flicking between us. Dario smirked and sauntered out of the closet.

I grabbed my things and ran for the car. "Get to my mother's house. Now!"

I yanked off my jacket and held a hand to my stomach, willing myself to breathe.

"What's the matter?" Fulgenzio asked urgently.

My hands shook as I dropped everything on the seat to look for my phone. "Oh, God, please be all right."

"Mrs. Bresciani, talk to me."

"Dario was here."

Fulgenzio looked around. "Where?"

I wiped the tears off my face. "He just—"

"Gigi, calm down and tell me what happened."

"He killed my mother." I burst into tears.

My phone rang. Finally locating it, I saw Ginerva's name scrolling across the screen. "Ginerva? God, I'm so glad—"

A sinister laugh cut me off.

"Who is this?" I whispered.

"Since we got interrupted, I didn't get a chance to tell you that Ginerva won't be available to take your calls."

"Dario, what have you done?"

"Taken everything from you."

My stomach lurched. "Ginerva has nothing to do with this."

Dario chuckled. "Really? Because from her screams, I think she wanted you to leave me."

I forced myself to speak calmly. "Think about what you're doing."

Dario paused as if weighing his options. "If I can't have you, then everyone in your world is going to die." He ended the call.

I dialed the number again, but it went to voicemail.

"Call Axel," Fulgenzio barked.

"Fuck! I can't believe him."

"Gigi, call Axel," Fulgenzio repeated.

We reached the open gate of my mother's house. That was a sign that something was wrong. Fulgenzio swerved around to the entrance and I hopped out without waiting.

"Gigi, stop!" he yelled.

The door was open, and I slowly creeped. A blood trail led to our house manager, who was face down on the floor.

"Oh my God!" I froze, whirling around the room in shock, hands shaking, heart pounding.

I ran into the kitchen and tripped over a body. "Aurora, no!"

I crawled to check her pulse. Her eyes were closed and blood leaked from her stomach and neck.

Fulgenzio appeared at the entryway, "Damn! Gigi, we can't stay here."

Tears poured down my cheeks. "I... I... can't leave her alone."

Fulgenzio tried to pull me away. "Axel is on his way."

"No! He needs to find Dario." I stood up and looked around the kitchen. Everything was a disaster.

I ran out of the kitchen dand up the stairs to my parents' bedroom. My eyes fell to her body on the floor.

"Mommy?" I dropped to my knees next to her. "Wake up, please."

I hated what she'd done. I said I'd never forgive her. Words that would haunt me for the rest of my life. She told me I was too weak for this world. She was right because this pain was unbearable.

"The neighbors called the police," Fulgenzio said from behind me.

"I want him dead," I said through numb lips.

"We have to go."

I paused for a moment and prayed for my family. I kissed my mother's forehead, and Fulgenzio helped me to stand, supporting my weight as we left the house.

"Get the jet ready," I instructed. "I need to rethink some things."

"Where are you planning to go?"

"America."

"*Breaking news. Prominent families are grieving tonight at the news of Rosa Carrington's death, along with her house staff, who were all found murdered. Many are speculating about a mob hit...*" the newscaster read off the report.

The man I was supposed to marry had wiped out my entire family.

Fulgenzio rushed me to the airport. Axel met and hadn't left my side since we'd boarded the plane.

"You need to eat, Gigi." Axel ran a hand up my leg.

"I'm not hungry."

"I understand. But you have to keep your strength up."

Food was the last thing on my mind, but I told the flight attendant to keep the drinks coming throughout the flight. There was still no word from Ginerva. I wanted to check before we left, but Axel put a stop to that. He thought it best we recoup and let Dario think we'd given up before we struck back.

The tears stopped flowing after a while. I was numb

to the pain and finally understood the place Axel was living in after the death of his parents.

I stared at the screen and watched the news report my mother's death over and over. I had no one now.

My gaze moved to our security team; Lazaro and Sandro whispered in a corner, and Fulgenzio and Turin were on their phones.

"Any update on Ginerva?"

Axel wrapped his arm around my shoulder and tugged me close.

"Turin is still checking."

I grew up in the church, but I stopped going when I turned sixteen. My decision caused a huge fight with my parents, but being Italian and not living by my religious standards felt like a hypocrisy. Still, I'd always believed in a higher being and right now, I needed my prayers answered.

Axel rubbed my leg. "Do you want to lie down in the bed?"

Fulgenzio sat in the corner of the plane with some of Axel's crew.

"No."

"Dario will be found."

I frowned. "How did he get through the gate?"

"What?"

"Dario. How did he get through the gate?"

"He has resources," Axel reminded me.

"Yeah."

I pulled the blanket up to my chin and laid my head on Axel's his shoulder. "How long long have you known Lazaro?" I whispered under the covers. "No, keep your eyes on me," I added when he glanced at him.

Axel examined me. "What are you saying?"

I tapped my foot restlessly. "It's probably nothing."

* * *

The plane landed hours later, and Antonio provided a security detail to escort us to our home. Our reach went up high, but most of our team were in Italy. In New York, we needed more support.

Lazaro sat up front, and I watched him out of the corner of my eye. He was behaving as if nothing had happened today. Maybe I was paranoid. Maybe Dario was working alone, but only a select few had the code to my parents' gate.

The doors shut, drawing my attention to Axel standing with Joaquin at the front steps. I opened my door and waved off the help.

"How is she holding up?" I heard Joaquin inquire.

"Not good," I answered.

"If you need anything, let me know," Joaquin responded.

"Thank you."

"Any leads?" Joaquin asked.

I glanced over my shoulder at Lazaro texting on his phone. "No."

"Talk inside," Axel said.

I held the phone up to the lock screen on the door and we headed inside, sitting in the living room.

"Antonio offered his condolences and talked to the police in Italy to keep the details under wraps."

"Thank you, Joaquin," I responded, sauntering around the home I would live in for the next few months while we regrouped.

"The girls texted and wanted to know if you're up for a visit," Joaquin expressed.

"Um, maybe in a few days. I need to get things squared away here."

"Understandable," Joaquin replied.

I looked at Axel. "Did you tell him my suspicions?"

"What suspicions?" Joaquin asked.

"Let's take it to the office," Axel commanded.

We went to his office on the first floor and I sat in the chair near the bookcase. "Everyone is going to think I'm crazy." I rubbed my hands.

"Tell him," Axel pushed.

"No one had complete access to my family's property except a few people we trusted."

"You think it was an inside job," Joaquin pried.

"At first, I thought it could be Fulgenzio, but he's way too loyal to Axel to betray him or me."

"Then who?" Joaquin asked softly.

I looked from Joaquin to Axel. "Lazaro. One of our foot soldiers. He's come to my family's home with Axel a few times."

"Dario has access, and she thinks they worked together," Axel explained.

Joaquin's eyes narrowed. "He's here with you now, right?"

I discreetly motioned toward Lazaro with my eyes. "Unfortunately, yes. And that scares me."

"We can't tip him off if he is working with Dario. It's our only way to find him," Axel reminded me.

Joaquin clasped his hands together. "You know I like to torture and kill to get information, but if you want to take things slow..."

"Normally, I would let you, and be the first one in line

to shoot, but it's Gigi's theory and I want her to have a say in what's going to happen." Axel showed me a long time ago how much he cared and listened when we talked. He was letting the world know I was capable of running a cartel like my father.

"Lazaro texted with someone in the car. We need to get his phone," I suggested.

"He won't give it up without a fight."

Axel smiled. "If he lost it?"

Joaquin answered with a mischievous grin. "Lost and found."

Axel cupped my face. "Right now, you need to act normally."

"Maybe I should hang out with the girls, then." I glanced at them both.

Joaquin encouraged, "Shopping and drinks at Ryde."

"Guards in and outside of the club," Axel demanded.

"Never worry. We always protect our women," Joaquin replied.

Sabrina rode with Janice to meet me at the mall, and the first stop was at a lingerie store to pick up some items Janice had on hold.

"Carlo is going to rip that off of you," Sabrina joked.

"Always the plan." Janice giggled.

"Gigi, you'd look gorgeous in this light-blue lace number." Sabrina pushed the garments into my hands.

"Axel would kill me for even thinking of buying something this risqué."

"He'll be grateful. Crotchless panties. Carlo almost had a heart attack after he ate me out." Janice laughed and high-fived Sabrina.

"Oh, Lord, you have to forgive Janice. The girl has no filter," Sabrina remarked.

"If you're hanging with us, Gigi, I suggest you get used to my mouth now, because I'll never change." She poked her lip out.

"Carlo knows that already," Sabrina jested.

"Don't let Sabrina fool you. She's crazy like me, but tries to hide her wickedness," Janice stated.

Sabrina chortled. "Here she goes."

"You two are hilarious."

Janice jested, "Do you and your best friend act the same way?"

"A little, but minus the mafia part."

"We traded our roles for being wives and mothers. That world will drive you crazy, but if my man needs me to ride shotgun, he knows I'm right there with my gun," Janice explained.

"Yep. Antonio is the same way with me. He hates knowing I'm capable of taking that risk, but I love my husband." Sabrina picked up two red gowns.

"Axel and I are still fresh and new in the love department and working together. Hard to separate the two."

Sabrina wanted our pick of which was cuter, and I pointed at the deep plunging gown. "Marriage is hard, but you have the double-edged sword since you're the boss and he's under you."

Axel's perception meant the world to me. "I know."

Janice looked at the price and put it back on the rack. "Has he ever tried to get you to step down?"

"Not really," I lied.

Janice tried on a long robe, standing in front of the mirror. "Lie to everybody else, but you can't lie to Sabrina and me. We've been in your shoes."

"Axel is great, but sometimes the age difference makes

me wonder if he'll love me beyond what people think about us."

"Everything will work out how it should." Sabrina showed me a silk leopard-print bra set.

"Tonight we're going to Ryde nightclub." Janice took the robe off.

The distraction would be good. "My first time going."

Sabrina said, "It's mostly young people. You'll like it."

Janice pressed her lips together. "I'm still young."

"Girl," Sabrina cackled.

"Sabrina wants to play like she's an innocent do-gooder. When we get a chance, I'll tell you about the time she almost killed a woman over Antonio," Janice whispered.

"Leave my business alone," Sabrina muttered, grabbing a few thongs and walking to the register.

"Anytime you want to shut her up, say that." Janice and I burst into laughter.

They continued to banter back and forth, reminding me of Ginerva, so I picked up my phone and dialed her number. "Shit."

"What?" Janice queried.

They both stared at me. "Nothing."

The thought of Ginerva being in danger hurt my heart. We still hadn't heard any news.

"Tell us. Maybe we can help," Janice suggested. She grabbed her purchases and interlocked our arms, strutting out of the store and around the corner.

It felt like Dario was punishing me for going against him. "I still can't get in touch with my best friend."

"Did you talk to her parents?"

"No. It's like they dropped off the face of the earth."

Janice said, "Maybe a vacation."

"No. I called her number and my ex picked up." I felt a tightness in my chest.

"Did you put a tracker on her parents' car?" Janice investigated.

A tracker should have been the first thing I figured out, but everything happened so fast. "No, but maybe I can get Axel to have our men in Italy do a search. Since we found out about my family, we flew out of the country quickly."

Sabrina proclaimed, "It will work out in due time."

"Don't stress yourself out," Janice implored.

The girls tried to encourage me, but I felt as time went by, things would only get worse. My nerves rattled more with no any updates. "It's hard with everything going on."

Janice laid her head on my shoulder as we walked. "As long as you have Antonio, Carlo, and Joaquin, you'll be fine. Just stay focused on the goals."

"Thanks, Janice. I appreciate you."

"You're welcome."

Sabrina walked onto the escalator and turned to face us. "It's time we head back to your place and get dressed for the night."

"Have you arranged the funerals for your family?"

"A family friend handled it for us."

Cyrus stepped up to the plate with his wife and made all the arrangements. Also, it released my trust fund to me. Now I was the sole surviving child of the Carrington name, everything from houses, cars, property, and accounts belonged to me. Money wouldn't bring them back, but I made donations to the families of our staff.

"I'm still grieving my father's death. And now my mother and all the people who worked with us were murdered. So it's still embedded in my mind when I walk through the house."

"Give yourself time to grieve. It's gonna all work itself out." Sabrina comforted me.

Janice pulled me into a hug. "In the meantime, we'll distract you."

I checked my phone for messages from Axel. "Where are we hanging out?"

"My husband's nightclub," Sabrina answered.

"Can I ask one more question?"

"Go ahead," Sabrina replied.

Fulgenzio took my bags, and we went to the car.

"How naïve were you to this life?"

Sabrina popped a piece of gum in her mouth, offering us one. "Extremely."

I motioned I was fine and Janice took a piece. "Both of us were, but that will go away soon."

Sabrina remarked, "And remember, keep friends close, but enemies next door."

"Enemies next door," I mumbled to myself.

Our car drove out of the parking structure toward the main road. I turned to see extra security behind us. Janice sat forward to get Fulgenzio to turn the radio on and Sabrina chuckled at her friend negotiating which channel to play.

Two hours passed in a flurry of makeup, dresses, and hair styling

Fulgenzio escorted us inside the Ryde nightclub, along with Lazaro and a couple of other guards. Axel was off working on Dario's whereabouts. He told me they captured Edmundo to figure out where his son was, but he hadn't talked yet.

All three of us stared up at the cocktail server.

"What do you want to drink?" Janice asked me.

"Whatever you're having."

"We will take two Aces of Spades bottles, Don Julio, Circo and Long Island Iced Teas. Just keep the bar open for us." Janice laughed.

Loud bass from the DJ booth reached all around us. The decor was modern and expensive, from the long drapes and each booth with its private bar.

I wasn't in the party mood, but I agreed to come to get out of the house. Every time I closed my eyes, I could see my mother and Aurora on the floor, covered in blood. I had to figure out what my life would be like without them. How could I be who I needed to be and remain true to the person I was inside?

Sabrina fiddled with her dress. "Do you want to dance?"

"No, I think I'm just gonna sit and watch people." I scanned the crowds; most of the women flirted with the men for drinks. I didn't miss those days of being single.

Janice clapped her hands in excitement. "We can start slow. All the kids are asleep and our men are working."

"Do you have babysitters?" I asked.

"Longtime babysitter," Sabrina replied.

"Took me a while. I never trusted anyone with my babies."

Sabrina clapped her hands when our drinks came to our table. "Janice said she's gonna be in a mood all night. So be prepared to drink and have fun."

"Thank you," I told our server.

All three of us toasted and took sips. Janice twisted in her chair in excitement and we laughed. My attention went around the room, seeing the men and women flirting and make out. I remembered those days of wanting to be accepted by someone. I rubbed my wedding ring. I was almost empty inside without Axel next to me.

Our guards surrounded our table, and I figured no guy would press us for our number. Even the backup protection made me feel a little insecure.

I removed my phone, seeing it was almost dead. I rose out of my seat, and Janice reached over to grab my wrist.

"Where are you going?"

I pointed to the hallway. "I'm gonna go and call Axel. Check in real quick."

Janice and Sabrina stood . "We'll go with you."

"Oh, no. You guys sit. I'll be fine. I promise I'll be right back."

I grabbed my purse and sauntered down the hallway until I saw the bathroom and an office next to it. I stepped in a corner and started to dial Axel's number when a familiar voice reached my ears.

"What do you mean, after everything I've done? I want my money," Lazaro muttered.

"Be patient," Dario responded.

I gasped, covering my mouth, and put my ear closer to the door.

Lazaro growled, "I put my life on the line for this."

I heard a scuffle.

"That's fucking bullshit. You knew the risks."

"Listen to me. I will give you up if you don't give me my money," Lazaro spat.

Dario cackled. "They'll kill you before you even get a chance to come find me."

"Fuck you, Dario."

"Where is she?"

It sounded like Lazaro choked on a cough. "Out front. Why?"

"Keep a close eye on her until I make a move."

Lazaro barked, "And my money?"

"You'll get the fucking money after I get her. She owes me for fucking up the plan."

Chapter 23

Axel

Fulgenzio sat in the car while I talked to Gigi, trying to get her calmed down. Janice and Sabrina were in the car with Carlo and Joaquin. Antonio was out of town, so we called for backup. When Gigi ran out of the club, Turin and I were twenty minutes away.

Gigi continued to take deep breaths while I rubbed her back.

"He can't hurt you," I promised.

Gigi muttered, "He's inside with Lazaro. They're still back there." She turned in her seat to look at the car behind her. "He doesn't know we left the table?"

I spun around to watch the door. "No."

Gigi cocked her chin up to face me. "Should I go back inside?"

I bent down to press a kiss on her lips. "I'm going in to grab him."

Gigi begged in a whisper, "Please be careful."

I pressed my forehead to hers and caressed her cheek. "Never worry about me."

Turin spoke. "Dario could have set a trap."

Gigi reluctantly released her hold on my hand. "It won't matter. Edmundo is gone and now his son will follow him."

I stood tall, shutting the car door behind me. "You see him?"

Turin nodded. "Lazaro's in the bathroom."

"Grab him, and we will take them both."

Antonio's guards allowed us entry. I heard the doors shut behind me. Carlo and Joaquin jogged to catch up. Music blasted as Carlo walked ahead to show us where the offices were. I kept a hand on my gun and walked through the dark hall. A few girls came out of a bathroom and waved at Carlo.

The door opened on our right, and Lazaro stepped back in shock. "Boss, I had to use the restroom."

"Where's Gigi?" I already knew where she was, but for him to leave her alone for so long would put a red flag in his mind.

Lazaro gulped. "At the table with the girls." He tried to step around me, and I cut him off.

"Anything you want to mention to me?"

He looked between from me to Turin and Carlo. "Tonight went fine."

"Lazaro, I thought we had an understanding."

He slid a hand to his hip. "Boss?"

All three of us moved in closer. "You know I don't like excuses."

Lazaro held a hand up, pleading, "I can explain."

"Why would you need to explain? Did something happen?"

Lazaro glanced around for help. The bathroom door

opened again and a few drunk guys stepped out. Lazaro pushed them toward us and ran to the front.

"Hey, man!" one of the drunk patrons yelled as I shoved him to the floor.

I chased after Lazaro and saw him run through the crowd of dancers. Turin motioned to the right, and I went left.

"Watch the entrance!" I shouted to Carlo.

"Stop pushing." One girl turned to smack Lazaro across the face.

He knocked her down and ran through the side employee curtains. I charged across the dance floor after him. I jumped and grabbed the back of his shirt as he reached the exit doors.

"I'm sorry! Please!" Lazaro panicked, trying to twist out of my headlock.

"Shut the fuck up," I seethed.

"Dario's not here."

"Where is he?" I barked.

Lazaro fell to the floor. "I don't know."

"Get up."

Turin pointed his gun at him and I reinstated a headlock until I could remove my gun and point at his back.

"Walk normally or you die."

He nodded, visibly shaken.

Carlo talked to his guards and passed me a pair of the zip ties they used on anybody rowdy.

I escorted Lazaro to the gray van we used for work and pushed him in the back, then slid the door closed. "Take him."

"If we kill him, we might lose sight of Dario," Turin remarked.

I watched people go up and down the streets. It

wasn't a crowded night in New York; most of the traffic was a few blocks over. Glancing down the street, something told me a busted Honda with expired tags was misplaced in this area. I moved toward it when it pulled off with a tall figure inside. Our eyes briefly held, and I caught the arrogant smirk on his face.

Soon after, we rushed Lazaro back to the destination we purchased to get answers—painfully.

"No, please. I didn't have a choice!" Lazaro screamed in pain.

I twisted the knife in his leg. "He promised you how much?"

His head hung low. "A million."

"What was that?" I gripped his hair and pulled his head forward, ensuring he stayed awake.

"A million."

My lips twisted with disgust. "You betrayed my trust and family for a million dollars?"

Snot ran down his chin. "I can make it up to you."

"A promise he didn't even keep. He wanted to give you the money at the end, right?"

He glared at me.

I chuckled.

His frown lines deepened. "Fuck you."

"I hope you're happy with your life." I raised the sledge hammer and brought it down on his stomach and he convulsed in pain. "Bring me the needle."

The two guards stood beside him to make sure he didn't squirm around too much. I took the needle out of Turin's hand.

"No, listen, we're family," Lazaro begged.

"Family! Motherfucker, you helped the people who hurt my wife and killed one of my mentors. You will die."

The syringe would numb him as I used the chainsaw to cut him up and drop him off at the bottom of the ocean.

I positioned the chainsaw over his foot, then knees. "Dario won't need to worry about that million now." I smiled in appreciation at being one step closer to ending Dario's life.

An hour went by until we boarded the boat and drove out through the river and finished out the night. The Meat Factory had a shower for us to change, then I jumped in the car while Turin drove.

Turin drove through the gate of Gigi's home, up to the side of the garage.

I opened the glove compartment and grabbed some wipes to clean my hand. "I think Dario saw me outside."

"He has too many resources. It's pissing me off."

"Now Lazaro is done, he's going to be even more frightened."

"I have to fly back to Italy and check on the farm," Turin reminded me.

"Hold off on that. I need someone I can trust here with me."

"How is Gigi?"

"A little shaken, but she'll be fine."

"Make sure you stick around here for the next day or two."

I turned my back to the door. "Are you an expert in relationships now?"

"Get out of my car, and act like you have some sense," he growled.

I stepped out of the car and stalked through the side garage door into the house. I placed my wallet and keys on the counter, reached in the fridge for a bottle of water, and climbed the stairs to our bedroom. The door opened to an empty bedroom, and I was immediately concerned about Gigi's whereabouts. I headed back downstairs to the man cave I had built, and found her lying on the couch with a blanket covering her lower half, watching a movie. I stood in the entryway and watched her for a few minutes.

"How long are you going to stare?"

I dug my hands in my pockets. "Long as I want."

Gigi lifted her hand for me to come forward. I came off the wall, approaching her on the couch and lay down behind her, wrapping my arms around her waist.

She rubbed circles on my arm. "Tell me what happened. And before you deny it, I can handle it if you killed him."

"Dario escaped."

Gigi tensed. "How?"

"I don't know for sure, but I think we saw each other."

She sat up, and I pushed her back down. "Meaning?"

I rubbed up and down her back. "Stop and relax."

"A crazy stalker has killed everyone in my life."

"Baby, relax for me." I cupped her cheek, pressing a kiss on her mouth.

Tears fell, but I kissed them away. Even though she was here in my arms, I knew her mind was a thousand miles away. To have so much taken away from her and the person still not caught would eat away at anybody.

"Dario wants the one thing he will never have."

"What?"

"You. Which means he's not that stupid to hurt you," I reasoned.

"He never loved me. He only wanted power."

"People get desperate when they have nothing to lose, but I will lay my life on the line before he ever hurts you."

"The regret I have sometimes is that my family would be alive if I'd given him what he wanted," she whispered.

The look in her eyes caused my heart to ache. She thought she should've given in to her mother's demands, but I needed her to understand her choices were up to her.

I breathed in her sweet floral perfume, caressing her hair. Being with her brought out the boyish affection I'd closed off at a young age.

Tonight, she felt powerless. Dario stole something from her a long time ago and I needed to show her that she held all the power and no man, not even me, could cause her to break.

I captured her lips in a gentle kiss, moving down her cheek and shoulder. I lifted my head and found her studying me and pleading for the warmth our bodies created together.

While the movie continued to play, I removed the top of her dress, kissing each of her breasts while she watched me. Her delicate breath caught in her throat when I slid my hand in between her thighs.

"So wet, baby."

Her eyes glowed with excitement as she brushed a thumb over my lips. I kissed the back of her palm, allowing her to push my shirt and jacket off.

Gigi kissed me with burning desire. My mouth sealed over hers. I deepened the kiss as our tongues moved in sync.

I eased the strapless bra down, then tugged on her thong to move it down to her feet, and she kicked it off. Her tongue made a path down my chest and stomach. With her teeth, she tugged on my belt buckle. Everything she did turned me on, even when we fought.

My hands slid over her back to her breast, and I flicked my thumb over her nipple. Deliciously, her warmth got wetter, and I eased a finger in and out before pushing it into her mouth to taste herself.

"Mmmm," she moaned.

The beauty of her like this made me even harder. Her moans prickled my ears. "Fucking goddess, angel."

I pulled her chest to chest, wrapped a hand around her waist, and pushed another finger inside from the back while she moaned into my mouth.

"Baby, that feels so good," she purred, grinding back and forth as I pressed my hand against her pussy.

I discarded my pants and boxers, and Gigi rubbed up and down on my shaft while I continued to please her.

Finally, she lifted her leg, easing down on my dick, and we both groaned in pleasure. She lifted her neck and pushed her breast forward so I sucked on her sensitive nipples. Locking eyes with my beauty, I focused on her tantalizing moans in my ear.

"Y-y-yes," she stuttered, shivering against me.

I moved in and out of my wife's sweet essence with purpose. Over time, I'd seen her become more comfortable with herself and demand how she wanted to be fucked. I gently stroked her neck, nipped around her ear, and added a little pressure.

Gigi closed her eyes. "Oh, shit, baby."

Her voice made me want to stay inside her forever.

She clawed at my chest, and the sting pumped me up more. With her eyes closed, she bit her bottom lip before her mouth dropped agape. "Baby, right there."

I made her feel this way, and she would own my heart even after I died. "No one can compare. You're the one for me."

The blanket beneath us was saturated with our juices.

My heart beat faster. I wanted to take her away and erase every negative thought in her mind.

"Ah, fuck." I grunted when she bent backward out of my grip and exposed more of our connected bodies, spreading her legs and grinding faster as I played with her pussy.

I thrust harder, and we had an unspoken competition of who would make who come first. She moved my hands away and turned around. Pushing herself back down, she tossed her hair back and rode me.

"Beautiful as fuck."

I could feel her ready to come. I surged up and grasped her hair with one hand, the other on her shoulder. My head lowered, and I licked and nibbled up to her ear. "Feel so good. Ready to come, baby?"

She nodded.

"Let me hear you."

Gigi gasped when my thumb slipped into her asshole. "Axel, please," she begged.

"Come for me, angel."

That was all I needed to say, and she came in a low moan, her juices dripping down her thighs to wet our couch. I held her as I stroked into her for a few minutes until I released fell back on the couch with her in my arms.

Her hair fell on the side of my face and I rubbed her stomach and thighs as her skin glowed with sweat. Silence drifted over us until Gigi turned around to face me, thighs parted to accommodate my length.

I closed my eyes and felt the comfort of her warm breath against my ear, and I knew all was right in our world.

* * *

My father sat with me while I watched TV. "Being in this world isn't about who has the biggest balls or guns."

I glanced up and ignored my toys. "What do you mean?"

He patted me on the head. "I know you understand what I do, son."

I kept my head down.

Father wasn't the typical father who had a lot of rules for me, especially being the only child.

"Look at me, son."

"Yes, Poppa."

"Everyone isn't your friend in my world."

His statement gave me pause. Something in me stirred with alarm. "What are you talking about?"

"While I do work for Laurent, we are friendly. Not everything is clear to be seen right away."

Even as a kid, I needed to figure out if something was wrong. "I don't understand."

"My job is to protect his business. Some people don't like that."

My brows bunched in frustration. "Who?"

He chuckled when I balled up my fist. "Calm down, Axel."

I was ready to go to war for my father. "Are you in trouble?"

"No, nothing for you to worry about."

"Well—"

"What I meant is that Laurent has enemies and friends around him at all times. My job is to protect his business from both. He's done a lot for our family, but people will try to cast doubt on me."

"To make you an enemy?" A frown covered my face.

"Enemy or friend to Laurent would be a terrible thing, but one thing I can say is he would never make a move without knowing the full truth."

We never finished the conversation when my mother came from the kitchen to make us come eat.

Those words from my father replayed in my mind. Casella made it known he was after Gigi. Dario and Lamberto partnered up to hurt her. So many enemies, and then we found out her mother was involved in her father's death.

After my parents' funeral, I had some of his work packed up. I dug through everything and saw Lamberto's signature on a few accounts. Laurent seemed to put a lot of trust in Lamberto, and I wondered if Rosa had influenced that decision.

"Life insurance policy," I mumbled, scanning the old accounting records of his offshore accounts

Turin stepped into my office and shut the door behind him.

I waved him over to sit down. "Anything new?"

"Carlo got rid of the security cameras that night. Lazaro's family thinks he flew out of the country with a girl."

"Good, if they continue to question—"

"I know what to do."

I held the papers out to him. "Check out these accounting records."

He cradled the papers in his hand. "Where did you get these?"

"My father's records. I had them all packed away."

Turin bowed his head. "I see Laurent had a lot going on."

"True, and Lamberto made it his mission to be in control," I replied.

Turin looked at me. "Surprised?" He sat forward, grabbing more papers from the desk, along with old pictures of my father with Laurent around town.

"No, I think Rosa has worked on this plan for a long time to get rid of Laurent."

"Damn." Turin went silent.

"Makes sense, even when Cyrus put her in charge of the trust fund."

"Man, she was really in control." He rubbed his chin.

"When Gigi finds out it went this far back…" I tried to control my anger.

"Maybe you should wait until Dario is caught." Turin was always the voice of reason; bringing more problems to Gigi wouldn't help her heal.

"Probably."

Turin pushed everything back on the desk and stood. "Plan for today?"

"Stick around for Gigi. I'm not ready to leave her alone after what happened the other night."

"All right. Let me get back to work and make some calls."

"Tell Carlo and Joaquin I said thank you." Both men came through for me and I appreciated the backup on short notice.

He tapped on the doorframe. "Sure. If you need me, I have my phone on."

I rose out of my chair. "Thanks. How are the rest of the guys?"

"So far, no one has asked about Lazaro."

"Good. We keep this to ourselves."

"Yeah. If more snakes are in the garden, I'll find out."

I walked Turin out of the office and to the front door, shaking hands with him before letting him out. I pushed my hands in my pockets and looked around the kitchen, then the living room for Gigi, but didn't find her. I heard talking from outside as I stalked through the house and into the backyard, and saw her talking with Quinn.

"Thank you, Quinn." Gigi pushed her shades over her eyes.

I watched Quinn grab the empty plate and head back into the house. I greeted her before moving out of the way and approached Gigi laid out under the cabana.

"Are you done with work?"

I sat on the edge, picked up her legs, and placed them in my lap. "For now."

Gigi's hand caressed my arm. "Is Turin gone?"

"Yes. How long have you been out here?"

"Not long. I did a little work and came out here for some sun."

"How are you feeling?"

She gave me a soft smile. "You don't have to keep checking on me."

"My job is to make sure."

"I know. You've explained multiple times over the past few years. Thank you for last night." Gigi grinned, leaning forward for a peck on the lips.

My fingers fluttered to her neck. "Never thank me for loving you."

She lifted her arms around my neck. "Loving you is the one thing I've gotten right in my life."

Since being with her, I'd felt more open to having

conversations about my family. "I had the time to look over some of my father's old files."

Gigi withdrew her kisses. "What did you find?"

"I don't think your father had anything to do with my parents' deaths."

I registered a change in her mood. "Are you sure?"

"Never a hundred percent, but my gut is telling me to look in a different direction."

She sighed. "Imagine that's how I felt when I found out about my mother's affair."

I wrapped my arm around her waist. "Stop beating yourself up."

"Hard to do when she plagues my mind."

"We'll get clarity in time."

For the rest of the day, we talked and reminisced about the old days when I was younger and growing up. Turin hadn't reported back any updates, so I took that as a chance to enjoy my wife and spoil her with food, movies, and shopping for her favorite things.

Chapter 24

Gigi

A month later.

"**Y**ou continue to play up the role of devoted soldier to Axel, and let me handle everything else."

"They have your father."

"I know. I'm working with Lamberto to figure out how to get them out. My mother is pissed off," Dario hissed.

"The hit on her mom was too much. It put a bigger target on your back," Lazaro confirmed.

"Just wait. She won't know what hit her."

I stepped back, covering my face, the call to Axel forgotten.

I sprinted down the hallway back to our section. "We have to go."

"Why?" Sabrina perked up.

"We have to go. He's here."

"Who's here?" Sabrina looked around the club.

"Dario," I whispered.

Janice scanned the crowd. "He's in here right now?"

I planted a hand on her shoulder. "Yes, and I don't want more people to get killed. We need to go."

She reached out and clamped a hand on top of mine. "Okay, just stay calm,"

"Let's walk out calmly so they don't suspect anything."

"Do you know who he's with?" Sabrina quizzed.

An air of dread came over me. "Yeah. One of my guards. I overhead them talking to Dario."

We sauntered out of the club.

"Fuck," Janice said, sliding into the passenger side of the limo.

"We need to call the guys," Sabrina suggested.

My heart beat fast. "Wait. Maybe we could follow him."

"No," Janice argued.

Noises from downstairs broke through my memory. I continued to be plagued with the events of the other night at the club. I shook it off and opened my eyes, turning to see the empty spot on Axel's side of the bed.

I was becoming more paranoid, even though Lazaro was gone. Dario was still missing, and Lamberto, last we heard, had killed himself. I should be happy and ready to live life, but I felt another problem would drop into my lap and interrupt our happiness.

I tossed the covers back, climbed out of bed. Grabbing my robe, I removed my hair wrap and combed through my hair with my fingers. Entering the bathroom, I brushed my teeth and did my morning routine to get ready for the day. It usually took Axel about forty minutes, but I needed an hour or more. It was why we had separate bathrooms and closets because he complained about me taking too long.

I finished up and went downstairs to a full kitchen of staff cooking and cleaning.

"Morning, Mrs. Bresciani." Quinn was all smooth skin and slim figured.

"Morning, Quinn. Have you seen Axel?"

Quinn answered, "No, ma'am. His car was gone when I got here this morning." She strode to the table and poured my coffee.

I had our dining room decorated in my parents' favorite colors and photos filled our home of my family and Axel's.

"Maybe he's working." I yawned, scraping jam on my toast.

"Do you need me to gather anything else for you?"

"That won't be necessary. I can handle it from here."

Quinn's oval face rose in a smile. "Sure, Mrs. Bresciani. I have a few errands to run."

"Thank you, Quinn. I left a list of items we need from the store."

"Yes, the first thing I picked up from your desk."

Quinn was referred by Janice, and she was fluent in Italian. She took care of her mother and wanted to pick up extra money since she couldn't be away from her for long hours. Axel did his usual background check, and we brought her on.

Our daily lives in America had come a long way over the past weeks. I'd gotten things off the ground for the business, and Antonio helped with locations to handle drop-offs and access to the ports. Today, I had a meeting scheduled with a new client who wanted to use our services. Axel hated when I suggested branching out from our normal operations, but things needed to expand.

The doorbell chimed and I tossed the napkin on the table, scurrying to the door.

"What are you two doing here?"

"Wanted to see how you're doing?" Janice and Sabrina hugged me, passing me a cup of coffee.

"Come in. Quinn has breakfast laid out if you're hungry."

Quinn stood behind me, ready to go to the store. "Don't forget to stay with your guards, Quinn."

"Yes ma'am."

Quinn climbed into the second jeep we'd purchased specifically for her use.

"Where's Axel?" Sabrina asked.

Still pissed he left, I waved it off. "Working. I woke up to an empty bed."

Janice rolled her eyes. "Husbands! How did you sleep?"

"I tossed and turned all night."

They followed me into the dining room.

"We wanted to take you out," Sabrina said.

I gestured for them to sit down. "I have a meeting."

Sabrina frowned. "How long will it take?"

"Maybe a few hours. It's been on my calendar for a while."

"Then call us, and we can get together for a spa day later." Janice took a sip of the orange juice.

For the next hour, I listened to them talk about their children, and how they had started to get disrespectful as they grew up.

Dressed in my best suit and heels, I checked my lipstick and came out of the house armed with my purse, gun, and phone. I hopped in my chauffeured car and saw a text message from one of our crew members at the Meat Factory.

Jesus: *Mrs. Bresciani, the packages arrived.*

Me: *Everything good?*

Jesus: *On the scale, it was short.*
Me: *How many pounds?*
We talked in code.
Jesus: *At least fifteen pounds.*
Me: *Make sure you let Axel know and tell them know we want full payment for wasting our time.*
Jesus: *Yes, Boss.*

Fulgenzio whipped around the traffic, parking out front of the mutual location we agreed to meet at for protection on both sides.

"Keep the car running."

He planted his hand on the steering wheel. "You have your gun?"

I smirked. "Fulgenzio, you don't have to check up on me."

He smiled. "Mrs. Bresciani, I will always check up on you."

We both burst into laughter.

"Fine. I should only be an hour."

He pulled out his phone. "All set."

The Meat Factory housed meat, but underneath, it was loaded with cocaine, while the guns were kept in another location. Axel set it in motion to fly under the radar with local politicians, and the businesses we set up in America came in handy to fund their lifestyles.

I shoved the door open, sauntering toward the closed furniture store that looked outdated. Both parties didn't trust each other, even though I had the upper hand. I marched in and looked around at the dingy furniture.

Someone stepped out from the dark hallway into the light.

"Mrs. Bresciani, thank you for coming." Officer Ronson extended his hand.

"Mr. Ronson. When I got the call, I have to admit it surprised me."

"Sorry for the confusion and the location. Thought it was important to have discretion."

"A wise choice. Are you into decorating?" I asked as we sat at a table.

"I dabble in it from time to time," Ronson explained.

I came to meet with Ronson through mutual friends. As a cop, he would never have my full trust, but the call came the other night, and I talked with Axel, who he agreed to see what it could be about.

"Billionaire business."

"I agree. I have something for you." He reached into his pocket and held out a yellow envelope.

I stared at it. "I hope you're not setting me up on our first meeting."

"Never. I wanted to give you a peace offering as goodwill."

I flipped it open, pulled out the contents, and saw pictures. I stared at Officer Ronson, then back to the pictures. Dario and his mother were boarding a plane.

"When was this taken?"

Ronson glanced at the picture. "A day or two ago."

"So, what do you want, Officer Ronson?"

It always came down to money with these men. "As a police officer, I know how to get around red tape."

"How did you hear about me?"

"Turin." His movements were slow and steady.

I stayed focused on him without reacting. "Turin knows you're here?"

"He does," Ronson responded.

"Do you know who my husband is, Officer Ronson?"

"Axel Bresciani."

"Tell me why I should take a chance on you because my husband hates when other men are around me unless he knows them personally?"

"Strictly business. We want the same thing."

I leaned in, bracing my elbows on the table. "What is that?"

He clasped his hands together. "Not only money, but Dario Ramini dead."

I needed to test his loyalty. "Why is Dario a concern for you?"

Ronson hunched his shoulder. "He's my brother."

My eyes turned cold and I stood. "If you think you're setting me up, I suggest you never speak about this meeting again."

Ronson looked tough but easily manipulated. "Mrs. Bresciani, nothing about me is a setup. Dario is who I want to bring down."

"Edmundo is a lot of things, but he would never have a side baby."

Ronson reached out and grabbed me, and I jumped back.

"How wrong you will be, Gigi."

Dario walked inside and I turned to face him, with Officer Ronson behind me.

"Do you think I came here alone?"

"Doesn't matter. You're not leaving alive." Dario grinned snidely.

"Think again."

Gunfire exploded and I dropped to the floor. Dario ran, and I wanted to chase him, but knew it would be safe. I saw Officer Ronson take his last breath and wondered how much Dario filled him in about me.

I took the stairs and came out of the front as though

nothing happened. Putting on my shades, I looked up to the top of the building across from me and saw a tall figure staring back.

My phone rang, and I dug it from my pocket. "Hello."

"You hit?"

"No." I looked from left to right as people scattered like rats to hide.

"Get in the car and go home."

I swung my head around to find him. "He wasn't hit."

"We scared him."

For Dario to get pleasure from my pain pissed me off. "I want him dead, Axel."

"Dario is dead. He just doesn't know it yet."

"Hurry home."

Police sirens and ambulances started to block off the area. People stayed on the ground to avoid any more shots.

"Don't worry. Just in the car," he directed.

"I hate leaving you here."

"Look up the block at the gray utility van."

I scanned the area and saw the van.

His tall figure mesmerized me. "Turin is driving. I have backup."

"Okay. Make sure you dump everything and I got a call about a shipment that was short."

He looked at me, then at the police and ambulance arriving. "I'll handle it later."

Suddenly, I felt the need to go to him, but he raised a hand for me to stop. "Be safe, angel."

Whenever he called me that, I knew to be strong. "I love you."

"Love you, too."

* * *

I was at the kitchen sink when strong arms engulfed me. Fulgenzio had brought me straight home, and I planned to watch a movie until Axel took care of cleaning up with his men.

"How did it go?"

"Turin is setting Officer Ronson up nicely with a background for stealing from the cases he busted."

"Good. He was ready to kill me without blinking."

"He's trained to do that."

"What are you trained for?" I turned in his arms, stretching my hand around the back of his neck.

He lifted me and placed me on the counter. "Many things, including making you happy."

I smirked. "I need to shower first."

"We'll get to that soon. I want to make sure I keep you informed." He slid his hands under my shirt.

Electricity crackled between us. "Informed, huh?"

"Dario is more dangerous than I expected. I need you to keep your eyes open."

"Yes, sir." I kissed him on the lips, rubbing the back of his head.

Axel's phone rang.

"Ugh, they can wait."

"Stop pouting." Axel reached into his pocket and pulled out his phone.

"Who's calling you at this time of night?"

Axel smirked. "Turin. What's going on?"

I watched his expression change from a smile to a frown. "You don't need to come here. I'll be there in a few minutes."

"Are you leaving?"

Axel dropped the call. "Turin has something lined up for us to inspect."

"A few more minutes before you go." I kissed him and melted into his hard body.

"Either I leave now or we don't get this deal done." Axel groaned, pulling back.

I wiped the lipstick off his mouth, and he pecked me on the cheek.

"Don't forget, we have a flight to catch tomorrow morning. Don't be late," I announced, following him to the front door.

"You take this boss role a little too far," he teased.

"Whenever the *Capo* is talking, you should listen," I teased, opening the door.

He chuckled. "I'll be back before you wake up."

"All right." I shut the door behind him and headed back into the house, laughing to myself. I paused, seeing he forgot his cell phone. Heading back to the door, I saw he had a text message.

Unknown: *My turn*

"My turn?" I muttered as I opened the door.

An explosion ricocheted around me, and a bright red fire rose in an instant. I was thrown back, hitting the ground hard, and darkness swallowed me.

* * *

I hope you enjoyed Gigi and Axel's story so far. Check the sneak peek of "**Claim**" on the next page. Follow my standalone, opposites attract, age gap, military romance "**Exposed**" https://books2read.com/u/bQyYZe. Are you a fan of sports romance? Then download one-night stand, billionaire romance "**Refuel**" https://books2read.-com/u/boDyDA. Also, follow it up with workplace, sports romance **"Pressure"** https://books2read.-com/u/3Ly1r7. If you love romantic comedy, fake relationships, enemies to lovers, find it here, **"Something Gained."** Click the link here https://books2read.-com/u/baGLYy. My stories of friends finding love started with the Heart of Stone series that includes a host of characters and family. **"Broken"** book 1 Emery and Jackson a sports, one night stand, workplace romance is here: https://books2read.com/u/3LoelX

Then you can continue with a fun side story of Emery and Jackson with "Valentine's Day short here: https://books2read.com/u/4jAypY

Jordan, her best friend's story, continues here in **"Rebirth"** book 2 a single dad, widow billionaire romance here: https://books2read.com/u/ba2OMx

* * *

Please also check out a second-chance workplace romance here, **"Renew Book 4"** https://books2read.-com/u/4NXyPG with a host of characters intertwined.

Follow Desiree and Gabriel in **"Temptation"** a standalone contemporary, sports, curvy girl romance. Check it out here https://books2read.com/u/mle1Vv

Check out dark mafia romance here that started my journey with Antonio and Sabrina in **"Ruthless Book 1"** https://books2read.com/u/4AxKLo

The relationship continues in **"Savage"** book 2 as they get to know each other and their families: https://books2read.com/u/bpED6g

Antonio and Sabrina have more work to do in

"**Beast**" book 3 right here: https://books2read.com/links/ubl/4AxKOd

* * *

Did you know Janice and Carlo have a book? Well grab this dark mafia romance with emotional scars, and betrayal right here: https://books2read.com/u/b6je6M

Any fans of forbidden romance, political? Check out "**Mutual Agreement**" https://books2read.com/u/mgzzWX a steamy romance. Pre-order the full novel of "**Nasir**" here click the link here.

Have you checked out "**She's All I Need**" click here https://books2read.com/u/49lkeW a sports, opposites attract romance. What about dark romance that has everything from steamy romance, opposites attract, suspense, thriller, celebrity, and more "**Stolen Book 1**" https://books2read.com/u/mvZlgV Don't miss the follow up Joaquin and Sofia's story in book 2 "**Saved**" https://books2read.com/u/4DWwLd

The conclusion for Joaquin and Sofia comes full circle in "**Betrayed**" here: https://books2read.com/u/4A5LGp

* * *

Catch up with favorite characters in this holiday short romance which includes spoilers. "**Holiday collection**" here https://books2read.com/u/bzd59G

For small town, single mom stories check out "**Until Seren**a" https://books2read.com/u/mej8vr. Always fun when you love billionaire romances so check in with

"**Cocky Catcher**" a sports romance, enemies to lovers here: https://books2read.com/u/bOxNgJ. Some familiar characters show up in "**Bossy Billionaire**" a workplace, enemies to lovers romance here: https://books2read.com/u/mvZoDq

All curvy girl, plus size romance lovers get into "**I Deserve His Love**" a standalone, second chance romance here: https://books2read.com/u/mVrGwP

The fantasy romance readers look no further than a "Red Light District" a curvy girl, fling romance here: https://books2read.com/u/m2RQ6G

Coming Soon!

Claim: The Carrington Cartel Book 2

They might have won the first battle, but the war is about to start.

When Gigi and Axel unexpectedly fell in love, the events that followed were expected yet terrible. Turning away from the match her father secured for her to strengthen the cartel, left Axel fighting for his life.

Balancing her new role as Boss becomes more complicated than she ever anticipated. But stepping down isn't an option.

Secrets from the past linger in the shadows and if they come to light, they will destroy everything.

Gigi has always been underestimated and it's time to show her true wrath and take revenge on her enemies.

Gigi wants blood to pay for what she lost.

Sneak peek: Claim (The Carrington Cartel Book 2)

Seven months later.

I tossed and turned all night, but nightmares continued to cloud my dreams. The rain descended for the third day in a row, and usually I could sleep if I had Axel next to me, but now it was different.

I felt a pinch in my stomach. "Shush," I murmured, then smiled. "You decided to keep me company again."

I turned over, sat up, and stretched. My stomach calmed down a little while I checked the time on my phone, which buzzed with an incoming call.

"Yes?"

"We're outside."

I stood and walked toward the window, seeing a few of my men lined up.

"Give me a few minutes."

Turin blew out a breath. "Boss?"

"Yes, Turin?"

"Are you sure you want to do this?"

My eyes brimmed with mist. "Positive. Please don't question me again."

"Have to look out for you, since he's not here."

I felt calm about my decision. "He would want me to handle business."

He was amused. "You're right about that."

"I'll be down soon."

"No heels this time," he grumbled.

I giggled and looked down at my swollen feet. "Let it go, Turin."

"No, because you need someone to watch over you."

"Only three-inch heels," I teased.

"Determined to drive me crazy."

Turin had become more of a big brother over the past few months. Our back-and-forth banter was the highlight of my days.

"As my friend, you should be used to it by now."

"Get dressed." He ended the call.

I shook my head and went to the bathroom to shower and dress for another late-night meetup.

Forty minutes later, Turin parked the car in the usual spot. Meat Factory had become the destination in order for me to not travel far out during my pregnancy.

Turin turned toward me and grasped my hand. "The moment I think it's too much, you're leaving."

"Who put you in charge of babysitting me?"

"I put myself in charge. What are the rules again?"

"Turin, I'm fine. Rules are for kids."

The look on his face kept me laughing; most people would think I was crazy to push a mafia guy around.

"You're pregnant and running a cartel. Sorry, but you need someone to tell you no."

"That someone is not here." I looked off into the dark night.

"Let's get this done so we can get you back home."

He pushed the door open and came around to help me. I stepped out in my long black stretchy dress with the split on the side—and three-inch heels. All you could see was my belly.

"Is he conscious?"

The guard opened the doors to on duty and Turin held his hand out for me to not miss a step. "Yeah. I told them to leave you enough to finish him."

"Thank you."

I scanned the room and took in my crew surrounding me as they waited for my words. I'd restructured Carrington Cartel after what happened with my family and Axel.

"Please! I don't know anything," Sandro whimpered.

I rubbed my belly, calming my baby. "Sandro, I thought we could trust you."

He lifted his head as blood trickled down his face. Seems they did more than enough. His clothes were torn, and his wounds were fresh.

"Gigi, I swear Lazaro acted alone."

"Did he?"

"Yes, I beg, whatever you need."

My frown set into a dark mask. "Dario is missing and I want his head." He lied, and I wanted to cut him up into pieces, but we didn't have enough time.

"He's never contacted me."

"I have a phone record that says differently."

With a shake of his head, Sandro turned away.

Turin's phone rang, and he pulled it from his pocket.

"Dario is my enemy and you're going to tell me what you know." I moved in closer, but Turin grasped my arm.

"Turin, let me go." I stuck my hand in my purse to pull out my gun.

"It's for you," Turin remarked.

I waved him off.

Sandro sobbed. "Gigi, I swear—"

"It's 'Boss' to you, Sandro, and I'm afraid you're no longer worth my time." I put the gun to his temple and pulled the trigger before taking the phone from Turin. "Who is this?"

"Angel," Axel whispered.

Reader Questions

1. Do you think Dario was wrong for going behind Gigi's back to work with her mother?
2. Do you think Gigi will survive as the mafia boss?
3. Should Axel have walked away from Gigi instead of going along with the plan of a fake marriage?
4. Will the other mafia families want revenge?
5. Do you think Gigi should forgive her parents?

Reading Order of Heart of Stone Series

Broken 1 Emery and Jackson
https://books2read.com/u/boWPAV
Heart of Stone Book 1.5
https://payhip.com/b/kWg7
Rebirth 2 Jordan and Damon
https://books2read.com/u/ba2OMx
Heart of Stone Book 3.5 Bottoms Up
https://payhip.com/b/HGP1
Reveal 3 Angela and Brent
https://books2read.com/u/31rx9l
Renew 4 Jessica and Joseph
https://books2read.com/u/4NXyPG

Reading Order of Antonio and Sabrina Universe

The Early Years-A Prequel
https://books2read.com/u/49Zjnw
Ruthless Struck In Love Book 1
https://books2read.com/u/4AxKLo
Savage Struck In Love Book 2
https://books2read.com/u/bpED6g
Beast Struck In Love Book 3
https://books2read.com/u/3LpgdJ
Janice and Carlo Captivated By His Love
https://books2read.com/u/b6je6M
Brutal Struck In Love Book 4
https://books2read.com/u/4NQyE9
Stolen-Fuertes Mafia Cartel Book 1
https://books2read.com/u/mvZlgV
Saved-Fuertes Mafia Cartel Book 2
https://books2read.com/u/4DWwLd
Redemption Struck In Love Book 5
https://books2read.com/u/b5kZ8O
Betrayal- Fuertes Mafia Cartel Book 3
https://books2read.com/u/4A5LGp

About the Author

Chiquita Dennie is an author of Contemporary, Romantic Suspense, Erotic, and Women's Fiction.

Chiquita lives in Los Angeles, CA. Before she started writing contemporary romance, she worked in the entertainment industry on notable TV shows such as the Dr. Phil show, the Tyra Banks show, American Idol, and Deal or No Deal. But her favorite job is the one she's now doing: full-time writing romance.

A best-selling author and award-winning filmmaker, her first short film, "Invisible," was released in summer 2017 and screened in multiple festivals and won for Best Short Film. She also hosts a podcast that showcases the latest in beauty, business, and community called "Moscato and Tea." Her debut release of *Antonio and Sabrina Struck in Love* has opened a new avenue of writing that she loves.

If you want to know when the next book will come out, please visit my website at http://www.chiquitaden nie.com, where you can sign up to receive an email for my next release.

Acknowledgments

I want to dedicate this to my team that helps me behind the scenes, from my editors, test readers, graphic designers, and the list goes on. Truly appreciate each of you for keeping me on my toes.

What's Next?

Want to know what happens next?

Follow me on my website to catch the next release.

Reviews are the lifeblood of the publishing world. They're read, appreciated, and needed.

Please consider taking the time to leave a few words on your review platform of choice.

Sign up for updates and sneak peeks at the site below. www.chiquitadennie.com

Catalog of Releases

Catalog Releases

    By Chiquita Dennie:

    The Early Years-A Prequel Short Story

    Ruthless: Struck in Love 1

    Savage: Struck in Love 2

    Beast: Struck in Love 3

    Brutal: Struck In Love 4

    Redemption: Struck In Love 5

    Broken Book 1 (Emery & Jackson)

    Heart Of Stone Book 1.5 Emery &Jackson A Valentine's Day Short

    Janice and Carlo: Captivated By His Love

    Rebirth Book 2 (Jordan and Damon)

    Temptation

    Reveal Book 3 (Angela and Brent)

    Cocky Catcher

    Bossy Billionaire

    Bottoms Up Heart of Stone, Book 3.5 (Jessica and Joseph Short

    Love Shorts: A Collection of Short Stories

Stolen: Fuertes Mafia Cartel Book 1
Exposed (Salvation Society Novel)
Saved: Fuertes Mafia Cartel Book 2
Refuel (A Driven World Novel)
Pressure (A Driven World Novel)
Until Serena (HEA World Novel)
Renew Book 4 (Jessica and Joseph)
She's All I Need
Red Light District (A Fantasy Romance Short)
The Carrington Cartel Book 1
Betrayed: Fuertes Mafia Cartel Book 3
Something Gained (A Romantic Comedy Book 1)

Thank you so much for reading and if you enjoyed the crazy ride and decide to leave a review, we'd truly appreciate the support.

304 Publishing Company

We showcase authors writing African American, Interracial, Women's Fiction, Erotic, and Contemporary Romance novels. Along with Thriller, Suspense, Poetry, Beauty, and Style Books. Thank you for taking the time out to visit. Join our mailing list to stay updated with new releases and blog posts.